Also by Ruth Boswell
EMMY
published by *Routledge & Kegan Paul*

Ruth Boswell

Out of Time

The Muswell Press

Revised Edition First Printing and Publication
Published by The Muswell Press
129 Rosebery Road, London N10 2LD, UK

A CIP record for this book is available from the
British Library.

Printed in England by Pims Publishing

ISBN 0-9547959-0-3

We may well ask when and where men do live.
The answer is that they live in the future and
in the past and now, or all at the same time;
or, more correctly, that when they live at all they
live out of time

.

The Third City by Borra Bebek

Time present and time past
Are both perhaps present in time future,
And time future contained in time past.
If all time is eternally present
All time is unredeemable

TS Eliot

—

Chapter One

Girls fancied Joe. He was seventeen, tall, dark haired, grey eyed, handsome though this was difficult to tell. A Gap jumper whose hood permanently covered his head and left his face in shadow served as a useful disguise and allowed him to see out but prevented anyone from seeing in. Torn jeans and trainers conformed to the political correctness current among his peers.

Joe and his mother lived alone in a red brick house in Bantage, an unassuming town in the Cotswold Hills. The odd Tudor front, a covered market in Weymouth Square, a few remaining narrow lanes, bore witness to a more ancient centre, almost obliterated by the usual parade of chain stores, a small shopping mall and civil facilities. Where Joe lived, nearer the outskirts, the thirties planners, or unplanners, had taken over and post-war architects added their indelible mark. Their house, three up, two down, small front garden, larger back, was what might have been called ordinary but served its purpose. It was home.

It was this that Joe was now trying to enter. His key refused to turn the lock and open the front door. He gave it a hard kick. This usually worked. Not this time though, this time the door remained obstinately shut. Typical of the day, he thought bitterly. It had started with a fight in which he beat up a boy weaker than himself for reasons he could no longer remember, it had continued with an argument with his best friend Martin who wanted him to go to Dick's Cafe after school, and it had almost ended for good with a heavy fall outside the local park gates which had left him unconscious for several minutes and with a pounding headache.

Dick's Cafe was where groups of friends gathered, hyped themselves up on caffeine, phoned friends and if seriously bored went on to punch a few video games at the local arcade. He suspected Sally would be lying in wait for him. He'd been going out with her in a half hearted kind of way for the past term, the last of a succession of girls with whom he had had vague relationships but who, as he had no inclination for commitment, eventually walked away. Sally was more persistent than the others and he was anxious to avoid her.

He wished his mother were back. It was Monday and she worked late at her secretarial job which she disliked but bore with stoicism. She had had no outside financial support since Joe's father disappeared and she was too proud and independent to pursue him for maintenance. Joe tried to supplement their income, or at least see to his own immediate needs, by working at the local Sainsbury's on Saturday mornings.

Mrs Harding's life was devoted to Joe. This Joe knew but instead of helping their relationship, he was left with a burden of guilt which made him resentful. Dimly aware of how unreasonable this was, he tried to express the genuine love he felt for his mother but failed, thus intensifying his guilt. Mrs Harding for her part, also guilty because Joe was being brought up without a father and the masculine guidance she thought essential for a teenage boy, could not break the cycle of tension that marked their daily life. It was an unsatisfactory situation but neither knew how to alter it.

Joe once again tried to open the door. He inserted the key into the lock and twisted and turned it with increasing frustration. It served him right. The lock had been temperamental for some time and he had promised to install a new one; but hadn't. He tried the side door leading into the back garden but this too unaccountably failed to open.

The air was hot and still and the street quiet. No one was about, blank-faced windows revealed no sign of life, no doors opened or closed, he could hear no voices, no sounds of children. He wondered where they had all gone in a street normally active at this time of day. He felt dizzy and faint and sat down on the front steps. When was Mum due? He looked at his watch. In four interminable hours. Should he go to friends? The idea repulsed him. He wanted to get indoors, flop down in front of the TV, watch a crap programme and go to his room, the only place in which he felt secure enough to relieve himself of being who he was. His head throbbed.

He dragged himself upright concluding that, befuddled by his fall, he had gone to the wrong house; easy enough to do, in these repetitive streets, after a blow to the head. He picked up his bag and walked back into the street. The gate, swinging half open, revealed two white numbers nailed crookedly to the gatepost. They stared at him with the familiarity of old friends and he stared back, remembering the pottery class at primary school where he had fashioned them, brought them home and laboriously screwed them on. It was a lifetime ago, a period he preferred to forget, a time when the house vibrated with shouted or unspoken confrontation between his parents, when he lay trembling in his bed, his ears sensitive to the slightest sound that could herald a storm breaking out either below or in the bedroom across the landing. This was the prelude to his father leaving home. Joe was given to understand he had gone to live with someone else, some 'tart' he heard his indignant grandfather proclaim. This his father denied, tried to explain to a puzzled eight year old that he had fallen in love with someone else whom Joe would like when they met. But they never had. His mother had forbidden the contact and eventually his father and new wife moved to Australia. After a time they heard no more of him.

Dots danced before his eyes and he shook his head to clear them but his vision, when he read the street name, was unclouded. Fairfax Road. That was where Joe lived. Twenty-two Fairfax Road.

His knee hurt. He limped back to the house, sweat starting out in groin, armpit and forehead. He needed tea, something to eat. He had, he suddenly realised, on this unsatisfactory day, dashed out in the morning on only a cup of tea. Should he go to a friend's house? He automatically reached for his mobile phone. The back panel had split, probably in his fall. The line was dead. He threw it in disgust into the nearest flowerbed.

He would have to get in through the bow windows but these, with safety locks in place, were impossible to open. His only hope was to break a pane and climb through. This seemed a drastic measure but he would square it with Mum, replace it himself if necessary. Joe no longer felt reasonable, his sudden and urgent need to get in the house overriding all other considerations. He picked up a stone from the garden, wrapped it in a dirty handkerchief - no point in raising the alarm with the shattering noise of broken glass - and prepared to throw.

The stone never left his hand because he now saw that, in place of the mirror that normally hung over the sideboard, was a charcoal drawing of a man's head, heavily framed in black and executed in strong, bold strokes. Joe gazed at it, mesmerised by its extraordinary power, by the dark malevolent eyes staring straight into Joe's. He drew back in alarm, his only wish to flee; but he had noted with astonishment that the room that he was looking at was not his, was not the one belonging to Joe and his mother, was not the room inside twenty two Fairfax Road. Averting his eyes from the hypnotic stare of the portrait, Joe drew near again and registered foreign furniture, heavy and dark, hessian curtains and, he now noticed, thick, roughly hewn wooden shutters swinging loose either side. How was this possible? He had checked the address. Were there two Fairfax Roads in Bantage? It seemed unlikely; yet there was no mistaking that the right address had brought him to the wrong house. He withdrew to the garden hedge where the portrait's eyes could not follow and tried to work out logically and calmly a plausible explanation for his predicament. He had no doubt that there was one but for the moment he was too bewildered to work out what it could be.

He was interrupted by a harsh voice.

'What the hell d'you think you're doing?'

He whirled round. Facing him was a small swarthy man, dark featured, heavily bearded, staring at him with hostility. Joe shrank back as the stranger laid a heavy hand on his arm.

'Take your hands off me!'

He responded by grasping both Joe's shoulders and giving them a shake.

'I don't advise you to be insolent,' he hissed. He was looking round furtively as though caught in some illicit act. Clearly mad, an escapee from the local hostel. On drugs probably. Joe decided to handle him with care.

'I am trying,' he explained, as though addressing a recalcitrant child, 'to get into my house'.

But it wasn't, from what he had seen, his house. Someone else's house, perhaps this man's.

'Your house?' the man whispered. His pushed his face into Joe's.

'The key won't turn in the lock,' Joe offered in a conciliatory tone. If he kept talking perhaps he could edge him onto the path, back him into the street, find help.

The man gave him a sharp push.

'Scram!' he said, 'before I call out the nets. Run!'

His mouth was pressed against Joe's ear, the word exploding from him in a tone so low Joe was uncertain he had heard it. The man again looked to either side and then, taking a key from the loose folds of his shirt, opened the front door. Joe watched with astonishment. Pausing, the man whispered again,

'I warned you,' and disappeared inside.

Joe stood stupefied.

A bell began to ring, tolling from near at hand. Then another, and another. Looking up Joe saw, outlined against the sky, wooden structures on all the roofs, two uprights and a crossbar from which, their clappers following the rhythm, dark bells swung back and forth. The summer afternoon resounded to their peals. This was not the comforting sound of church bells but threatening, alarming, an imperious summons… to what?

The front door opened and the man came out carrying a long pole with a large net suspended at its end.

'I told you to run!'

Joe needed no second bidding for the sound of other doors opening, other people shouting, galvanised him into action. He took off down Fairfax Road, turned left at the corner into Sydenham Road and on into Forest Lane. Behind him pounded a gathering momentum of feet, shouts, bells and whistles. More people emerged from their houses. All were holding man-sized nets.

He had had nightmares like this before, intensified after his father left. Always he was being chased by men out to kill him and he running, running but waking at the point of death, sweating and shivering - but safe. He had perfected a technique for dealing with these attacks from his unconscious by realising that he was asleep, knowing that he had only to run long enough and hard enough before waking up in his own bed, in his own room, the normal world solidly around him. Now he waited for the moment of release.

It did not come. Instead a sharp blow caught him on the back of his neck and stunned him. Joe stumbled and then ran on in an agony of bewildered despair. He could see the park railings where so recently he had stood, contemplating the possibility of a cup of tea. Should he run in? He decided against it, fearing to be surrounded. He raced on, uncertain of the direction he was taking.

A warm liquid trickled down his back, sweat ran down his chest and into his eyes, preventing his seeing ahead. Lost in a vortex of sound, of breathlessness and terror, the throbbing in his ears was indistinguishable from the clamour behind him. If only he could wake up. Hate was at his heels.

He zigzagged to avoid the nets and as he did so his body hit wall either side. Out of the corner of his eye he saw the legend 'Cat Walk'. So that was where he was. The local graveyard for cars lay beyond. As he hurled himself to the end of the passage another blow caught him on the back of the head. He threw himself forward, expecting a net to close over him, and braced himself for a final struggle. There was no need. His pursuers had not followed.

He fell to the ground, into silence and oblivion, a blank, black abyss.

It was dark when he woke, not the dark of his room but the dark of a night sky. He was lying in the open. No stars but a pale moon occasionally obscured by moving clouds cast a thin light. He tried to rise. Movement was agony but he staggered to his feet and looked around. The tall beech trees of a nearby wood rustled in the warm breeze; on the other side of Cat Walk he could make out the pitch outline of houses pressed one against the other, their belfries like gaunt gallows pointing towards the sky. His senses now more attuned to his surroundings, Joe heard a chorus of creaking sounds, moans, thuds, squeaks, rattles, not regular but persistent and alive, like an old house talking at night. He held his breath and waited and then moved a step forward, colliding painfully with something tall. He pushed past it and moved towards the town, preparing to negotiate his way through abandoned cars but, looking closely, was shocked to discover that they no longer existed. The object with which he had collided was a wardrobe leaning crookedly like a drunk, its doors swinging in the wind. The waste ground was the depository for discarded furniture, chairs, tables, benches, planks piled on one another in crazy confusion. This could not be.

Cold and trembling, he wrapped his arms around himself in a futile attempt at comfort. The Gap jumper stuck to his back. Blood. He was wounded, needed help. He had to get home. He stumbled towards Cat Walk but tripped over an obstacle in his path which, he realised with a jolt, was one of the nets, its pole broken in half. Joe kicked it aside and moved cautiously forward until he reached the far end of the passageway. There was neither light, movement nor sound in the town but clearly visible in the moonlit sky were the stark outlines of the belfries, each suspending a now silent bell, the agents of evil that had made him a fugitive.

He walked through the familiar streets, the park to his left, he turned into blessed Fairfax Road, his eyes fixed apprehensively on the houses but they were shut up, silent. He read the nameplate with deliberate care, tracing the letters with his fingers.

Nothing had changed, the front of his house was as he had always known it, squat, undistinguished, home;

only the bell was unmistakably on the roof, a malevolent, alien guard. He looked up at his bedroom window and wondered if he was lying in his bed dreaming that he was standing outside, wondering if he was lying in his bed... If he threw a stone would it wake him? Would his mother be inside, asleep, in a house that appeared to belong to a fiercely hostile stranger? Should he wake her, assure her he was all right, had not been drinking or caught up in a fight, though he wondered how to explain his torn clothes or his wounds. Mum could be fierce. He did not relish the idea of confronting her with an absurd explanation of the state he was in.

He put his hand on the gatepost, his pottery numbers reassuringly still there, slipped the latch and pushed it open, bracing himself for the familiar squeak. The gate made no sound, swinging on well oiled hinges. At the front door he took his key out of his pocket but after a moment's hesitation decided the risk too great. He stepped instead into the flower bed that still held his imprint from the attempt, an eternity ago, to break the window. Closed wooden shutters obscured his view of the interior.

The garden door was now unlocked and he stole into what had once been familiar green space. There were no flower beds now, no lawn and, worst deprivation of all, no old, gnarled apple tree, in earlier years his tree house, his fantasy world, his hiding place. Instead, rows of poled beans, carrots, cabbages, cauliflowers marched in subdued rows towards a garden shed. Inside, an array of garden tools, a scythe and a sickle were dwarfed by two man-sized nets reaching from floor to ceiling. Joe saw them with a shudder and felt his wound. The net so carelessly kicked aside in the waste ground must have been the one that hit him. He picked up a sack from a pile, put it round his shoulders and stepped out.

He looked long at the house, studying its darkened windows, wondering if normal life continued inside. Had he ever got home? He could not remember. He had surely returned from school, eaten a meal, watched TV, gone to bed. And if he had not, had his mother missed him on her return from work, had she wondered where he was, tried to reach him on his mobile, asked round his friends' houses? He could imagine her anger and anxiety building up as he failed to appear. No light shone from her window, but then if the evidence of his eyes could be believed, it was no longer her window, it was the man's. Joe resisted an overwhelming temptation to call out in the hope that she was there but to reveal himself was too dangerous. He moved to the back hedge and burrowed through to the lane that ran parallel to the houses. As he walked along it towards the town centre he considered whether to seek help from neighbours. Then he heard footsteps. Perhaps it was someone he knew, perhaps it was Mr Bernard, a large pot-bellied man who worked at the local hospital returning late after his night shift. Perhaps he could explain...

Joe shrank into a wall. Three figures emerged from the end of Fairfax Road, making towards Acacia Avenue, two men dressed in long, straight, black coats, heavy boots on their feet, either side of... whom?

Peering more closely to make sure he was not mistaken Joe saw with astonishment that, between the two guards, for that was clearly what they were, was the man who claimed to own number twenty two, his face stricken, ashen grey. A shirt with sleeves tied tightly back, Joe presumed it was a straitjacket, imprisoned his arms. What had he done, what crime committed to be picked up in the middle of the night and brutally taken away? This, like everything else that had happened to Joe since his fall, seemed evidence of some tangible evil. He watched with apprehension as the men dragged their prisoner away and out of sight, leaving the unlit streets empty and silent. He hesitated. If the man had gone, dared he go inside the house? But what if he had a wife, or someone else lived there? He was not prepared to risk it.

The park gates were locked but at the side two railings, in his own world, were worn thin by countless generations of schoolboys. Now they stood straight and sturdy but Joe found, to his surprise, they still yielded to his pressure, allowing him to slip inside and walk across to what was called The Field though it was no more than a grassy area. It looked wild and forlorn. Joe made his way to the copse on the far side.

It was as he sought the shelter of the trees that he heard steady drumming as though someone were beating the ground. He inched forward, bracing himself for another surreal image. What he saw was hardly surreal, merely inexplicable, laughable in its ordinariness. A small girl of about eight or nine was skipping with frightening intensity. Skip, skip, skip. Her face, he could see even in this dim light, was taut and grey, her body so thin it was almost transparent. Her hair fell in thin strands to her shoulders, now moving with the rhythm of the rope. Skip, skip, skip.

A rustle. To Joe's alarm a couple emerged from his far right, the man's face tight with fear, the woman's hunted, drawn and weary, eyes darting from side to side as though expecting retribution. They approached the girl, took the skipping rope from her, wound it round its handles and moved silently away in single file, the man first, then the child and lastly the mother. Joe followed at a distance, reaching the railings in time to see them go down Rose Avenue and into Jarvis Road. They disappeared inside number fifty six but as he turned away he noticed a twitching curtain in the house next door.

Uncertain what to do next, he retraced his steps to the corner of Fairfax Road and again studied the nameplate with painful longing. He looked back at the familiar streets where he had spent his childhood. He could remember walking as a toddler down the then never ending Fairfax Road, his small hand comfortingly in his mother's. 'Then' was his time of innocence, of hope, of a golden world with mother, father and dog, Ricky a cocker spaniel, now long dead. They had had to put him down because he had contracted leptospirosis, a disease deadly to humans. His murder, as Joe thought of it, coincided with the beginnings of his parents' break-up and his first taste of the relentless loneliness of misery. Nothing was ever the same again.

He experienced now a similar sense of closure, of terminal alteration to his life. Why this should be he could not understand, knew only that a desolating sense of loss left him unable to move. Fairfax Road, ordinary, pedestrian Fairfax Road seemed like a lost paradise that he could never regain. He looked at it with longing,

19

etching its contours into his memory, then silently retraced his steps to Cat Walk. He stopped only to grab the broken net in the hope that, with it gone, they – the townspeople who had hunted him like an animal – would forget.

Shivering now, Joe clutched the sack round his shoulders, made his way through the sea of furniture and, throwing himself down on an old creaking bed, fell into an uneasy sleep.

Chapter Two

JOE woke to the early morning sun and the improbable vista of an open sky. He searched in vain for familiar sights, for his crumpled duvet half trailing on the floor, for window curtains blowing in the wind, posters staring down from his pock-marked ceiling. He could see only dark stacks of unfamiliar furniture, hear only the call of birds, sounds and images to which he could not connect. He grasped at memories from the previous day and slowly, like phantoms from a dream, the happenings that had brought him to this improbable place came into focus. His aching limbs, the dried blood on his neck, a throbbing headache, bore witness to the reality of his predicament.

Joe's was not an imagination in which wild fantasies took place; only in dreams and sometimes lying half asleep was he invaded by images with scant connection to his humdrum life as though an alien world, concealed in his unconscious, needed to make its presence known and pull him into its orbit. The sense of dislocation this produced often left him bewildered, unable to pick out threads that would restore reality. So it was now. The alien world had taken over but instead of the changing, disconnected world of his dreams, the place in which he found himself was clearly defined, substantial.

The furniture, now that he saw it in daylight, was weather-beaten, crumbling and old, beetles munching into its heart, he could hear their million jaws. It must have once been imposing for it was dark, solid and occasionally finely carved. What kind of houses had it come from? It resembled no furniture Joe had ever seen, except in Gothic horror films. It had the same exaggerated quality.

He felt exposed, the only human in the absurd panorama of wooden detritus going to waste. He put his hoody over his head and painfully made his way towards the nearby wood. This at least was territory he knew and he climbed over the alien contents of unknown homes towards it. He reached its welcoming shade gratefully and paused a moment to look back. The waste ground looked incongruous, a Stonehenge of ghostly, rotting sculptures. Nearby a staircase climbed into nothingness.

A stream flowed through the wood. One carefree spring weekend he and Martin had traced it to its source, their first independent foray, camping two nights en route. He looked for the well worn footpath. That this too had ceased to exist was all of a piece with what had gone before but he struggled on through tangled thickets and fierce bramble bushes until he reached the stream's cool waters. He drank, stripped, cleaned his wounds and lay submerged. The throbbing in his body subsided and he rolled onto the bank and lay unmoving as he tried to unravel the fantastic events of the past day and night. They did not yield to logic, nor to any remembered experience. Only in the most outlandish video games did he inhabit places of such wild improbability. Absurdly, he wondered if he was caught inside one, a figure manipulated by electronic impulse. He pulled himself back sharply. That was the stuff of science fiction, yet the game was the same, the challenge to escape, to find a way to take him back to where he rightly belonged. This was not a matter of pushing buttons but of using every mental resource to find an exit point. He searched for a gap in events, a point at which his own volition could empower him but could see none. Circumstances beyond his control were in command and he would have to play their game, follow their signs.

Was he being tested by some unknown, malign god, were these happenings a trial of strength? If so, he had to meet the challenge or else....die?

Joe did not favour speculation. It seemed to him a vain and useless waste of mental energy. His solutions to problems were purely practical.

He remembered now that he had been to a school camp at a farm which lay some five miles northwest. The farmer and his wife had been welcoming, they might remember him, might help. He dressed, brushed himself down and set off. He would cut through the wood until he reached the main road; it would be easy going after that. But once under the canopy of trees, without a path to guide him, he lost his sense of direction. The way was barred at almost every step by rioting bushes, fallen tree trunks and branches obscured by thick moss and lichen. He pushed his way angrily through long ivy tendrils that hung in thick, twisted ropes from overhead. The wood, like the townspeople, was attacking him and he was powerless to fight back.

Each step released a volume of sound, twigs snapping, the crunch of rotting wood beneath his feet, quick slithers in the undergrowth. If he stood still the silence was oppressive, relieved only by the chatter of birds high above and the scraping of countless insects below.

Only small plants could thrive in the lush dark of the wood; white wood anemones, sorrel and, here and there, glossy green leaves where earlier bluebells bloomed. He found an anthill, two feet high and poked a stick into its summit. The ants, red, large and fierce, scurried to rebuild. He felt panic rising, alone in this wild wood, and sat down on a nearby tree stump. What had he been taught to combat it? - take a deep breath in and then a long one out. He tried, but it did little to still the pulse beating in his throat. He pushed on.

It was impossible to know where he was heading. Everywhere looked the same, an endless forest of gnarled trees and undisturbed vegetation. He was probably going round in a circle, would stay here forever, never be found. Panic gripped him again as he thrashed through with brute force, tripping and falling constantly. What was once a wood had become a forest, unyielding in its cool, somber light.

Sobbing with frustration, he forced himself to stand still and let his heartbeats settle. He had time, it was still morning, ten o'clock by his watch, and there was surely a way out to the road. 'Keep calm,' he told himself, 'think laterally.' The obvious answer presented itself almost at once. Grasping the low branch of a nearby oak he hauled himself on and climbed laboriously to the top. He broke through to sunshine and the blue canopy of the sky. Scanning the horizon in every direction he was amazed to see nothing but acres of trees, their undulations in every possible and impossible shade of green; only the distant roofs of Bantage broke through the quivering carpet. Of buildings, roads or cultivated fields there was no sign. Man had left no mark on the landscape. Nature held sway, untroubled.

Joe climbed to the ground no longer able to think or reason or make sense of the insane universe imprisoning him. He wandered, directionless, in numb despair. Later, he found himself again by the stream.

He fell asleep, waking only when the sun lay low. The day was fading and with it came a desperate longing for home. Joe crept to the edge of the waste ground and parted the bushes to get a clearer view, praying to see once again the lost paradise of his youth, the cars' rusty and jagged edges; but outlined against the sky was the same rotting furniture. In a forlorn desire to touch a familiar object, he made his way to the broken bed on which he had slept, wondering for a wild but hopeless moment if stopping here again for the night would dissolve whatever fantasy he inhabited.

The pole and net that had so nearly caught him lay on the ground beside the purloined sack. He picked them up and slowly made his way back to the wood.

*

In the town a gaggle of men are gathered in a low, oak beamed room. It has no windows and is lit by braziers on the walls and two flickering lamps. The men's skin is grey, as though rarely exposed to light. One, a tall man of indeterminate age, is sitting at a long refectory table. Ten heads incline towards him. This man, known as Helmuth, exudes a deadly power. No one dares speak as he gives short, sharp orders. Four guards who have been concealed in the shadows come forward, listen and then leave by a central door.

Helmuth nods. The meeting is dismissed. The Councillors rise and with an obsequious bow follow the guards. Helmuth remains seated.

Opposite him, on the wall, his portrait observes him thoughtfully.

*

Joe was hungry. This was real hunger, gnawing hunger that made him feel sick, faint and unsteady. He had seen on television, read in the papers, learned in geography, that millions of people were starving, a statistic that, until this moment, had evoked little beyond a brief stab of pity. Now the images of stick people with swollen bellies grew into sharper focus; but while they died in their barren and desolate landscape here, with abundant nature all around, he ought to be smart enough to survive. He lacked the know-how. Pity, he thought wryly, he had always scorned joining the boy scouts. It might have prepared him for this bizarre and inexplicable ordeal.

A hedgehog and four small young scuttled past. He had once been told that gypsies ate hedgehogs, baking them in clay. He looked at them with interest. Delicious evidently. But where would he get a clay pot? Shocked and amazed at the impracticability of his situation - he had nothing, out here in the wild - he turned out his pockets. They revealed the house keys, a few coins, about £2.75 in all, a calculator, a box of matches, a broken felt-tip pen and an old, two bladed penknife. It had belonged to his father, a tactile contact Joe valued. Crumpled into a tight ball at the bottom of one pocket he found a sheet of glossy paper, a page from an old copy of The Face with an article on what was termed 'the biggest star of 2001, Andrew WK.' He could no longer remember why he had kept it so long but shoved it back. He switched his calculator on, played with it for a while and wished again he had his phone, though he doubted that it would have worked in this mast-free wilderness.

The stream was teeming with fish, silver minnows darting in and out of the shallows, now and then larger fish that looked like trout. The net that had so nearly caught him, a neat construction made from thick, wispy rope knotted loosely and attached to a knobbly pole, would now be put to better use. How many people had it captured? Joe brushed the image aside. Without food he would be unable to continue, might lie helpless until 'they' found him. He cut off the broken half of the pole and, weighing the net down with a stone, placed it in the stream's bed. He waited for the ripples to fade and fish to swim into his trap. But they knew better and swam past or straight through. His stomach turning on its juices he finally caught a big, silver grey trout. Joe lifted it out and watched it thrashing inside the net, helpless but with surprising strength. Then it slid through a hole and hit land. The extra purchase gave it lift and it leaped high and forward, teetering at the water's edge. Joe pounced and, holding the slithering fish with one hand, reached for a stone with the other. The fish flapped its tail in a last helpless gesture as, eyes half closed, Joe bashed its brains out. He picked it up and it lay wet and slimy in his hands. His gorge rose. He was tempted to throw it back.

Having learned from countless Westerns that smoke would reveal his whereabouts, he knew better than to light a fire within limited distance of the town. He placed the fish inside the sack and walked further upstream until he came to a secluded clearing. Here he gathered handfuls of dry grass, small twigs and rotting branches and built them into a pyramid in best boy-scout style. Thankfully he had matches. These he had always hidden from his mother, taking them carefully out of his pockets before the trousers were washed, for he and his friends smoked out of school, in local cafes and in homes that tolerated it. Joints were passed round regularly. This now made him pause. Was he, could he be on a shitty weed? He had taken Ecstasy once or twice and had watched others habitually on harder drugs. Had someone laced his drink? He didn't quite see how. He had not been to Dick's and it was not the kind of thing his friends did, making it unlikely that this experience was drug induced; in any case, no matter how bizarre his surroundings, his thinking was too ordered, too logical.

He lit a match impatiently and put it against the dry grass. The fire, smouldering at first, sprang to life. Skewing a twig into the fish, he hung it over the flames and, after an agony of impatience, tore into its flesh, burned and half-raw. He caught another, swiftly dispatched and swiftly eaten. Then another. Satisfied at last, he doused the fire and sat beside its embers, preparing for the next part of his journey. He had to keep going. Death in a dream, if such it was, might spell death in life.

*

Four men and four dogs advance along the stream,
dogs straining at the leash. Each man carries a man-
sized net. No words are spoken but their determined
tread and their cold eyes express an implacable desire to
subjugate whoever crosses their path, an uncom-
promising determination for mastery untouched by pity.
They move forward.

*

Clearing away all traces of the fire Joe trekked on. In
other circumstances he would have appreciated the
wildness of this countryside, untamed by man, so
different from the neat fields and bordered woods to
which he was accustomed. He remembered now with
wistful pleasure a cycle ride some years ago in the
Chiltern hills with his mother, one of the many rambles
they had enjoyed together in the days of short haircuts
and neat clothes, before being uncouth became
necessary for survival. They had approached from
Hambledon, coming on it by chance and seeing, lying
snugly at the foot of a steep incline, a small village of red
roofs and curling smoke. As they stopped, looking
down, Joe had felt a rush of affinity with this land as
though he had inherited its memory, aeons ago from
another life. No sense of that now. Here nature was
untrammelled, stretching to he knew not where.

Faintly at first, he heard dogs barking. Was he
approaching civilisation at last? His heart beat with
hope. But not for long. The dogs were behind him,

downstream in the direction of Bantage. This could mean only one thing. They were after him. His mind told him he must flee but his body refused to move. He crouched instead in the undergrowth, the hood well over his head and waited to be captured.

A blackbird, disturbed by the noise of the approaching dogs, launched itself from a nearby branch and Joe, released from his trance of terror, sprang forward, falling over branches and dead trees in headlong flight, feet and frayed trouser bottoms caught by long grass, ivy and twisting convolvulus. Out of breath, slowed by a painful stitch in his side, he fell over a tree trunk that blocked the way and plunged into the water, slipping and slithering over wet, mossy stones on which his worn out trainers failed to find purchase. His way was barred by the overhang of a tree growing sideways from the far bank.

Joe hesitated. The baying was moving closer and he was exposed, in the open. He grasped a branch above his head and with his last breath hauled himself up. Crawling on all fours, he reached the tree trunk. Here, huddled into a fork and shaded by leaves, he was for the time being out of sight.

Four men cleared the trees, their dogs, noses to ground, inexorably following his trail. He realised with sudden panic that he had dropped his net and sack in the grass, a clue so telling that he must be discovered. He closed his eyes and waited for the end.

The men stopped at the point at which he had slipped into the stream. Tongues lolling from heat and exhaustion, the dogs lay in the grass. One man and one dog crossed the stream immediately below Joe. Pressing his back against the tree trunk until the hard crusty bark hurt his skin, he saw his pursuer hesitate, shake the short chain on which the dog was leashed and, with low grunts that were clearly commands, walk up and down. The dog looked up at its handler with fear, head down, tail drooping, slinking behind as he was dragged through the wood. On the far side another dog stood alert, pointing towards him, a huge wolf like animal. It seemed impossible that, bathed in a sweat of fear, he could avoid detection.

They waited, three men and a dog, the boy camouflaged in a tree while the wild world went its way. The hunt, the predator, the victim. It was the way.

No one moved until man and dog emerged below him without warning - how close had they been? - recrossed the stream and joined the waiting party. Joe expected them to confer and perhaps fan out, but they moved off, back towards Bantage. Joe watched them go until they disappeared. Unable to believe in his escape he remained in the tree long after they had gone. The chase, for the time being at least, was over.

Later, much later, he unlocked himself, clambered to the end of the branch and jumped. He grazed his knee and all the aches from his initial flight returned. Blood poured from his wound into the water. He waded back across and found, miraculously, the sack and net hidden in the topmost tangle of a bush. He picked them up with relief, plunged once more into the water and stumbled upstream. Progress was slow. Uprooted trees, their leafy branches growing upright from fallen trunks, formed an almost impenetrable barrier. He had to give up, return to the grassy bank and hope his scent was lost. He was intent now only on putting mileage between himself and the town. He urged himself forward.

In the late afternoon he collapsed in the shade of a tree and lay, semi-comatose, until twilight fell. It was quarter to five. Joe studied his watch in amazement and disbelief. Eleven hours only since he had woken that morning. He had lived an eternity and covered, according to his reckoning, some ten miles in this wild country which stretched ahead without a break.

*

The four men return to the town. Their journey has been in vain. They know they will be punished and try to make themselves invisible by keeping close to the wood's shade but as they emerge from Cat Walk they are seized by rough hands and dragged to a heavily fortified building. A thick wooden door is wrenched open and the four are thrown down stone steps into a dark, dank cellar. They cry in protest but the door is clanged shut and bolted from outside. Their shouts are ignored. The dogs are led away.

In the Council Chamber Helmuth listens disdainfully to what has occurred. What fools these men are, not worth their keep.

He is puzzled by accounts of this boy. He does not appear to be like the usual fugitive, but older, cannier. Helmuth wonders whether it is by chance that he is going in the direction of the community. He suspects not. This suits him well. Its stubborn dissidents are a thorn in his side, the last remnants of his erstwhile enemies. If they are harbouring the boy they will in time be eliminated. But not quite yet. There is a reluctance in Helmuth for this final deed.

*

The moon cast a clear light above the wood. Joe spent the night in a tree, the mysterious pads and rustles, the odd painful cry of an animal, the hoots and screeches of birds, preventing any hope of sleep. A grey owl, sharing his eyrie, brushed his face with outspread wings. Once he thought he heard hounds baying.

With the first light he jumped to the ground, relieved to be on the move. He walked all day, pausing only occasionally to gather berries at the forest's edge. The ground was rising and the stream changing into a fast flowing torrent, tumbling headlong towards its destination. Broad-leaved trees gradually gave way to darkening conifers, firs and pines. Their tangy resin smell reminded him of other places, other times.

When night fell he tried lighting a fire but the matches were still damp from his plunge into the stream and failed to ignite. Angry and frustrated, he threw them to the ground, unable to combat any longer the misery and fear that overwhelmed him. He sat in the enveloping dark for countless hours while invisible night creatures bustled round, slithering, creeping, flying, an unheeding world at his feet and above his head. Eventually he fell into a light slumber, only to be invaded by nightmares in which he saw his mother's face loom over him while he lay, pinned to a bed, imprisoned in a straitjacket, trying to explain, to speak, feeling his lips move but knowing that no sound came. He strains to warn her that there is danger, danger but he is gagged and as he struggles against his bonds an unearthly cry, a long, low howl, pulls him back into conscious thought. A tremor starts in the base of his spine, speeds through his body, his eyes bulge, his skin prickles and his hair stands on end. The cry rises again and again, culminating in a long high crescendo like the howl of a banshee, predatory and primeval.

Six pairs of yellow eyes glower through trees. Joe stares at them. Wolves. The leader of the pack crouching low, creeps towards him, growling, tail sweeping the ground, fangs bared. Mesmerised, Joe watches its savage shadow approach. Others in the pack are circling round. He is trapped.

Joe springs to his feet and advances on the wolf. Raising arms and head to the sky he lets out a primordial shriek that reverberates through the forest; then with the pent-up terror of his plight, another and another.

Man and beast are locked in confrontation and, as he has always done, man wins. The wolves turn tail and slink into the forest.

Chapter Three

—

THE morning found Joe scrambling for his discarded matches. He recovered twenty-three and the box, damp but still intact. Pushing them gratefully into his jeans pocket he set off up the hill. Conifers converged on either bank, somber, impenetrable and threatening. He hurried on along the thin strip of sunlight beside the stream and stopped at midday to rest and allow his matches to dry. He needed urgently to light a fire in the coming night and cook more fish but made do with handfuls of wild raspberries and small, sharp strawberries. It was a sparse meal; he did not want to stop a minute longer than was necessary.

Nothing in Joe's existence had prepared him for the ordeal he was now experiencing. There had been no premonition, no warning that his ordinary life, spent in a kind of scowling indifference that, he knew well enough, masked other deeper and unrealised feelings, could be disrupted and destroyed. That he was one moment in a normal day, in an activity as tame as going home from school, and the next in this wild improbable country hunted by packs of men, was the stuff of nightmares, part of the confused jumble that haunted him at night. But this time he was not going to be released by waking to his old surroundings because this time he was not asleep.

He trudged on, on automatic pilot. In the late afternoon as the shadows lengthened, the trees, releasing their resinous smell, pressed closer, lines of pine, fir and yew.

The forest filled him with terror. He had never succeeded in banishing its mythological figures, familiar from fairy tales that used to people his imagination. Though their power faded as he grew older, he realised now that they had been lying in wait, ready to take revenge for their dismissal. Here, they had him at their mercy and they taunted him, witches, warlocks, demons, hobgoblins. He kept his head well covered by his hood for if he looked he might see, and if he saw succumb to their power. The impossible had already happened. Anything could follow. He broke into a run, hoping to escape, but the forest stretched as far as he could see, on and on, perhaps forever, perhaps it covered the whole world. Its evil spirits were closing in on him. He felt their hot breath on his neck.

Though he was unaware of it for it had never been put to the test, Joe carried inside him a reservoir of courage. This now came to his rescue. He stopped running, he stood still, he faced the enemy and he sang. He sang every song he could remember, he shouted out the words, he bellowed his defiance, his confidence growing with every note. Joe felt the forest's inmates shrink before his onslaught, conceal themselves in the darkness to which he had banished them. He walked on steadily, along the thin strip of bank, towards the summit of a hill. His repertoire exhausted and his throat aching, he kept command over his fears by playing mathematical games, number one, double it to two, then four, eight, sixteen, thirty-two. Iteration. He did the same with square roots, pushing them higher and higher until his mind reeled; then primary numbers that stretched to infinity. These he had always relished. Because they went far beyond any calculation made either by computer or by man, they had served to give him a sense of eternity, symbols of the immutability of existence, a safeguard against mortality.

He stopped as the light failed, gathered dry grasses, branches and twigs, lit a fire and flung himself gratefully beside its Promethean flame, his guard against wolves and unholy spirits. Sensing that he was no longer easy prey, they left him alone.

*

There is no moon tonight. The park is dark. Skip, skip, skip. Susie is taking her nightly exercise. Her mother watches anxiously, her father walks the perimeter of the grassy clearing, then nods. The girl stops skipping and the procession, man, child, woman, moves stealthily forward, past the trees and to the park's railings. Here a small gate is opened. The man looks to right and left and beckons child and woman to follow. Keeping low, they cross Bridge Road, walk stealthily up Rose Avenue and across to number fifty six Jarvis Road.

A face appears briefly at number fifty four but Susie's parents do not see it. They are desperate to reach their home.

The girl sits on a high stool in the kitchen and eats hungrily from a plate of meat and vegetables. She drinks a mug of milk, eats some fruit.

'Time to go, Susie,' her mother says.

The girl shrinks away but the parents, grasping her firmly by the shoulder, march her upstairs to a third floor attic and push her unwilling form through a small door. The mother follows into a windowless room that contains a truckle bed, chair, table, some wooden toys and a doll. Susie lies down on the bed and the mother caresses her forehead but the father gestures impatiently. The mother leaves, closing the door firmly behind her. Susie listens to the familiar sounds of a large cupboard being placed against it.

Once she is alone, she picks up the doll her mother has made from a wooden spoon. She is called Susie Two and is dressed in a wide blue skirt and yellow top. Susie tucks her in beside her, cradles her in her arms and goes to sleep.

In the morning, when light filters through the roof, Susie looks at her for a long time. Susie Two is smiling today. Susie removes a brick from the wall under her bed, pulls out a sheet of parchment and a stick of charcoal. She draws lips that curve down at the corners. Susie Two is no longer looking happy. She is put into the bed and covered up.

Susie begins to write on the parchment. She has never been taught but she has invented her own symbols. These follow a simple pattern with an upright stroke and one, two or three shorter horizontal strokes added respectively for different sounds. In some cases the horizontal strokes run left to right, in others, right to left of the upright. Over a period of time Susie has added circles and diamonds for vowel sounds. She is now able, though it is a laborious process, to express her thoughts and feelings with some sophistication. Susie is as resourceful as Joe is courageous.

*

Joe woke at sunrise. The forest still cast its looming shadow but he ignored it and set about catching fish in the now turbulent water. He was lucky. Two were idling in a pool formed by the eddying water and he scooped them up with his net, cooked and ate them, doused the fire with water from the stream and dispersed the ashes. He set out again, still anxious to put greater distance between himself and the town. The land was rising sharply and the trees were thinning. By mid-morning he had seen the last of the conifers.

The comforting greens of deciduous trees, now in the full bloom of summer, welcomed him. He threw himself down gratefully under the generous branches of an ancient elm, exulting in the terrors vanquished. Later, as the sun reached its noonday height, he caught more fish and hung them from a stick to dry, he picked berries and what he hoped were harmless mushrooms which he ate raw. Then he pushed on, uphill. The stream increased its force with every rise, cascading over boulders and stones, its roar dominating the landscape. By mid-afternoon he had reached its source, wilder and more fierce than when he and Martin had last seen it. He sat beside it and dangled his feet in the water, regretting that he had to move on and away. The stream had been his friend, it had given him food and water, it had saved his life.

In the late afternoon the tree-line stopped abruptly as though drawn with a ruler and he emerged onto soft springy turf on the green summit of a chalk escarpment studded with thorn trees, shrubs and gorse. On either side hills rose in long undulations, some wooded, others bare. Birds of prey, harriers and hawks wheeled overhead. Tired but triumphant, he surveyed a broad valley stretching into the distance, blue hills rising at its furthest edge. Of human habitation there was no sign. He was alone, the only person in this lush countryside.

Joe climbed down the cliff, using sparse bushes and stunted trees as footholds on the steep incline. A grassy plateau a little lower down, a sapling beech growing at its edge, offered an opportunity for pause. He rested, lost in contemplation of the luminous perspectives below. Here, safe from predators, he would stop for the night and press on in the morning.

The plateau was damp from a thin ribbon of water trickling out of the rock. He put his face to it and drank thirstily and, stripped bare, showered with a sense, if not of happiness, at least of satisfaction and relief. Behind the waterfall a narrow fissure opened in the rock. He moved closer and, on hands and knees, crawled through. Inside was dark but as his eyes adjusted he saw that it concealed a bigger cave, high enough to stand in, spacious enough to allow movement. Some daylight filtered in. It offered perfect shelter from wild animals, from humans that might be lurking and from the elements. Here he would stay until, until… he knew not what.

He laid the sack and his meagre possessions carefully inside the cave and climbed to the top with the net, seeking food. A patch of bilberries yielded a sparse meal but the rabbits that hopped carelessly around him offered better fare. His net, patience and ingenuity should keep him in meat for an almost indefinite period. He climbed down again, gathered dry twigs in the fading light from beneath the beech and, under the narrow overhang of rock, lit a fire. This he resolved to keep alight. That night he slept inside the cave while it kept guard.

Early next morning he was back on the escarpment, gathering wood. He cut bracken for his bed and set out to stalk rabbits in the clear morning light. Unused to the ways of humans they offered little resistance. Guiltily, he caught a small one, killed it and took it to his fire. Skinning it was messy and difficult and made him retch but he was learning the ways of the wild world. He dug up stones, laid them round the fire and cooked his prey. Essentials were now provided for. He had water, food and shelter, he had eluded his pursuers and he had unexpected company. Its morning song revealed a thrush nesting in the beech. Sometimes Joe sang back. He took to talking to himself aloud, or to the thrush, the tree, the grass.

Days passed in a timeless progression of hunting, gathering firewood, cooking and making his eyrie habitable. This, to his surprise, he found satisfying, imagining himself as a latter-day Robinson Crusoe. Wild housekeeping, he called it and wondered what his mother would say if she could see him cleaning his cave, shaking his bracken bedding.

Sometimes he ventured further afield in ever growing concentric circles, exploring the terrain above the cave, familiarising himself with its teeming wildlife, trekking on one occasion as far back as the source of the stream. He felt exposed without the cave's protection and hurried back. He spent many hours in which he did nothing but contemplate the shimmering land below while he tried to grasp the reality of what had happened. His attempts to find an explanation were futile. His situation was not explicable. He gave up trying.

One morning he woke to find that all his energy, all his elation, had drained away. He could not rise from his bracken bed, his limbs too heavy to move, his head throbbing with a dull, steady rhythm. Perhaps he was ill and was going to die in this lonely place. Would someone one day find his skeleton and wonder who he was? He contemplated the possibility without alarm. Suffocated by the immensity of his loneliness he could find no reason for the daily struggle to survive and marvelled at how energetically he had been labouring. What was it for?

He struggled onto his platform for a drink and to relieve himself - he had dug a loo up above under some trees but was too weary to climb to it - and noted vaguely that the landscape had lost its wild beauty. Its colours were washed away, the sky, the trees, the grass, reduced to a uniform grey. Joe crept back into the cave and closed his eyes.

He lay, half awake, half asleep for days without number, ate no food and now and then roused himself to drink. The fire went out while he stayed motionless, oblivious to his surroundings, absorbed by recollections from his past life replaying in a continuous, vivid loop with himself not as protagonist but as observer of friends past and present, now lost to him, of his mother. He thought about their relationship, conducted since his father left, in a pool of unspoken emotion. Unable to admit to their mutual feelings of loss and rejection, they took refuge in a sang-froid in which neither believed. He recalled with profound regret the rare occasions on which his mother had tried to break through the barrier he had erected and he had turned away, rudely rejecting her advances. The isolation that had been his choice was now his prison.

Above all, he thought about his father, a tall, comforting and exciting presence that had suddenly vanished, for whom he had felt at times a burning hatred, at others sorrow and love. His image, with the lengthening passage of time, had assumed heroic proportions. He would probably never see him again. Perhaps he would never see anyone again, not his mother, not his friends, not his home. Perhaps his life was at an end. Astonishingly, he did not care.

*

Susie is accustomed to her home imprisonment and she has learned to escape it by dreaming. She dreams of being out in the open, in the light, under the sky, the sun warming her skin. She imagines she is a bird flying over the land, away from this vile existence to a place where she will always be free, where there will be no evil men stalking her and her parents. She is frequently so absorbed in her wish-fulfilment that time passes without her noticing. It is a rude awakening to return to her real circumstances. But the mind is not easily imprisoned. They cannot put her imagination in chains.

*

A small white snail, leaving a sticky trail, climbed laboriously up a long stem of grass growing immediately outside Joe's cave. He watched it obsessively, measuring its slow but steady progress. It took all day to reach its pinnacle and, having finally arrived, remained motionless. There was no discernible purpose to its laboured journey. Had it attained a goal invisible to Joe? It appeared satisfied with its minuscule universe, unaware of the giant eye observing it. So many universes for so many creatures. Was there a giant eye watching him? And if there was, was its owner responsible for his plight, was there some joker up there, laughing his head off? The thought made Joe angry and for the first time for days he sat up but the world spun round, for he still had eaten no food. He quickly lay down again and returned to contemplating the snail which, he now noticed, had several companions on the ground. Lucky old snail, he thought.

If this tiny mollusc could expend its energy and strength on the modest ambition of ascending the stem could not he, with his infinitely superior strength, rouse himself? He debated this coldly as though the problem were not his. It depended on how he evaluated his life, whether he considered he was worth the trouble or whether anyone, apart from his mother, cared. Did God, that mythical Being, love him or the apocryphal sparrow that lay dying in the street; did He care for the snail or was it acting of its own volition, for its own secret purpose? And what of the rest of the teeming life around him, the untold number of insects that scraped and burrowed under him every day, the worms that worked the soil, the thrush on the beech, what life force kept them going, what allowed them sufficient joy in their own existence? If a clue to these metaphysical problems existed he could not fathom it. He fell asleep.

But the next morning, with the first rays of the sun hitting the cave, with his thrush in full song, with larks rising, and kites and hawks planing the air currents in search of prey, the first stirrings of a sense of self returned. Joe crawled out of his cave and, holding onto the tree for support, stood at the edge of his promontory, a lone figure between sky and earth but no longer a lonely one. The world, which so short a time ago had been a place of desolation and despair looked new, pristine, washed clean. He felt its beauty and it pierced his heart. He had almost, with careless abandon, thrown it away. He thanked whoever was out there for this translucent morning, for the glorious revelation that life had to be cherished. It was all he had, and it was enough.

He did not, in the days that followed, go far afield but clambered up and down the cliff face, studying the tiny flowers growing out of its clefts. He admired their air of independence, a quiet assurance of their place in the abundant universe, vaunting an infinite variety of colour and form, some yellow thistle-like flowers, others pale blue miniscule snapdragons. Leaves in different shades of green grew everywhere; one long plant with seven thin sacks at each head sprouted red spiky

45

flowers, reminding Joe of the structure of a virus illustrated in his science book. Ivy luxuriated where it could find a foothold and even where it could not, some dark green with six starred leaves, others a lighter shade, and over all the fresh, faint smell of mint and thyme.

He contemplated the shadowy valley below and in his imagination created a river flowing gently towards the ocean, a wide, light-reflecting shimmer, edged with reeds. He imagined plunging into its clear depths, he invested it with magic properties, with healing waters that would sweep away the stark images of his flight, he pictured beyond its far bank another land in which the privations and loneliness of the present would be banished. The mythical river offered a vision of Elysium, it promised salvation and hope.

He was not ready for the journey to reach it, did not yet feel the need to prove that it existed, that it was real. Through some deep connection with a mythological past of which he was unaware, Joe felt he must prepare for baptism in the river, to subject himself to a purification rite before approaching it. Unable to guess what this might be he waited, sensing that it would announce itself. It was enough that, for the time being, the river of his dreams flowed in his mind's eye.

He stayed, and time ceased to have meaning, days passing without end, not in neat bundles containing allocated tasks punctuated by clocks, watches and bells. Here, in this cave, in this country time, like a Moebius strip, had neither a beginning nor an end, its passing relating not to an almighty clock but to his own perception. It was unquantifiable; there was night and there was day and there were moments of enchantment between the earth awakening and settling into sleep. Twilight and dawn. These were the only time keepers. He discarded his watch, a recent birthday present from his mother, placing it with the meagre reminders of home in the far recesses of the cave. Its best feature, a programme that recorded past, present and future for forty years - he would be fifty-seven when it ran out - had become irrelevant.

It rained all one day. Joe moved the fire under his roof and watched swathes of water cascading past him into the valley. The cave, though smoky, was warm and dry. In the evening the clouds lifted and the mist rose from the ground in tattered wisps, the refreshed land reflecting a sky striped green, violet and red. The invigorating smell of renewal went to his head like champagne and as he lifted his arms in a spontaneous benison a tremor started in his spine and an electric current sped through his body, leaving him trembling; but elated. Tears pricked his eyes. He wiped them away impatiently. He could not afford to weep.

One restless night an image from his childhood returned: a pile of hollow picture bricks, like a set of Russian dolls, one filling the other. But unlike the dolls they could be built into a tower, the biggest brick at the base, the smallest at the top. He had been building inwards. He must build upwards or else disappear. It was time to start on his quest to the beckoning river.

The next morning he woke before dawn and, purified by a cascade of water, dressed in his now ragged clothes. It would be the last journey for his trainers. They had done well by him.

The cliff was steep and difficult to negotiate, slippery with dew. The sun rose. Swallows circled, serkins and blackbirds, bullfinches and yellow hammers, the whole host of creation was awake on this translucent day. Looking up from the valley floor he could barely make out his tattered T shirt, placed as a marker on the longest branch of the beech. He built a cairn of stones at the point of his descent and forayed into the prickly bushes, trees and saplings, that formed a barrier between him and the river of his fantasies. Using his penknife, now sadly reduced, he hacked a way forward, stopping only at midday for some morsels of dried rabbit meat he had brought with him. He had no water and his river, if it existed, was too far to reach on this first day. In the evening he trekked back and scrambled to his eyrie, exhausted but triumphant. The journey had begun.

He returned the next day and the next, cutting an extending path. He stopped the first night in a small clearing and lit a fire. He felt exposed but not overcome; indeed, nothing disturbed him except passing deer, wildlife rustling in the undergrowth, midgets and mosquitoes descending on his skin. Did they presage water? This he fervently believed and he pressed forward next morning with the first sunlight.

It was not until the second day of his journey that the river of his longings lay before him, neither a mirage nor a figment of his imagination. It existed, it was real, surpassing in its tranquil beauty. It seemed to an exultant Joe that he had waited an eternity for this moment, that this God given expanse of water would, like the Red Sea, part before him. He ran forward, ready for a baptismal plunge into its waters.

Far to his left came a piercing cry. Joe stopped his headlong flight and turned. Nothing moved. It came again, then faded. All his elation gone, Joe waited, vulnerable in the lone landscape.

But when he dived in, the water washed away all fear. A flock of widgeon took off into the air, whistling loudly. Red breasted geese, shelducks and mallards scattered, disturbed by this strange creature. On the bank, two black cormorants hung out their wings to dry in sun and breeze. Diving, floating on his back, looking into the sky and at the soft outlines of the hills on either side, Joe twisted and turned in the clear water, splashed arms and legs, followed small schools of fish swimming with the flow. Finally exhausted, he waded to the bank. Bulrushes and reeds flourished and to his surprise, tall all embracing willows trailed their fronds in the water, giving the wilderness the ordered look of a suburban riverside garden.

The river was wide, far wider than in his dreams and the current ran strong. On its further bank the land stretched flat and overgrown to the foot of the next hills. It would take several days to reach them once he had swum across.

He returned to the cave in time to find shelter from a thunderstorm. The sky turned black and banks of dark cloud rolled across the heavens, lightning flashed and wind-swept rain invaded the cave, pushing Joe into its innermost recesses. By evening it had cleared but the next day the temperature dropped. Joe waited for the hot, sunny days that had distinguished the summer but they did not return. Morning and evening he caught the sharp chill of the coming autumn.

It was time to leave and to consider how to survive the winter. He had only his Gap jumper with which to ward off colder weather. At least he had rabbit skins. The rabbits had grown wary of him and were increasingly difficult to catch. Joe had abandoned the net and devised a sling, using gut as string. With practice he was able to hit and stun prey from several yards away. Now he calculated how many skins he needed to make a jerkin and a pair of shoes. He caught eight rabbits with difficulty over a period of two days, hung the meat and spread the skins to dry.

Travelling constantly to the river he managed to cut the journey down to one night's stay either way. He built a permanent bivouac, strengthened his swimming and explored the river's banks. He saw a herd of cattle come down to the water, dun coloured, long-haired. The bull looked fierce. Joe kept out of its way. He saw reindeer coming to drink, he watched kingfishers skimming the water, their brilliant blue flashing in the sun, he came to know the profusion of wild life, otters, beavers, water rats, that made the riverside its home.

Then one day, clearly imprinted on the sand, he saw footsteps.

Joe hurled himself into a bed of nearby reeds. A female teal, disturbed from its nest, scuttled away with a cry. He inwardly cursed it and himself for carelessness for it would give away his position. Joe crouched, immobile, ears strained to catch the slightest sound. Nothing stirred, only the insects humming in the still air. He parted the reeds and, heart beating, crawled out.

'Hello,' he called.

There was no reply.

He moved forward cautiously, scanning the branches of trees, moving stealthily behind bushes, stalking an unknown prey in the long grass. He inspected the footprints once more. There were six leading inland. Joe placed his own foot in one. It was bigger than his own. The adversary, if such he was, might be formidable.

His pile of clothes, his sling and a bunch of reeds he had cut to use as ropes were untouched, exactly as he had left them. Dressing quickly he made for home, arriving next day on the plateau after dark. He approached the entrance to his cave cautiously. The fire was untouched, its embers glowing consolingly inside the circle of stones. His treasures at the back of the cave, when he later examined them, were intact.

*

Helmuth is holding a meeting round the refectory table in the Meeting Room. He is listening to a citizen, standing deferentially before him. The man is gesticulating wildly and saying something that he thinks important. He waits to be thanked or rewarded but Helmuth is impassive and dismisses the man with a nod. Though he has left them little alternative he is tired of these people ingratiating themselves, tired of the stupidity with which he is surrounded, tired of the necessity of constant plotting. He almost wishes there was someone to challenge him, someone strong and clever. He forgets that he has conveniently eliminated anyone who posed the slightest threat; and many who did not.

Three men are brought in. They are in uniform, black tunic, black trousers, a knitted hat concealing all but their eyes and mouth. They receive orders and leave.

Helmuth rises and goes. The gaggle of grey men waits respectfully and then disperses. The Meeting Room is left in shadowed depth.

The three men move swiftly through the night-still town. They tread softly. They go first into the park and stand behind the trunks of the same trees that recently protected Joe. They too are watching Susie skipping. As her parents wind up the rope and move towards Jarvis Road they follow on silent feet.

The neighbour is keeping watch. He sees Susie and her mother and father walk unawares up Rose Avenue. He sees the men following, he sees them pounce on the family who struggle helplessly against their attackers, he sees them being marched away. The curtain falls and he gives what one may think a little sigh of satisfaction, or perhaps it is something else.

*

Joe slept uneasily. He was no longer alone. Other people, probably hostile, lived in the wilderness. He no longer felt safe on his cliff.

The next morning dawned clear but white cumulus was gathering. He spent the day making a jacket from his rabbit skins. Sharpening his knife on a flint he cut out several pieces, three for the back of a jerkin, two each for left and right fronts. It was hard and difficult

52

work and he was left with uneven, unwieldy sections of hide. Cobbling them together took all day. He shaped armholes and pulled clumsy strips of hide through holes that tore, but he finally had something that resembled a garment. And it was warm. He made rough shoes but knew they would not last. Something tougher was needed, the skins of goat or reindeer, and that necessitated returning to the river and killing one from the herds he had seen. It also meant returning to the threatening presence of another human who, Joe almost hoped, would show himself, even if only to attack. He would at least know his adversary.

A thin drizzle turned by midday into windswept rain. He spent most of the day by the fire, climbing upward only to fetch wood that was too damp to burn. He stacked it in the cave.

The sky cleared next morning and he set out at dawn to bag a deer with sling and stone, a tricky operation without certainty of success. He slept warily in his bivouac, ready to spring up at any moment and defend himself. No one came. He reached the river before midday. The footsteps in the sand had gone.

Diving into the water, he swam far out into the current, turned and looked back. Both banks seemed alarmingly far away but, fitter than he had ever been, he knew that he was ready to reach the far side. He floated and let the current carry him, then struck sideways. By the time he hit ground he was a good mile distant from his clothes and sling and walked back, cold in the now constant wind. He dressed and turned into hitherto unknown territory. Coming to a steep incline beyond a group of birch, he climbed to the top and scanned the area ahead. In the distance, close to where the hills turned sharply inland, a reindeer herd grazed. Getting close enough for a shot meant going further than he had ever been for they were at least an hour distant. Joe trudged on, hoping that with the wind blowing in his face the animals would not pick up his scent.

He came on them suddenly, on the other side of a copse and approached silently, sling and stone at the ready. One shot would make or mar the hunt for, once disturbed, the deer would be away. He concealed himself behind a bush and fixed his target, a small doe, grazing immediately outside the herd. Somewhere to his left the grass rustled. A wild animal. He hoped it would not disturb his prey. Discarding his unwieldy rabbit shoes he advanced slowly. The doe's belly was white, a delicate brown darkening towards her neck and to her dappled back. Her ears, relaxed, flopped sideways.

Joe took aim. The heavy stone, sent with force, hit her on the head and she fell, stunned. The herd, alarmed, flew away and, as the doe struggled to stand, Joe ran to her, pushed her down and, ignoring the appeal in her eyes, beat her again and again with a heavy stone until her legs ceased to twitch and her head lay open, scattering blood and brains on his arms.

'Well done.'

Joe stood up, electrified, blood spattered, clothes torn, the doe bleeding between his legs. A tall young man with light brown hair, dark eyes, freckled face and a short gingery beard stood before him.

'It's my first one.'

Joe wiped his bloody hands on the grass.

'What did you want to do with her?'

'I need the hide.'

'We'd better take her back before you skin her,' the young man said. Joe looked at him, uncomprehending. Take her back?

'Who are you?' he asked 'Randolph. And you?'

'My name is Joe. Joe Harding.' 'I'll carry it.'

Randolph slung the carcass over his left shoulder and started towards the hills, not doubting Joe would follow.

'You can't take her, she's mine!' He could feel his anger rising. 'I need her here.'

Randolph stopped. 'You're coming, aren't you?'

'Where to?'

'Back to the Manor, of course. Surely you're joining us?'

Joining them?

'Who?'

'We're a group living together.'

'How many of you?'

'Five, including me. You'll make the sixth.'

Who the hell was this stranger? Joe resented his confident manner and the assumption that he would meekly follow. He teetered between a nuclear response and total compliance but came down on the side of the latter. Randolph did not seem overtly aggressive and the prospect of human company was tempting. He doubted in any case that he had any choice. If he refused the man might attack him and there might be more, hiding in the bushes.

'How far is it?'

'Far,' Randolph said shortly.

'I've got my fire to attend to.'

'You'd do better to let it go out. It can be seen for miles.'

'I've kept it low.'

'Not low enough. Come on,' Randolph said, 'it's getting late.'

He started towards the far hills. Joe followed reluctantly, stepping carefully in bare feet.

'No shoes, boots?'

Joe looked enviously at Randolph's skillfully crafted leather boots. He was well if roughly dressed, a woven tunic falling over a pair of knee length trousers.

'They're back there. They're not very…'

'You'd better get them.'

Randolph watched him coolly.

'You'll need better ones than that.'

Joe bridled.

'They're good enough.'

But they weren't and he was embarrassed as they walked on and he had constantly to adjust them on the rough terrain, flat but overgrown. They stopped only once to drink water from Randolph's leather bottle and then moved on at a fast pace.

'How long since you escaped?'

The question immediately made Joe suspicious. How did Randolph know that Joe had been hunted and had escaped? Was he part of a plot, luring him to his death?

'I'm not sure.'

He was not prepared to give away information that might later be used against him.

He regretted nevertheless that he had failed to keep a count of the days, he felt defeated at abandoning his long-planned journey across the river and he regretted leaving the cave and all that it had meant.

Chapter Four

—

THEY emerged from the tree line as the sun was setting. Wooded hills rose on their left towards the far end of a semicircle, forming a bow shaped valley. Here Joe expected Randolph to turn further inland but he kept parallel to the river, across sporadic marsh, its vivid greens contrasting grotesquely with the more muted colours of a long dry summer. They regained the wooded hills by nightfall and stopped. Randolph pulled a hunk of bread and a piece of white cheese out of a leather bag carried over his shoulder, gave them to Joe with a drink of water and ordered curtly,

'Wait here.'

He was soon out of sight.

Joe felt exposed and alone. He fell asleep and in his sleep the chase at Bantage re-enacted itself with all the vividness of the reality. He woke abruptly, shaking with terror, astonished that he had allowed himself to be led into unknown territory to join a group of people unheard of and unknown. He had always despised his craven tendency to fall in line with the herd, to conform to political correctness in the way he looked, dressed and behaved. It was never what he had wanted. An image of himself far removed from what he appeared to be had always hovered uncertainly in his mind but even now, in the bizarre situation that had become his life, he had been unable to stand firm. He was now in an impossible, a probably dangerous situation. Worst of all, he had been forced to abandon his meagre possessions, the only tokens from his erstwhile home. Home… The word had acquired a different meaning. Home now meant the cave, the cliff, the river. He had left home twice this summer and could no longer define the base to which he belonged. He had become a stranger in a strange land.

And a fool. What proof had he that Randolph was not an emissary of the townspeople, sent to succeed where the nets had failed? At this moment he could be getting reinforcements while he, Joe, like a tethered animal, waited to be captured and taken away. He sprang up, ready to retrace his steps, but flight was hopeless. He was exhausted, his shoes had disintegrated and his feet, bruised and scratched, would carry him no further. It was impossible, in any case, to hide in the dark in unknown territory from people who knew every inch of the ground and would have no difficulty in following him, no matter where he went. Could he reach the river and swim across, as he had so long planned to do? He was too tired, too confused, and no longer certain that he cared; he half hoped that a pack of wolves would come out of the trees and tear him to pieces, relieving him of the necessity, unbelievably tedious and irksome, to survive.

As though on cue a twig snapped with a sound like gunshot. Joe leapt to his feet and felt for sling and stone. Someone was closing in on him. He pulled the stone back, ready to release it. A shadowy shape emerged from the bushes and stopped, a long snout sniffed the air, slit eyes from a face covered with long bristly hair stared at him. Wild boar. It had no interest in Joe and ambled on. Joe collapsed in a heap of unnatural laughter.

The stars came out, brilliant in the clear air, and a half moon rose on the horizon. He felt numb, unable to think or reason. Nothing made sense, he did not make sense. He wondered if he was he insane, a schizo inhabiting a world that did not exist. He sank into the ground as though wanting to bury himself.

Footsteps crashed through the trees and roused him. Randolph appeared and with him a younger boy, shorter, slighter, pale, clean shaven with a mop of black wavy hair and, his most distinguishing feature, black penetrating eyes.

'This is Otto,' Randolph said.

Otto examined Joe carefully, scrutinising him for an uncomfortably long period. Then he gave a nod. Randolph produced a pair of serviceable leather boots and these Joe put on. They proceeded, single file, Joe in the middle, through the wood. Stark images filled his mind, reminders of bygone days at the cinema with just such a trio, the middle man's hands tied behind his back, the lining up, the shout of 'Fire', the body lifeless on the ground. Was this his fate?

They walked uphill for some two hours. It seemed to Joe like ten. The way continued thickly wooded. Eventually the trees thinned.

'We're here.'

The moon was high now. Stars swirled overhead. Joe wondered yet again at how much larger and brighter they were than at home, shedding an unnatural brilliance over the landscape.

They cleared the wood and came at last to a large, rambling house. No light showed. He was ushered through a wooden door, down a dark stone flagged corridor and into a kitchen lit by a flickering lamp casting shadows into far corners. Three people sitting round a table turned expectantly towards him.

One boy, two girls. They shook hands as though he had returned from a victorious exploit.

'You're hungry.'

He nodded and stood awkwardly while food was brought to the table, cold meat on a thick wooden platter, a cooked root vegetable akin to a potato but with more flavour, small yellow tomatoes, spiked green leaves. Into an earthenware mug someone poured milk. Joe emptied it in one draught and, despite ten pairs of eyes watching him, wolfed down the first real meal he had eaten for countless weeks. He felt he ought to say something, make the equivalent of polite conversation, but nothing came to mind; and the young people round the table made no contribution. An uneasy silence reigned and he was relieved when Randolph lit a second lamp and led him out of the kitchen and down a corridor. His stomach full, exhausted from his day, Joe could barely walk but swayed from side to side as he stumbled up countless flights of stairs, through echoing rooms and collapsed somewhere on a bed.

*

Susie is alone in a cell. It is small. It has no window but she is used to small windowless spaces. The cell has a straw mattress on the floor. It has a bucket. That is all.

She does not know where her parents are, there is no one to let her out and no one to take her skipping. She is a prisoner. She misses Susie Two, her charcoal and parchment. She sits on the mattress and imagines all that she would write.

From time to time water and food, thin soups and soggy potatoes are brought in by a female guard. She is large and impassive, her eyes dead, registering nothing. The first time Susie speaks to her her face is slapped. She does not try it again. Susie wonders how long she is going to be kept a prisoner.

Susie expects, after the first day, that her slop bucket will be emptied. But it is not. The smell is intolerable. Susie bangs long and loud on the door but no one takes notice. The bucket is emptied only after several days. She tries to be brave but finally she lies on the mattress and cries. It is all more than she can bear.

*

Joe woke to the unaccustomed luxury of a bed, a pillow, a light duvet. He thought he was back in his room at Bantage and need only wait for Mum to call before he was up and off to school. He drowsed lazily and thought about the coming day. What lessons had he got? What had happened the day before? He could not remember and eventually opened his eyes to the bare timbers of a sloping roof. Memory came flooding back and with it grief and longing. His former life, which had been near enough to touch, had once again slipped into the past.

The room he was in was bare, the only furniture a bed, a table, a chair. A window looked out on a roughly cut stretch of grass, a green bank, and above it a wood dominated by silver birch shimmering in the rays of the early sun. He put on his jeans, reduced to shreds, T shirt and hoody but did not cover his head. It seemed inappropriate. He opened the bedroom door which led onto a narrow, wood panelled corridor. There was no sound to guide him and he wandered through the rambling house which once must have housed a large family but now echoed to silence. He happened on a flight of narrow stairs and a small landing that swept, grander and larger, into a hall. This Joe descended and continued through a door to the left, down a corridor and, following the mouth watering smell of freshly baked bread, into the sunlit kitchen that faced the same grassy area as the room in which he had slept. It was large, dominated by the long refectory table at which he had eaten his meal the previous night. Heavy chairs ranged round it were elaborately carved, not unlike those he had seen rotting in the waste ground, though of superior craftsmanship. This Joe admired. It was, as far as he could see, the only concession to luxury. The rest of the kitchen was functional, bare brick walls mellow with the patina of past years, a wood burning stove, above it a bread oven. On the inside wall a generous fire burned below a spit. Shelving round the walls was laden with heavy earthenware pots. It reminded him of the ancient kitchens of country houses he had visited. He wondered if he was in a time warp.

Only Otto was there, of the others he had met last night there was no sign.

'Food?'

'Yes please.'

Milk, fresh bread.

Otto seemed the kind of boy they would label studious at school, bad at games, perhaps inclined to be bullied though he did not have the air of a victim. Joe made several attempts to draw him into conversation but Otto had a shut in quality that made open questioning embarrassing.

Breakfast finished Joe took the earthenware mug and plate he had used to a deep white sink by the window and rinsed them in a bowl of water. Otto watched and nodded, then led him outside into a small area scented by thyme. The kitchen garden. To their left, a tall trimmed beech hedge surrounded a spacious formal garden, landscaped into five triangular flowerbeds, their apex pointing towards a well which was protected by a convex wooden roof.

'Haul up some water and bring it to the house.'

The tone was commanding. Joe turned the wooden handle, getting a firm grip on an elaborately carved face. A full bucket rose to the top, the water cool and clear. He carried it into a scullery opposite the kitchen. This had a brick floor and brick pillars supporting a stone slab on which rested two basins. Here he was left to strip and wash with a bar of gritty soap but before he could put on his clothes Otto brought a new set, a woven light brown tunic like his own, a darker pair of trousers, a leather belt, thonged sandals and a used pair of boots. This seemed to be the uniform they all wore. Otto picked up the Gap jumper and Joe's Marks and

Spencer pants, whose resistance to wearing out was absolute, and examined them curiously.

'Do you want to keep these?'

'Yes.'

'You can't wear that hood here.'

'Why not?'

Otto looked at him with contempt.

They returned to the kitchen.

'Where are the others?'

'They will be back by nightfall.'

As an answer it was inadequate. Then, dismissively,

'You can have today free.'

Free from what? Joe hovered but Otto turned his back. Joe left the kitchen and found his way back to his room. He hid his hoody under the mattress and wondered what to do. He felt aimless and disoriented and, for lack of any other activity, decided to explore the house.

On the landing below two heavy oak doors either side led to rooms facing the front. He pushed one open. He was in a large, rectangular room. Heavily boarded windows let in a modicum of light, enough for him to proceed and see that it contained no furniture, hangings or rugs. A door at the far end led into a second, larger room. Here too the windows were boarded, not even the faint daylight from the landing filtering in. The layout was the same, a long inner wall on his left, windows from floor to ceiling on his right and a door corresponding to the one he had entered. One room led into the other, corridor fashion. He went into the third room. This was the most spectacular, dominated by a

65

huge mantelpiece over an open fireplace. He groped his way towards it, attracted by elaborate carvings of an extraordinary intricacy, even luminosity, for what had first drawn his eye towards them were pinpoint reflections of the sparse light. He ran his hands over the polished wood, felt the round heads and elongated bodies of carved animals, sharp pointed ears with intricate veining on the inside, the spiky leaves of ilex, circling one into the other in infinite complexity. He longed to tear the boards from the windows so he could feast his eyes on such remarkable workmanship. Instead, he touched it all over like a blind man, felt the shapes and sensed its life.

Other rooms had similar carvings but none as magnificent. All were boarded and empty.

It was eerie, alone in the semi-dark in the huge mansion.

A corridor running left and forming the corner of the house revealed a wing. Four doors corresponded to four unshuttered windows overlooking a yard. Joe opened one door. A wild young man looked at him in surprise. Joe muttered excuses and slammed out. Who could that have been? Randolph had said there were only five inhabitants, with him making the sixth. And he had seen them all. None looked like this boy. Yet there was something familiar about him, something that made Joe open the door again. The boy stared back. Joe moved further in. The boy moved too. With a galvanising shock Joe recognised himself reflected in a long mirror. He was tall, much taller than when he had last seen himself. The schoolboy had metamorphosed into a young man, tough, rough, hair jagged where he had tried to cut it, falling below his shoulders. He was thinner. Stubble covered his chin. The new clothes, the tunic hanging gracefully to his thighs, were not displeasing. He lingered, absorbing his new image.

That he was in someone's bedroom he now noticed. Two beds stood in the corners, two chairs beside them, a small table and colourful, handmade rugs on the floor. He hastily withdrew and descending a narrow, winding staircase, found himself back in the kitchen.

Otto was still there.

'Where do you come from?' he asked, not turning towards him.

Joe was shocked by the unexpectedness of the question. He hesitated.

'I have been living in a cave,' he said.

An inadequate reply but it was all he was prepared to give away. He did not trust these people.

'And you, where do you come from? Who are you?'

Otto ignored the questions as though they had not been uttered and Joe felt too intimidated to repeat them. He turned away, uncertain where to go or what to do. He wandered outside and sat on a tree stump facing the house whose worn red bricks glowed through lush creepers. It was even larger than he had surmised the night before. He counted eight shuttered windows on the first floor, another eight on the second, one of them the room he had slept in. They were bisected in the middle by four long, narrow windows reaching from top to bottom. These were clearly over the stairwell. Elaborately built brick chimneys adorned the roof. No belfries, he noted with relief. Two wings extended at right angles either side, symmetrically facing one

67

another. More windows, more shuttered rooms. He found at the back a set of crumbling stables, doors swinging loosely.

Joe had had little truck with horses. His grandparents had given him riding lessons when he was eleven as a birthday present but he had enjoyed neither the riding nor the associated equine myths and conventions. The people who looked after horses seemed like a different species. He preferred football and footballers. But now, faced with empty stalls, he felt the absence of a horsy presence. Stray bits of straw and hay lodged in corners, scattered grains of corn, the pommel of a disintegrating saddle upended on the cobbles, a stirrup rusted with age, were the only mementoes of the life there had once been. All that remained was silence and hollow emptiness. It filled him with desolation and despair. He sank into a corner and wept, mourning his past and fearful of the future marching inexorably into the present.

Lonely though it had been, he regretted leaving the life he had carved out for himself on the cliff and contemplated his new situation with growing resentment. He had no wish to stay with these people who were off-hand, unwelcoming and rude, insensitive to his plight. He made a half-hearted attempt to return to the river but failed to find his way through the thick woods. It was useless, all useless.

He returned to the kitchen as the light was failing. Otto and Randolph were preoccupied, attending to an iron cauldron bubbling on the stove and a hunk of meat roasting on the spit.

'That's your deer.'

Randolph pointed towards it and threw more vegetables into the pot. A wave of nausea overcame Joe and he bent down to hide it, swallowing the vomit that had risen, sickly and sweet, into his throat. He felt embarrassed by his squeamishness, accustomed as he had now become to killing, skinning, cooking and eating animals, his only companions in the wild nature he had inhabited. But there had been a plea in the deer's eyes as he bashed its brains out that haunted him. He would have preferred never to eat meat again but knew this was impractical. God, or whoever was in charge, had willed that living things preyed on one another. Divine distribution. He remembered with nostalgia the neatly packed lines of supermarket meat that concealed their association with the animals from which it had been cut.

'You don't have to eat it, if you don't want to.'

Joe looked at Otto in surprise. How did he know? The other boy came in, relieving Joe of the necessity of replying.

'I've hung the rest.'

Meredith was short, stocky and tough. He had a ruddy complexion, clear blue eyes and reddish hair; his hands were horny and calloused. Like Randolph, he sported a short beard, the same colour as his hair. He looked like a Viking.

'I'll help the girls finish.'

He spoke with the same soft burr as they all did, lengthening the vowels and lingering on last consonants.

Joe felt ill at ease. Towards dusk the two girls came in and everyone sat round the table. The one beside him, Belinda, was extraordinarily pretty with pale blue hooded eyes, fair hair that curled gently, a face like a doll's and a smile that showed her gums. This might have been ugly. In her it was an attribute. Perhaps here was somebody he could talk to. He tried a few opening gambits and she was affable enough; but not forthcoming.

The meal over, he offered to help clear up. This was refused.

'You start work tomorrow.'

Belinda left the room and he followed her into the scullery. She was putting on warm, outside clothes.

'Where are you going?' he asked

She looked at him in astonishment.

'On guard duty of course. It's my turn.'

'Guard against whom?'

'Don't pretend you don't know.'

She turned away. Joe, rebuffed, went back to the kitchen. Otto was again on his own and Joe could think of nothing to say to him. After an awkward pause he made his way in the dark until he found his room and, more puzzled and bewildered than before, watched the moon rise behind the hills.

The other girl, Kathryn, fetched him at sunrise.

'I'm to show you the farm.'

She took him, in the early light, past the house. He paused by the carved front door.

'It's beautiful.'

She waited impassively and made no comment.

Her loosely bound fair hair swung on her back as she went ahead. 'What one would call well built,' he thought. Her face was round, high cheekboned but well covered and too fleshy for his taste. She had blue green eyes and a repellant air of self-sufficiency. He wished it were Belinda showing him round. She was closer to his vague, undefined model of femininity.

Had she been on guard duty all night?

They turned right down an incline. A fast-flowing stream running into lower pastures, where cows and oxen grazed, fed a mill race below a water mill, smaller and squatter than others Joe had seen. Its sails were furled. Kathryn continued downhill, Joe following, to a network of barns and sheds, old but well maintained.

Four dun coloured calves inside a palisade set up indignant, high pitched bellows. Kathryn patted their outstretched noses but walked on under a wooden arch into a cobbled yard. She fetched a bucket and three legged stool from a dairy and motioned Joe to follow.

'You have to get the cows.'

Trembling with uncertainty, unwilling to make a fool of himself in front of this commanding girl, Joe boldly opened the field gate. The cows, thick set and shaggy with horns curving upward in a generous sweep, Joe noted that they were the same variety as those he had seen by the river, walked sedately to a paddock where Kathryn was shaking feed into wooden mangers.

'You're to milk them,' she said.

Joe had been taken round enough farms to know the routine, but only with the use of machines. As far as he knew no one ever milked by hand, his only model for this extraordinary activity being from an illustration in a childhood book nursery rhymes. It was not the ideal model. He walked tentatively to one cow, seized the stool and set it down, well distanced from her back legs, the bucket balanced precariously between his knees, his head well away. The cow swished her tail across his face. Kathryn watched him sardonically and he felt himself flush as he tried pulling at the two teats facing him, with no effect.

'Don't you know how?'

No, he bloody well didn't.

'Yes, of course I do!'

He gave them a hard, simultaneous pull. The cow stopped feeding, turned to look at him, and kicked her back leg into the bucket which fell to the ground. Kathryn picked it up, rinsed it in the stream and took the stool from him. She placed it close by the cow, murmured quietly, and rested her head intimately against the animal's flank. Joe, feeling inadequate, stood back and watched her expert movements.

'You do the back two first.'

She pulled at the teats with thumb and forefinger until a trickle of milk came out, then bunched her hands into closed fists, opening and closing them in a quick rhythmic motion. The milk spurted out, making a billowing foam. It smelled strong and sweet.

She handed him the bucket and he took her place, imitating her as best he could. He succeeded in extracting only a small trickle.

'Not like that.'

'You bloody well milk it then.'

He kicked the stool aside, threw the bucket down and stalked off.

'It's not an it, it's a she!' she called after him.

Joe went downhill with as much dignity as he could muster, past fields of upright stooks of corn marching in neat lines, over the stream spanned by a narrow bridge, and into the wood below the farm. He kicked a tree as hard as he could. This was a trick he had used to good effect at home, forcing his mother to give way on whatever issue was at stake, but he hurt his toes and with no one to impress it was a pointless exercise. He turned along the stream, wishing once again that he had refused to follow Randolph into this hornets' nest of imperious people who seemed to take it for granted that he would work for them like a slave. This, he now decided, he was not prepared to do, even if they housed and fed him. But what options were open to him? He was isolated in a country whose inhabitants, whether here or in Bantage, were hostile. More, those in Bantage actively wanted to kill him for reasons that were unfathomable. Where could he go? The cave high on the cliff, subject to wind, rain and snow, would be uninhabitable in the winter, prey would be difficult to catch and his fire impossible to keep alight. He could easily die of exposure. Nor could he rely on finding help elsewhere. The country, apart from Bantage and here, appeared to be uninhabited. He had no option other than to lie low and wait at least until the winter was over.

He reached a high knoll that gave him a view of the farm. On the other side of the stream lay a well tended park-like area, oak, ash, birch and willow growing singly over patches of long, waving grass. He assumed it was where they spent their time off. He had still to discover that this was a concept unknown to the community.

He returned reluctantly to the farm.

Kathryn greeted him nonchalantly.

Later, with an air of insufferable superiority, she showed him round, familiarising him with the routine of feeding, mucking out sheds, piling the manure onto a heap, sweeping the yard; countless jobs to which he would not have objected had he been left on his own.

Kathryn reminded him of the girls in his class he disliked most, contemptuous, superior and tough. He could feel the assurance he had gained over the lonely summer in danger of disintegrating under her scorn. At least she had no wish to talk to him. Her conversation and murmured endearments were reserved exclusively for the animals.

They penned the sheep.

'No dogs?' he ventured.

'And have them bark and give us away?'

'To whom?'

She looked at him coldly.

'Don't pretend you don't know.'

The same words as Belinda's. What did it mean? The townspeople? It seemed the most likely but they were far away, surely too far to be a threat. There must be other enemies. He resented the assumption that he pretended not to know something he knew.

'But I don't.'

Ignoring him as both Otto and Belinda had ignored him, she said,

'There are logs to be split.'

She gave him an axe and took him to a pile of branches and tree trunks.

'Once they're done you stack them up against the side of the house. There's a wheelbarrow over there.'

She paused,

'I suppose you know how to do it?'

He did not deign to reply.

This at least was a satisfying activity which avoided contact with Kathryn and allowed him to pursue his own unproductive thoughts; and there was satisfaction in sheer physical activity. By evening when he joined the others for a substantial meal, he was tired. Conversation was sparse. He escaped to his room as soon as it was over, there to brood on his fate. He was exhausted and angry at the loss of his independence. He slumped on the bed and eventually fell asleep.

'He isn't used to working,' Kathryn later told the others, 'but he's not an escaped dissident. Too fit. Can't imagine what he's been doing - or where he's come from.'

Otto was equally puzzled.

'I found some faded writing in his clothes.'

'How bizarre. What did it say?'

'Couldn't read it properly. All I could make out was that his pants had 'St. Michael' on a label tacked to the back, then a lot of stuff underneath, letters and numbers. That hooded jumper was really odd. GAP stitched in the front in huge letters, you saw it last night. A tag that had been cut in half on the inside, at the base of the hood, done perhaps to stop us reading it.'

'What does it all mean?'

'Impossible to know,' Otto said, 'but we'd better watch out.'

*

Susie has found a small stone in her cell. It has an edge sharp enough to make marks. She uses it as her charcoal and writes stories on the wall. They occupy much of her time and become more and more fantastic.

One day while she is writing she hears tapping through the wall. Someone is trying to communicate with her. She signals back. At first, the tappings appear to be random but after a while she discerns a pattern. The pattern perhaps forms words. She makes some up for each set of taps and replies. She does not know if she is making sense to the other person but it does not matter. She has human contact.

*

It was impossible to make contact. Joe was sharing his life with a group of young people whom he could see, hear, even touch but who had nothing to say, either to Joe or to one another, for each one appeared to be absorbed in ceaseless conversation with himself. He sensed that they had been together so long words were superfluous.

Angry and resigned by turns, he pursued the daily tasks he was allotted and, under Kathryn's reluctant tutelage, quickly acquired farming skills; but no sense of companionship developed for there was disdain on her part for his ignorance of the most practical tasks and resentment on his for her disdain. In any case, he was too absorbed in his own problems to attempt drawing her out. His victory over loneliness and depression in the cave had induced a certain euphoria which made him, however irrationally, believe that his return home was imminent, even though he could not imagine how it would occur. He visualised his homecoming, tried to imagine what it would be like, wondered whether his mother, friends, teachers had despaired of seeing him again. Had the police been informed, was he a missing person or had they given him up, adding his name to the long list of young people who disappeared, never to be seen again? And would they recognise in the strong young man he had become the much punier boy he had been? How had his friends developed? Were they unchanged, absorbed by the same pre-occupations, still going to gigs, following favourite bands, smoking weed, going after girls, drinking, gathering at parties? Not that he had been away long, a summer and now the autumn but it felt longer. Time in this place did not have the same progression as it had at home. Calendars and diaries had no meaning. Wearily he accepted the inevitable.

He was, in any case, soon too occupied for long periods of contemplation. Farm work kept him busy. He helped gather dry stooks from stubbled fields, piled onto carts pulled by oxen and brought to the edge of the home field that lay beside the farm. He learnt to throw the stooks by pitchfork to Meredith and Randolph, precariously balanced on a fast growing rick. It was hard, dusty work but he found satisfaction in it; or would have if he had felt some sense of companionship. But there was none. Joe wished with longing that there were other people to meet or friend-ships to cultivate, but the community, relying entirely on its own resources, had no outside contacts. The good life, glamourised by television, was a hard taskmaster which left no time for thought or play or even the relieving jolliness of banter. Remembering the robust relationship among his mates Joe was puzzled at these young people's unrelieved seriousness like older, disillusioned adults.

Each one had their allotted tasks, Randolph and Meredith in the fields, Kathryn on the farm, Belinda in the house making and mending clothes. Otto cooked and saw to provisions. Everyone took their turn keeping watch at night, with the exception of Joe and Otto, the latter spared most physical activity. Joe had offered, although he had no idea what to watch for. He hoped that they might tell him. They turned him down without thanks, excluding him from an activity they clearly considered important. He felt it keenly.

His sense of isolation grew, greater now than during his solitary period in the cave. There he had been his own man, here he was merely tolerated, an outsider in a close and tightly knit community.

Joe longed for home with a with a painful ache in his heart.

Chapter Five

———

S U S I E is still in her cell but her circumstances have changed. Her food has improved, small extra morsels appear on her plate. She looks forward keenly to her meals. Then one day her guard points at the slop bucket and motions Susie to follow. Susie can scarcely lift the overflowing bucket but manages to take it as far as a small room of overwhelming stench. She almost passes out. She lifts a wooden lid and empties the contents into the foetid hole below.

She is led to a small paved patch. It is not closed in. There is sky, there is light. It is blissful. The guard, expressionless, hands Susie a skipping rope. Susie skips though she is weak and cannot skip for long. But the routine is repeated daily. She is allowed to empty the slop bucket and then to skip. Her strength improves.

She never sees another person but the tapping through the wall has continued. She makes up what she cannot understand and imagines the other prisoner is a child, older than herself. She does not know for certain.

*

The days grew shorter. Sheds were repaired, roofs checked for leaks and loose tiles, more logs cut and piled against the house. Making good took up most of the time. Joe felt as if they were preparing for a siege; which indeed they were.

The trees shed their leaves. One morning sheets of rain battered at Joe's window. Struggling into his clothes in the cold room he went downstairs, to find Otto in the kitchen, twigs and tinder box in hand, before an unlit stove.

'Doesn't Randolph usually do that?'

'He won't be here today.'

'Where has he gone?'

Otto looked stricken but said nothing.

Kathryn was sometimes ahead of him at the farm. Forced to work together over the long weeks he had been at the Manor, they had arrived at an uneasy truce. While she tolerated him, he had grudgingly learned to respect her resourcefulness and skill. Her close relationship with the animals, closer than with the humans with the possible exception of Belinda, intrigued him. He imagined it hid other, deeper entanglements.

A cacophony of noise met him. Hungry beasts stood impatiently at gates. No need to look for Kathryn. Clearly, like Randolph, she had gone elsewhere. Nor was there any sign of Belinda or Meredith. He was alone.

It was not a day to linger. He fed the animals, milked the cows, cleaned the stables and dealt with essential jobs; little else was possible in the deluge of rain that seeped through his clothes, trickled into his boots and ran down his neck. He returned to the house wet and cold.

He again asked Otto where the others had gone but knew it was a waste of time. These people only answered questions if and when it suited them and stopped their conversations at his approach. He had been worked hard and now felt they owed him some trust and loyalty. But no matter what he did or how conciliatory he appeared, they regarded him with the same wary suspicion as the day he walked in. Joe wondered for the hundredth time if he should leave and for the hundredth time was met by the same impenetrable barrier. There was nowhere to go. Helplessness and frustration brought the blood pounding into his head. His Furies were once again in command. He kicked hard at a wall. It hurt his foot but altered nothing. What was, was. Randolph, Meredith, Belinda and Kathryn had left farm and house without prior warning and for all he knew they might never return, leaving him in this wilderness with only Otto, a weak boy who could give no help with gruelling daily tasks. It was a dismal prospect.

Perhaps they were on some kind of expedition, hunting or... shopping? The idea was ludicrous. But they could have gone for supplies, though what these could be he could not imagine. Stationery? He had seen no books, no paper, no pencils, pens. Only now did this strike him as significant. Apart from the portrait at twenty-two Fairfax Road he had not seen a written word nor a drawn line since his arrival in the new world.

He and Otto ate alone.

'Who keeps guard tonight?' Joe asked.

For once he did not get a blank stare. Otto was looking at him long and intently. Joe stared back, determined not to falter under scrutiny, then felt ashamed for in the flickering light Otto looked old. His face was withered, eyes shrunk in his head.

'You can.'

Was this an honour bestowed or a mark of Otto's desperation? Joe took it as the latter and, supplied with the usual guard duty clothes, thick jumper, cape and a blanket, followed Otto into a fierce night of rain and gusts of wind that sent the trees dancing. They climbed steadily until the beechwood gave way to a group of tall pines.

'Up there,' Otto said. 'Any movement, light or disturbance you report to me straight away. I'll be waiting.'

Joe looked up at the pine Otto had indicated. The tallest of a clump of ten, its smooth trunk climbed into what seemed to Joe mere nothingness. A watchtower built onto the hill he had expected, not this high eyrie. His spirits quailed at the thought of ascending it. The oak he had climbed in the wood had presented few difficulties, for its sturdy branches were within reach and leaves obscured the height above and the drop below. But this pine had shed many of its lower branches as it grew to its commanding height. He could not see the top. He recollected with a shudder an unexpected bout of vertigo when, on a school trip abroad, the party reached the summit of a mountain. Admiring the panorama of snowbound mountain peaks he suddenly felt the earth move and rotate like a spinning top as though the hand of God had given it a twist. It spun faster and faster, threatening to whirl Joe off its edge and plunge him into the void below. Fearing ridicule from his friends, he closed his eyes and pretended nothing had happened but the intensity and suddenness of the experience shocked him, a warning of unknown demons hiding in his unconscious.

Joe thought of the consequences of not climbing the pine, of ignominiously returning to Otto to tell him he had failed; or even pretending that he had been up the tree all night but had seen nothing. Otto, with his uncanny instinct, would know that he had lied. It would count against him and endanger his already precarious position. It was, Joe thought with resignation, another Herculean test set by malign gods, for reasons he failed utterly to perceive.

A rope ladder descended to the ground. Joe hauled himself up and climbed swiftly, daring to look neither above nor below, ducking and diving between the ends of sharp fanged branches that hindered movement, scratched his face and arms and impaled the blanket tied across his shoulders. Footholds had been hammered into the bare sections of the trunk, leaving him exposed to the drop; but he climbed on with desperate determination, knees shaking, until at last, at the swaying top, he emerged onto a wooden platform. He collapsed face down, offering prayers to he knew not whom. He lay there, unmoving through the dark hours until the dawn, grey and undramatic, heaved itself unwillingly from the night.

Panic seized him once more at the prospect of the descent. Wriggling backwards his legs searched for the topmost branches. One foot found purchase and he lowered himself fearfully while still clinging to the platform with his fingertips. Hugging the trunk, holding tightly to any solid object within his grasp, he climbed slowly down. The impossible was taking place. With every step Joe's confidence increased, fear left him and, once on the glorious ground, he hugged himself in an excess of ecstasy and relief. Another demon conquered.

Otto was standing by the kitchen door, waiting. An unearthly silence reigned. Joe reported that nothing untoward had happened during the night. He break-fasted, then worked outside, doing all Kathryn's tasks on the farm and Randolph's and Meredith's in the fields.

He lingered in the kitchen in the evening in the hope of some communication from Otto, if only to thank him for his labours. In vain.

Long past the last barrier of fatigue, Joe climbed the pine with manic energy, triumphant at the victory over his fears. Once on the platform, a sturdy structure with four poles supporting a wooden roof that gave limited protection from the elements, he braced himself against the wind and holding onto an upright, looked down on the valley which he had traversed weeks ago with Randolph, and at the meandering river. His cave lay at a far bend to its right and he peered into the dark towards it with wistful longing, hoping that it guarded his few belongings, calculator, pen, the house keys he doubted he would ever use again, and his watch. Was it still going, stubbornly recording passing time? He wondered what day it now was, what date, what time. It no longer mattered. He was in a timeless zone in which days passed but did not move forward.

He brought his father's knife out of his pocket, and ran his fingers along its serrated edge, glad of its comforting touch. The old question returned. Why had his father deserted them? Was 'falling in love' with another woman just an excuse because he wanted to get away or was he bored with his life, disappointed in his son? Conflicting feelings of anger, loss and love once again left Joe limp with confusion. He pushed them aside and kept careful watch for an enemy who had neither face nor name.

Guard duty at night, breakfast, work all day, that was the pattern of his days. He found he could manage on three hours sleep until exhaustion found him one day almost at breaking point. But he battled on because Otto too was clearly suffering, becoming daily more inaccessible, eyes sinking into dark pools.

They spoke rarely to one another. Conversation, if such it could be called, was kept to a bare minimum. Joe found their uncomfortable silences occupied his thoughts. He was constantly anxious about what did or did not go on in Otto's head or if he, Joe, had failed to say or not say or do or not do something that was the cause of the impasse.

That the others were not coming back was his greatest fear, the prospect of being left alone with Otto a haunting threat. He made countless plans against the eventuality, for he saw that it would make him a virtual prisoner, chained by moral obligation. It was impossible to abandon Otto in this vast landscape, tantamount to a death sentence though, he thought bitterly, this was exactly what the others had done. They had used him, the newcomer, as a hostage. The outlook was bleak, utterly without hope.

Then, one late afternoon, he found a pile of food encrusted plates abandoned on the kitchen table. He called and searched but there was no response. Puzzled, he cleared the kitchen. If Randolph and the others had returned it was unlike them to leave a mess, for the accepted law of the house, strictly maintained, was that no dirty crockery was left about. He waited for Otto to appear, wondering with a sickening moment of panic whether he too had gone. But he had not.

'Are they back?'

No response.

Over the next few days he noticed that someone was taking food and leaving Otto to clear up. Then he saw Belinda in her night clothes walking upstairs, on her face the look of a somnambulist. He took a step forward, preparing to speak but she moved past, neither noticing nor acknowledging his presence. He followed. They were upstairs, in their rooms. What they were doing or why they refused to come down was impossible to discover.

One morning the wind dropped and a pale sun shone. Joe, dry for the first time since his nightly watch had begun, lingered outside, kicking dead leaves into coloured clouds. The air, cold and fresh, brought with it memories of home, the expectation of the smoky smell of bonfires from neighbouring gardens, of fireworks and burning Guys. How easily one fell into old moulds of thought.

Voices were coming from the house, loud and animated, as though a party were in progress. His first impulsive thought was 'visitors' but he soon realised what an absurd, fantastical notion this was.

He went cautiously inside.

They were back, sitting round the table with the complacency of a suburban family on a Sunday morning. Only the papers were missing.

'Where the fuck have you been?' he said.

'Breakfast?' Otto took a fresh loaf from the oven.

'All quiet up there?' Randolph asked.

Joe's anger flared.

'I've been coping by myself -that is Otto and I have.'

'I'll see to the animals today,' Kathryn said.

It was as much acknowledgement as he was going to get. He went outside, banging the door behind him, and sat on the embankment overlooking the house, wondering if he could bear another minute of this hard, frustrating existence. If only these young people were normal, if only they shouted, laughed, quarreled, demonstrated that they were alive.

He did not go near them for the rest of the day, slouching around the fields in rage and frustration at his helplessness. By nightfall his anger had reached a pitch he could no longer contain. His Furies had once again sunk their claws into him. He marched inside, determined on a confrontation; and stopped dead. The kitchen had been transformed. Floor and table were scrubbed, a huge fire burned in the grate, a leg of pork roasting on the spit was being constantly basted by Otto with a sauce of such spicy fragrance the entire herb garden must have gone into its making. The table was laid for six, glazed goblets by each place. Jugs of steaming mead stood in the middle, giving off their heady redolence. On the stove vegetables boiled and, wherever there was space, tall branches added to an air of festivity.

'Here.'

Randolph handed him a mug of mead and in a defiant gesture Joe drained it. The sweet hot liquid flowed like fire through his veins. After that, all was confusion and his memories of the night were to remain fragmented: the unexpectedly animated faces of the young people round the table, the talk, the laughter, his clumsy attempts to dance with Belinda, the complicated patterns traced by her feet; and over all enchanted notes from Randolph's flute, joyful, plaintive, haunting. This was no ordinary music but came from the great God Pan, from time beyond recall. It wrenched Joe's spirit from his body and sent it spiralling into the air. He watched himself in the shimmering room below, he saw a stranger that was Joe, behind him a phalanx of ghosts, not from his world but from this. They too were rejoicing, celebrating their release. He felt an exultant joy, a moment in eternity. He could not know that this was the brush of an angel's wing.

They went to bed that night as dawn was breaking.

Joe wondered whether he had been dreaming but the kitchen next morning showed unmistakable signs of a party. At least the evening proved, he later reflected, that these young people must once have led a more carefree life. They were accomplished musicians and dancers, they drank, they feasted, their lives were not after all exclusively dedicated to work and survival. And someone among them was a great artist, a master craftsman who had carved the mantelpiece in the long room. He felt a sudden, urgent need to see and feel it again and the next evening, when life had returned to its normal routine, crept through the dark silent house, letting his hands travel over the wood's breathing surfaces.

Some days later Randolph asked,

'Have you ever felled a tree?'

Joe shook his head.

'I'll show you.'

He fetched a two ended saw and axes whose shiny handles indicated many years' use.

They climbed the hill behind the house, beyond the garden and the well, stopping halfway to look back. They were high now, the surrounding hills outlined against the cold clear sky. Below, the bare branches of deciduous trees merged into one another in a continuous flow, obscuring the house.

Later, they stopped to drink from a stream, the same that flowed into the valley and the farm. They shared bread and cheese.

'Why do you go so high to fell trees? Wouldn't it be easier below?'

'They're less likely to come as far as this.'

Joe took a deep breath.

'Who?'

Randolph looked at him in surprise.

'You escaped them. You know who they are.'

He looked at him accusingly.

At last, the explanation Joe had been seeking.

'The townspeople,' he said now, 'they chased me with nets.'

'Yes.'

It was clear from his tone that Randolph knew.

'I don't know why.'

'Don't know what?'

'Why they chased me.'

'Because you're young.'

It was said as though it were the most natural thing in the world.

'That's why they're after us, here?'

'It will be winter soon. That's when they come.'

'Why in the winter?'

'Don't you know anything?'

'No.'

Randolph shook his head.

'Because the landscape is bare and you can see for miles. And we have to burn fires. Fires make smoke, smoke is a signal. And when it snows we leave tracks.'

'Do they know we are here?'

'Sometimes they find us, sometimes they don't,' Randolph said.

'How long have you been here?'

'Almost four hundred years.'

Not long. Aristocratic families back home reached back some seven centuries.

The business of tree-felling was more complicated than Joe had imagined. Randolph chose an oak, five foot in diameter, leaning slightly towards the ground. They laboriously removed large rocks and protruding obstacles from the fall path. This done Randolph showed Joe how to make three cuts, one diagonal and then horizontal on one side of the tree, a second horizontal almost to meet the second cut.

As soon as they heard the tree creaking as it started its descent Randolph pulled Joe away, well out of reach.

'Easy to get killed,' he said.

With gathering momentum, it toppled into place with a thud so mighty the ground trembled.

They lobbed the branches off, working until the sun was sinking.

'I'll use them to camouflage the roof,' Randolph said.

'And the trunk?'

'The oxen will haul it down.'

Joe assumed it would be used for firewood and, coming from a culture that had learned to value trees, felt a sense of pity for such waste for it was an old, majestic oak, reaching back into history. He had aided its downfall with mixed feelings. Randolph, intuitive, said,

'Can you carve in wood?'

Joe had never been aware of artistic leanings. While he was competent at drawing and painting, he had never considered taking up any form of creative endeavour either as a hobby or a career. His future plans were unfocussed, advice from career masters hollow and meaningless. Yet he suspected that an undeclared ambition lurked in the shadows. Too indifferent to tease it out he had let it lie, sensing that it would declare itself. This perhaps it had now done. The carvings in the long room had filled him with wonder and a yearning to fashion wood. He could imagine nothing more satisfying.

Randolph noted the look of excitement on the boy's face and wondered once again who he was. Joe was an aberration, fitting into no known mould. They could not place him, no matter how hard they tried and this made them wary. The group lived in a hostile world, clinging precariously to their existence and Joe unsettled them, made them fearful that they were harbouring a cuckoo in the nest.

'No, will you teach me?' Joe asked.

Was there a hidden purpose lurking behind this artless question? Should he prevaricate, guard the ancient art that had been handed down; but Randolph had not the heart to refuse him.

'I'll save you a piece from this oak,' he said.

Unaware of Randolph's dilemma, Joe looked at him with gratitude and pleased surprise, unused as he had become to spontaneous gestures of friendship. Perhaps the feasting and the breaking of bonds between them, would herald a new relationship. His spirits soared at the prospect but Randolph was embarrassed by Joe' enthusiasm, open as it was to contradictory interpretations.

They bundled up as much brushwood as they could drag by hand and proceeded back to the house. Life resumed its normal pattern of work and sleep.

From the sparse information Randolph had given him one thing at least was clear. The townspeople were the enemy, both of his companions and himself. This Randolph had stated with such an utter lack of ambiguity, that Joe could take it as reliable fact. Further, Randolph had supplied a reason. The townspeople wanted to kill him, and presumably them, because they were young.

Why?

Impossible to answer, possible only to treat the question as he had treated the many other insolubles - put it away, wait until someone, somewhere, offered an explanation.

In a corner of the cobbled yard Joe discovered a disused stable that housed big blocks of wood, ready to be transformed by a skilled hand. An ancient wooden bench, on which various appliances were screwed, took up the whole of one side. A large treadle grindstone stood beside it. On a bench opposite lay, in immaculate order, an array of chisels, gouges, saws, rasps, files and knives of many kinds and sizes; all with the worn look of tools that had experienced years of usage. They looked inviting. Joe longed to get his hands on them. He waited impatiently for an opportunity to remind Randolph of his promise.

The first frosts hardened the ground, the sheep were brought down from the hills.

'What do we feed them on in winter?'

'Mainly hay.'

'The cows as well?'

'Hay, maize and worzels when we've grown them. It depends on the crop rotation. Sometimes we have to slaughter, if the winter is long and we run out.'

The group's recent animation had given way to a quiet thoughtfulness that made Joe wonder with a sinking heart if they were going to revert to their previous silence. He sensed, as the winter closed in, a growing tension in the atmosphere.

*

The two prisoners either side of the wall have, with the desperation brought on by their confinement, evolved a rudimentary language. One loud knock means a guard is coming, two that they are free to communicate, three stands for girl, four for boy. Short and long and the strength of each knock have their respective meanings. It is a hit and miss affair but Susie has at least learned that her neighbour is called Rose and that she is fourteen years old and has been in prison even longer than Susie. Neither knows when or indeed if they will be released.

Susie has asked if Rose knows where her parents are but Rose has no other neighbour and no news.

One morning the unexpected happens. Susie's grim guard speaks to her. But what she has to communicate is brief and alarming.

'Your trial is being convened,' she says.

'When?' Susie asks but gets no reply.

Susie is uncertain what this means but she hopes it will give her a chance to see her parents. She taps her news to Rose but this time there is no reply. This leaves Susie devastated. Rose has been her mainstay, now she has gone and Susie has no idea where to. Is she alive or have they killed her?

Susie sits in a corner, her arms wrapped round her drawn-up knees, and rocks gently.

*

'Meeting tonight,' Otto said. Joe suspected from the prevailing mood that something serious was on the agenda, perhaps laying down plans against the hardships of the coming winter and a possible raid from the townspeople. He hoped they would allow him to contribute more than hard labour. He wanted above all to be in their confidence.

'Who is on watch?' he asked experimentally, needing to know if this meeting was valued sufficiently to dispense with guard duty. He had not been allowed to take part in the night watch rota when it was resumed, again for reasons he could not fathom; only that they still did not trust him.

The evening meal was cleared away, the shutters were put in place and the lamps lit. Otto sat at one end of the table, Joe opposite, Kathryn to his immediate left, Belinda next to her. Randolph and Meredith sat opposite the two girls. For a time nobody spoke and Joe felt the tension mount. As his gaze slid over the faces round him, touched by the flickering light, he realised with a shock that all were turned towards him. He stared back puzzled, hoping for a lead.

There was none.

He now saw how mistaken he had been. This was no planning meeting. A Star Chamber was in session, an inquisition, and he was in the dock. He felt it in their hushed silence, from their grouping together. Those on either side of him, Kathryn and Randolph, had drawn their chairs closer to their neighbours, leaving him isolated. He looked at them with rising anger and fear. How unpredictable they were, friends one moment, enemies the next. Were they expecting him to say something? The blood was drumming in his ears and his fists were tightly clenched.

Only then did Otto speak.

'We want to know the truth. We want to know where you come from. We want to know what you are doing here.'

—

Chapter Six

WHERE did he come from? They could not, would not believe him and might think him mad.

He looked at Otto, the sole witness to his unwavering loyalty when it was most needed. Otto looked away. Joe turned to Randolph, with whom he thought he had developed a steady relationship, cemented by the felling of the tree and his promise to teach him to carve but Randolph regarded him with cold indifference.

Belinda? Troubled and uncomprehending as though a favourite toy had been broken.

Kathryn? Her eyes were lowered, her body slumped in her chair as though wishing it were anywhere but here.

He tried to speak but the words would not emerge and it was only after a long, expectant pause that he said,

'I used to live in Bantage.'

Joe hoped that this would satisfy but a conspiratorial look went round the table, his answer confirming every suspicion the group had ever harboured. This boy, in an unusually cunning move, had been planted by the townspeople to spy on them.

Randolph and Meredith sprang to their feet, stepping threateningly towards Joe. Violence he had not expected and his fists went up in self-defence. His Furies hovered.

'Don't threaten me!'

'Then tell the truth.'

'That's what I'm doing, you stupid sods. Telling you what happened, trying to make you understand. I come from Bantage, I was born there, lived there but it's not the Bantage you know. It's another Bantage, different. At least the people are...'

How was he to explain?

'Don't lie to us!'

'I'm trying to tell the fucking truth!' Joe shouted back.

Meredith and Randolph closed in on him. The Furies descended. Joe landed a forceful punch on Meredith's stomach and an upper cut on Randolph's chin. Both reeled back in shock and surprise and then attacked from either side. Joe brought up his knee and caught Meredith in the groin, crippling him but Randolph seized his arms and, despite Joe's frantic struggles, pinioned them back.

'Who knows you are here?'

'No one. I wish they did.'

'When did the liaison with the townspeople begin?'

'There is no liaison with the townspeople.'

'Who kept you informed while you lived in the cave?'

'I saw no one until I met Randolph - and wish I hadn't. It's you who are traitors and hypocrites, all of you, pretending to be friendly and now this.'

He tried to bite the imprisoning arms and kicked backwards with enough force to bring Randolph to his knees but Meredith was on his feet, landing punches on chest and shoulders. Joe staggered sideways and fell.

'Leave him!'

The sharp command came from Otto who had risen from his seat and towered over them, suddenly an impressively powerful figure, unlike the Otto Joe was used to, puny and weak. Perhaps it was a trick of the light or a measure of his panic but Meredith and Randolph too were cowed and returned to their places. Suddenly deflated, Joe sat down. The questioning resumed.

'How did you know which direction to take?'

'I followed the stream.'

'Who are you working for?'

'Fuck off!' he shouted.

*

Helmuth sits high on a dais above the court. He is presiding over yet another trial, now nearing its conclusion. These have become routine for they follow a course long ago laid down by him. All prisoners are either condemned or put to hard labour. He could dispense with these kangaroo courts but it does not suit him. They serve to create the illusion that some kind of justice prevails. Helmuth knows about justice. He used to dispense it a long, long time ago.

The prisoners, Susie, her mother, her father, face him. He looks at them wearily, surprised that once again these insignificant people have the strength to defy him. But not for long. He will crush them as he has crushed all opposition. He is aware that danger lurks in the most unexpected places, plots threatening his position are hatched by even the most cowed citizens.

He begins the routine questioning.

'From whom did you receive instruction?'

'I have received no instruction,' Susie's father replies.

'You and your wife acted on your own initiative?'

'Yes. No one else was involved.'

Susie can hear her parents but she cannot see them. Her head is covered with a grey cowl, no slits for eyes, only a sliver of light seeping past the edges of the muffling cloth. Susie is used to the dark. She has rarely been out in daylight, though this morning, in a moment to be savoured, she was led out of her cell into intoxicating breathfuls of fresh air.

'We know that there is,' Helmuth thunders.

'There are no other conspirators.'

'There is a boy.'

'I know no boy.'

'You were seen with him in the park. He took instructions from you and left.'

' I have given no instructions. I know no boy.'

But Susie did. Susie knew whom they meant. Susie had seen Joe. She had told no one but she had written it in her diary.

'You and your conspirators knew you were acting against the law.'

'There are no other conspirators and yes, my wife and I, we knew.'

'It is strictly forbidden to keep children. They have to be handed to the Council.'

'We wanted to keep our own child.'

'You will be punished, your daughter put into the service of the town and the boy captured and executed. We will find him.'

Joe felt the community's hostility like a dark beating host. How could he ever have thought he could live with them as a friend, that they would provide shelter and comfort? He cursed himself for his naivety. All these young people were and probably always had been his enemies, feigning friendship or at least tolerance but, it seemed clear to him now, they were allied to the townspeople, in an outpost strategically situated to capture those who had evaded the nets. He was trapped, imprisoned.

Otto was asking him a question. Joe tried to focus on what was being said but, yet again, the words made no sense.

'Were you selected?'.

'Selected?'

'Yes.'

'I don't know what you mean.'

*

'You are aware of the selection process in the town?'

'Yes, we are aware.'

'You deliberately flouted our most important law.'

'We were doing what we thought best for our child.'

'It's not for you to think. It's for you to obey.'

'We are individuals. We cannot help but think.'

'You are, or were, a part of this community. You will be excommunicated.'

'It was a risk we were willing to take.'

'You will bear the consequences of that willingness. So will your daughter.'

*

What were they talking about?

'Selected for what? The school, the football team? What?'

'Don't prevaricate! '

Prevaricate? No, he was not going to. He was going to give it them straight. The time for pretence or pre-varication was over.

'Where were you living?'

'Twenty two Fairfax Road.'

'Who with?'

'My mother.'

'Alone?'

'Yes.'

'Where is your father?'

'I no longer know.'

'Exterminated?'

Joe stared.

'Exterminated?' he returned. Though it was many years since he had heard from him it had never occurred to him as a possibility. He examined it now. Extermination was not a concept with which, in his daily life, he was familiar but he read thrillers, saw films, watched the news, kept up with world events. These provided no shortage of extermination on a number crunching scale that this group of five people could not conceive. So why not his father?

101

He replied carefully.

'I don't think he's been exterminated.'

But suddenly he was no longer sure.

'He left.'

'To go where?'

'Away.

Perhaps the story of another love was a decoy, perhaps his father's absence was not voluntary but decreed by some outside agency. Perhaps MI5, MI6, or some secret organisation had used him in a special capacity Joe could not even begin to imagine. His father had been a civil servant and Joe was never clear what that entailed. He could have been sent on a mission abroad and taken hostage. Was he allowing his imagination to run riot? Joe put the question to one side to be considered at a later date, if such there was.

'He just left,' he repeated.

'To join the junta?'

'There is no junta where I come from, not in England anyway, and there are no townspeople, not as you know them. We live among decent citizens who don't chase and kill one another. We live in a law abiding country, not like it is here, everyone at one another's throat and young people like you living in isolation…'

'You've been sent to spy on us.'

'No!'

'We have proof!'

'What?'

'The jumper with the hood. The one you're hiding under your mattress, waiting for the right moment to put it on. Only Helmuth's guards wear hoods like that.'

His Gap jumper. His hoody. Joe burst into hysterical laughter.

'You cretins! It's just an ordinary jumper. Everyone wears them where I come from. It's you who are spying on me, searching my room where you have no business to be. You're like the secret police they had in Russia, using some insignificant detail to incriminate me.'

He could see they did not know what he was talking about.

'You're treating me as though I were on trial! You twist everything I say, just biding your time before you hand me over to this Helmuth whom you pretend to hate. Well, you can bloody well listen to the truth for once. Not that you'll believe it. But it's this. I don't know what I'm doing here, I don't know how I got here. And I no longer care. I wish I were dead.'

He sat down with an awful kind of finality, as though nothing else needed saying.

'Are you a spy?' Otto asked again.

'No I'm not! Why would I be? Who would I spy for? Those terrible people in Bantage who tried to kill me because I'm young? What reason is that? In my world young people are treasured and looked on as the hope for the future, not hounded to death. What happens if there are no young people? You'll all die out.'

No one moved, no one spoke.

'And you've sheltered me and I've tried to help you always, show I'm grateful. I kept watch and looked after

103

everything while you buggered off, leaving Otto to cope. He would have perished but for me. That's true Otto, isn't it? And anyway, where did you all disappear to without word or warning?'

They did not reply but went on the attack again.

'You're waiting for a signal for the right moment to destroy us, you want to put an end to the last spark of civilisation, the last hope for mankind.'

*

'You are part of a conspiracy. You were waiting for the right moment to stage a coup.'

'We have stated that there is no conspiracy. We were not planning a coup.'

'Why else would you defy the state?'

'For the sake of our daughter.'

'Who is now a prisoner. You must have realised that you would be discovered. You were using her as a hostage for your own dark purposes.'

'No!'

Susie can hear the anger and despair in her father's voice and tries turning towards him but firm hands hold her back.

'It was my fault!' she shouts. 'I asked them…'

A hand over her mouth silences her.

'Leave her alone!' her mother cries. ' She is only a child… only a child.'

*

Joe was beyond understanding, foundering in a welter of misconceptions that bore no relation to anything he recognised as reality. He felt as though he had become a character in someone else's fantasy, that his own individuality had ceased to exist, he felt that some essential part of him had gone missing. He felt that he had lost his being.

'If,' he said in a voice of utter resignation, 'if you think I'm here to destroy you, why don't you kill me? It'd be easy enough. There's five of you and only one of me. Go on, do it. There's nothing here for me anyway, just growing old and dying without having achieved anything, experienced anything….'

A murmur went through the room.

What had he said now?

'Look,' Joe said with controlled calm, 'I was coming home from school…'

'There's been no school here for four hundred years,' Meredith said

'There is where I come from. Hundreds of schools. People learn to read and write. Can you read and write?' he asked accusingly.

'Of course. But writing's been banned. And we have learnt to do without it.'

'Well, lucky you,' he said sarcastically.

'Go on,' Otto ordered.

'It was an ordinary day like any other. Same old routine, breakfast, school, home. Mum always leaves tea out for me, she has to earn you see….'

He faltered, seeing the incredulous looks on their faces.

'She has to earn a living with my father gone and never contacting us or sending money.'

Money. How were they to understand money? Joe saw that he was digging an ever deeper hole for himself.

'There's just the two of us. She's in an office. Not a very exciting job, she doesn't like it much.' He was talking to himself now. 'I've promised myself that as soon as I have my 'A' levels I'll train in some skill, don't know what at the moment. Don't think I'll manage university on account of the cost, though I would have liked to. We don't have an ancestral home, not like yours with family roots reaching back four hundred years. Ours is a three up, two down, rather poky….'

How could he possibly explain?. ·

'It's so different from the life you lead. Children live with their parents.'

Another murmur round the table.

'Everything is different. In my Bantage people live ordinary lives, in ordinary houses without bells on the roofs; and there are people in the countryside, there are farms and houses and villages, cars, lorries, tractors and no one wants to kill anyone else. Not as far as I know anyway. Here is like a foreign country even though we speak the same language and even though the houses in Bantage haven't changed. Or at least don't look different from the outside.'

He noted their disbelieving faces but once started on his tale could not stop.

'I was walking back from school and I had an accident. I fell. And when I got up to go home everything had gone quiet. There was no one about though I wasn't taking too much notice. I felt dizzy and odd. I thought I

106

was probably suffering from concussion. Then the front door key didn't fit and I thought I'd gone to the wrong house but I checked and I hadn't. And some strange guy who thought he owned our house chased me and the whole nightmare began.'

He told them about the chase, about how he had spent the night in the waste ground. He described his escape from the guards and tracker dogs, he told them how he had gradually learned to survive on his own. All the pent-up fears, hopes and speculations of the weeks since he had lost home, family and his once familiar life poured out of him in a torrent. He stopped only when he saw that their faces were still hostile.

'If all you say is true, how did you get here in the first place?'

'I told you. I don't know.'

'That's difficult to believe. We think you were brought up in the dark and have turned traitor.'

'I don't understand!'

'Yes, you do. There are parents in the town who hide their children.'

The image of the girl skipping in the park; that was it. She was hiding from the townspeople because she was young.

'We don't believe your fantasies.'

'They're not fantasies! They're real!'

'They're the ravings of a madman.'

Perhaps they were right. Perhaps it was he who was mad, making up a life that had never happened.

'Joe, how old are you?'

This was a question so irrelevant that it caught Joe off guard. For a moment he could not remember. When was his birthday? June seventeenth. It had passed without his noticing. He must be eighteen. He said so.

'I mean your real age.'

'That is my real age.'

Confusion round the table as they looked at each other in dismay. What now, Joe wondered with an indifference born of despair.

*

'Step forward!'

Susie's cowl is torn away and she is given a push. She confronts an impenetrable, silent court and the terrifying face of her persecutor, Helmuth. She has courage enough to look him in the eyes. His anger is implacable. She knows there can be no mercy from this man.

'How old are you?'

Susie tries to prevaricate.

'I'm not sure.'

'That is a lie.'

'She is ten years old,' her mother cries out, 'you have no right to put her on trial. She is an innocent victim.'

'Victimised by your actions. You have defied the state and escaped justice for ten years. You will escape no longer. The court will decide your sentence.'

But Susie knows Helmuth has already pronounced it.

*

108

Kathryn, distressed, said in an abandoned voice, 'He's a new born.'

'Have you taken the drug?'

What drug? Medical? Recreational?

'The drug,' Otto persisted.

Joe looked at him helplessly. What was he talking about?

'Cocaine, Crack, what?'

'L.L.'

'L.L? I've never heard of it. Is it something you lot take?'

That was probably it. They were all on drugs, the inmates of a loony bin playing out a morbid, obscene game in which he was cast as victim. But no, he'd got it wrong, it wasn't them, it was he who was mad, the people in this room the product of his ravings, personifications of his disgust for himself. He was shut up in a madhouse, drugged by white coated men with syringes. He could feel himself going faint, the faces before him blurring into grotesque shapes. He pushed past the two boys hovering beside him, ran into the corridor and out into the open. No one followed. Joe leant against the wall and took in great gulps of air. The wind howled round him, a potent symbol of his stricken confusion. He scooped up a clod of earth and held it in his hands, then rubbed it over his face and pushed some into his mouth, savouring the roughness and the bitter, gritty taste on his tongue. Running to the nearest tree he tried to dislodge one of its waving branches which held until, with strength born of despair, Joe tore it from its trunk and with these, branch and soil, ran back indoors.

They were still sitting round the table and looked silently at the wild and mud bespattered figure placing his trophies before them.

'They're real, aren't they?' he shouted and ran out again, retching up a stinking black mess in painful spasms as he staggered to the well and looked into its reflecting waters. A rippling, sickle moon looked back.

He jumped.

The dark and slimy walls went past him in slow motion, the sliver of moon broke up into a thousand silver fragments and the water closed over his head.

*

The court is dismissed.

'Get them out!' Helmuth orders. 'And the child!'

He rises and goes. Another set of criminals dispensed with. Will these citizens never stop trying to overthrow him, never leave him to savour his high position, so long fought for? They have forced him to plot and plan, to lay bare treachery even before they have thought of it.

Susie weeps bitterly as she tries to fight off her guards who again place a cowl over her head but they are too strong for her. She is dragged out, kicking and screaming, her heels beating a tattoo on the ground. She is walked for what seems like hours but at least she is outside, in the fresh glorious air. She would like to go on walking forever.

All too soon she is halted and hears a door clang open. She is pulled down what she thinks is a long tunnel for the air is fetid and thick; then she is given a push and falls down a flight of steps.

Her hands now free, Susie tears the cowl off her face but quickly covers her nose with it against an overpowering smell of decomposition, decay and human waste. She looks around. She is in a large dungeon, water dripping down its walls. It is cold and she is shivering in her light clothes. She is alone and, for the first time, terrified. She has been left to die in this desolate place. She has no more fight in her. Her only option is to accept her fate. She sits on the wet floor and leans against the dripping walls, hoping for a swift end.

Sometime later Susie hears a noise at the far end of the dungeon and a door which she had not noticed is opened and in streams a group of children of all ages. They are dirty, cold, hungry, skeletal. Some can hardly drag their feet across the floor and slump down, regardless of the wet.

The children are too tired and exhausted to take notice of this newcomer but one boy, less degraded than the rest, comes up to her.

'What have you been accused of?' he asks.

'Being alive,' Susie says.

The boy's name is Ian. He is two years older than Susie, tall for his age, with brown hair and hazel eyes. He has not been a prisoner for long. Though she is wary at first, Susie likes the look of him. Perhaps he will become a friend. She has not had a friend before.

'Have you been tried?' Susie asks him. But he has not. Ian, like Susie, was hidden by his family but one day his father fails to come home from work. His mother tells him that she is going out to look for him. He waits

111

and waits but she does not return. After several weeks, when food and water have run out, Ian decides to take his life in his hands and run away into the country. He has heard that somewhere there is a dissident community and although he has no idea where he will try to join them.

But he does not get far, only to the outskirts of the town. He is picked up by two guards and thrown into this dungeon.

'What do we do here?' Susie asks. 'You've been gone all day.'

'We clean the sewers,' Ian says.

—

Chapter Seven

JOE struggled to consciousness.

'Who am I?' he asked, panic stricken, 'Where am I? What am I doing here?'

He could not remember. He was no one, nowhere, a lost soul without identity.

'Joe, it's all right, you're all right now.'

He felt a soft hand on his forehead. A face framed with fair hair was leaning over him. Kathryn. Partial memories returned, his plight, the hostile group of people he had thought his friends, his overwhelming isolation. He tried to sit up, to get out of bed and flee but, overcome with dizziness, fell back.

'What are you doing here?'

'Looking after you.'

'Why?'

'You've been ill. Here.'

She handed him a mug of milk.

'She's tending me like a sick animal,' he thought bitterly and pushed it away.

'How long?'

'Days, nights.'

'You've been with me all the time?'

'Others have visited.'

He wished she'd go away and leave him alone.

Yes, I've been with you all the time, watching you, trying to read the thoughts flickering over your face, as I tried in that terrible meeting to reach out to you. I knew you were telling the truth, at least as you saw it, at least how you had experienced it, and I wanted to say, leave him be, leave him, I don't know who he is but he is not an enemy, he's a strange boy, ignorant and sullen but not harmful. He's strayed into our community, not infiltrated it for an evil purpose. The others knew it too, but we have to be so careful. We don't, even now, know who you are.

Days passed in an indeterminate progression of half sleep, half wakefulness in which, suspended in no man's land, Joe saw replays of his old life mingle with dreams of the present. Always he woke to the reality he least desired, his bare room, Kathryn. No exit signs anywhere. He felt trapped.

'Who's looking after the farm?' he asked, hoping that necessity would call her away. He needed peace and time to think, and would have preferred Belinda by his side.

'Belinda and Randolph, between them.'

'Hadn't you better help them?'

'I will eventually.'

Not soon enough.

She nursed him night and day and he gradually regained his strength until, one morning, he woke with his mind clear and sharp. The meeting and its aftermath came back to him with startling clarity.

'The well,' he said. 'I jumped in. I tried to kill myself.'

' We followed you and lowered Meredith down. He brought you up.'

'Am I a prisoner?' he asked.

'No, of course not.'

Of course not?'

'Why not?'

'We had to be certain…'

'Certain of what? That I wasn't going to, what was it, destroy the last spark of civilisation? Meaning you, I suppose?'

'We had to be certain that you hadn't been planted by the townspeople,' she replied with dignity.

'What would be in it for me? Certain death.'

'We couldn't know that.'

'I tried to tell you who I was but none of you would listen. There was no need to try me as though I were a criminal.'

'There was no need for you to be so violent. You've appeared out of nowhere, or at least somewhere we couldn't believe in, and we were worried and uncertain. We live on a knife-edge.'

'And now?'

'We think you're telling the truth.'

'Well, that's something to be grateful for.'

She ignored the sarcasm in his voice.

'We still don't know how you got here.'

Neither did Joe.

Kathryn returned to her duties and Joe resumed life downstairs. The weather had changed to early winter with sharp, cold days and a clear light that raised his spirits. He wanted to go outside but Otto advised caution for a few days. Joe was glad of the respite, did not feel ready to cope with the demands of daily life, though he calculated that he could not have been ill more than ten to twelve days; but he detected a change in himself.

Unconscious forces had been at work, busy traffic between neural synapses sifting, sorting, processing, the instinct to survive altering his pattern of thought and reaction. He felt better adjusted, more able to deal with circumstances that, before his suicide attempt, had seemed intolerable. There was in any case little alternative, he had either to accept or flee. The only other remaining route open to him had failed. Joe was a pragmatist and he accepted.

He wandered round the house, making himself useful where he could. Otto, he discovered, did not work exclusively in the kitchen, being busy much of the day in a set of rooms facing the yard. They looked like the kitchen quarters of a former stately home, large with high ceilings and flagstones which felt cold underfoot. Dried rushes served as matting.

One room, larger than the others, housed two looms. Here Otto and Belinda wove textiles, clothes, blankets and rugs. The others from time to time took their turn. Wide thick rugs covered the floor and though worn thin in places retained their original colours, warm reds, blues, yellows and browns woven in geometric patterns of open squares fitting into one another with the infinite intricacy of an Escher drawing. These were designed, he learned, by Meredith. This surprised him. Meredith did not strike him as the artistic type.

A spacious room contained vats for dying. Others were used for leather work and sewing. Here Belinda spent most of her day. She had a natural gift for handiwork and made most of the clothes. She fitted Joe out with a new set, thick woollen trousers and a baggy shirt tightened with an elaborate leather belt. Under her tuition he made himself a pair of fur lined boots. She was the only one among this serious crowd with a lightness of touch. Working with her was fun. It was almost like being with one of his friends back home.

One afternoon he wandered, light in hand, down to the cellar. The door, usually locked and bolted, was close to the kitchen in a small passageway leading to the back of the house. He had seen others going in and returning with various stores but had never ventured down. Today, surprisingly, the door was unlocked. Stone steps led into a deep vault, the echo of his footsteps indicating its size. Even with the light held high he could not see the far walls. He moved forward carefully, awed by the gloom and silence.

Partitions either side were used for storage. Strong smelling hides hung from rafters, hunks of wool were suspended from hooks, lumps of salt rock piled along the far wall. Slatted wooden shelves housed various stores, bundles of rushes, straw twisted into ropes filled the floor space and shelving above. In a corner, standing alone, Joe found four wooden pillars, hieroglyphic markings on each though one was incomplete. He could not interpret their significance.

He tripped, almost extinguishing his lamp and cursed himself for a fool, coming down alone without flints or without telling anyone. Later he mentioned what he had seen.

'It's our store room. We keep it replenished in case of a siege.'

'And those pillars with markings on them?'

Randolph looked up in surprise.

'Our calendars, of course.'

Of course, he thought bitterly. They told him nothing but expected him to know everything. He forbore from asking more details but once again this insignificant incident emphasised his otherness, his separation from the community whose aims and interests remained alien no matter how hard he tried to adjust. But he went to the cellar again and studied the pillars. They were easy enough to interpret now that he knew their purpose, each one clearly representing a hundred years. Three were completed and one awaited its final markings. The house had seen almost four hundred years of family life. If family they were. Joe had no idea whether or not these young people were related.

'Why don't they just tell me?' Joe muttered to himself.

When at last he felt strong enough to go outside he was glad he had made his boots thick and strong. Winter had taken over. The trees stood bare against a sky the colour of steel and the earth, whitened by frost, crunched underfoot. The exhilarating air, hard and cold, cut into his face.

The windmill's huge sails were turning boisterously in the wind. Inside the noise was deafening.

The windmill was smaller than the occasional ones he had seen at home. It stood on a squat brick foundation about a yard high and consisted of only one large wooden room. Joe was faced with a mass of turning wheels, hoists, pulleys and governors whose functions were a mystery. Meredith, who had built and now maintained the mechanisms, explained how the stones worked, how they ground and how they were driven by wheels with interlocking teeth.

'Look,' Meredith showed him joyfully, 'the best hornbeam, hardest wood there is.'

He glowed with enthusiasm.

'And the pulleys and governors - all controlled by carefully balanced weights. You have to get it exactly right or it won't work.'

'We have the same but in metal.'

'Won't last as long as hornbeam.'

'Maybe not.'

He showed him the smooth flour pouring out into sacks, later to be stored in bins.

Joe considered the community primitive in many of its aspects but he was impressed by the technology that had gone into the workings of the windmill and by Meredith's meticulous craftsmanship. For all the computerised machinery he doubted they could do much better back home; and the flour was of superior quality, the bread more delicious than any he had ever tasted.

It snowed and though the white covering melted in the sun it presaged what was to come.

Joe found Kathryn disconsolate in the dairy.

'The cows are drying up,' she said.

'Will we have to slaughter them?'

We? The word automatically uttered surprised him for it assumed that he would remain here in the foreseeable future. If Kathryn noticed she made no comment.

'Not unless the winter gets worse. Usually we manage to hold out with the fodder.'

She looked away as though she did not believe what she said.

One evening after supper was cleared away Randolph said,

'I've got something to show you.'

He took him into the wood carving shed. Among a pile of stripped wood lay a large section of oak.

'That's yours.'

Joe passed his hands over the surface. It felt rough to the touch but alive. He could hardly wait to pick up the tools arrayed before him and create an object worthy of the tree they had felled.

'We brought it down a few days ago. But you'll have to practise on softer woods, yellow pine or lime.'

It was the first of many evenings. Randolph showed Joe, an avid pupil, the quality of different woods, sycamore, rosewood, walnut, the way their grain ran, their advantages and drawbacks. Soon Joe could tell from the feel alone which wood he was touching and could, like an insect, identify them by their pungent aroma. He wondered why women used perfume made from flowers instead of trees. He could imagine nothing more alluring.

'These tools are very old, aren't they?'

'Been around for generations.'

Perhaps they had been used to carve the mantelpiece in the long room. Joe handled them with awe.

Life resumed its normal pattern, the fateful inquisition apparently forgotten. Although no further explanations were forthcoming the general attitude was amicable. Joe had no wish to revive memories of the interrogation, nor did he want to dwell on the community's previous alignment against him. It made him feel the outcast that he knew he was. Unanswered questions remained but Joe had come to understand that the community took the view that events would follow their course. They knew the wisdom of not forcing issues, gathering themselves before the next leap. He would one day have to explain the inexplicable and they would have to declare themselves; but it could wait.

The days were short. A blackout was observed. Shutters were put in position at dusk, lights doused as soon as meals were over, no lamps to light the way to bed. Joe learned the sound and feel of every room, every corridor, every turn in the stairs. The house acquired a new familiarity.

He was aware of other, more significant changes; the relationship between Kathryn and himself.

She had watched over him night and day while he was still unconscious, and most days while he recovered. He resisted her presence by not talking to her. She reciprocated by concentrating silently on tasks that she could do by hand, making clothes, mending, repairing. Yet, despite their unwillingness to communicate, an indefinable intimacy grew between them. It was as though, merely by being there, Kathryn released some of her privacy and drew Joe into her orbit. He sensed, beneath her calm exterior, an emotional vortex as heady as his own. He found it increasingly difficult to resist.

They sought each other out, working together as often as they could though it was Belinda who taught Joe to weave, dye and sew. Kathryn would come in and see them, heads bent over work, laughing together and Joe would find himself comparing the two girls. Belinda was pretty, entertaining, feminine, alluring in her own way. Katherine made no such concessions. Her personal magnetism was strong, her enigmatic manner attractive. Joe was surprised that this attribute had escaped him for so long.

He noticed a thousand details about Kathryn, how she walked with a spring in her step, head erect, her fair hair bouncing on her back, the unusual colour of her green-blue eyes, how they shone when she laughed. He noticed her trim figure, her high rounded breasts, her small capable hands, magically soft and pliant. He noticed her and she, he knew very well, noticed him. Life acquired a new dimension and it was wholly pleasurable.

Some days they did not see one another from dawn to dusk. This should have been of scant significance but Joe minded, minded not being near her, minded not hearing her laugh, missed her sparky rejoinders, the sense of exhilaration she gave him, a heightening of perception when they were together that excited, even exalted him.

Early one morning while it was still dark, knowing she was on guard duty, he stole downstairs. Otto was in the kitchen.

'Where are you going?' he asked

'Up the hill to meet Kathryn.'

Otto nodded and Joe sensed, not disapproval but unease. He wondered at it for the others, if they had noticed his and Kathryn's burgeoning relationship, had made no comment even by implication.

He reached the foot of the pine and heard her climbing down.

'Hi! What are you doing here? '

'Thought I'd bring you some bread and something to drink.'

They sat together on the guard duty blanket and watched the sun rising over the hills, an unusual hard clarity illuminating every stone, every bush, every plant. It took Joe's breath away and sent a tremor down his spine. Kathryn looked at him as though he had called.

One winter at home, while he was still at primary school, when a nearby lake had frozen, the town had come out, wrapped in gloves and scarves, cheeks red from the cold, like hers were now, to slide and skate. He, Martin and some friends had arranged to meet at midnight and, to the sounds of long forgotten tunes, had skated on a frozen pond. He could hear the absurd waltzes now.

He wanted to tell her, so vivid was it.

She turned to him.

'What is it?' she asked.

How could he answer? They had no past in common, no connecting link, no mutual reference points. An unbridgeable gulf lay between them.

'I love you,' he said.

He was trembling and he could feel the blood rushing to his face. The words had come unbidden, they had said themselves, had revealed a mine of emotion that had been concealed. He experienced a moment of pure and exquisite joy.

Kathryn took his hand and with her eyes acknowledged what she had not dared declare.

He's said it now. 'I love you.' Did I want him to? I don't know. All those long hours I sat by his side his presence grew into me, his strangeness, his otherness. I have never met anyone like Joe, a bewildered animal that has lost its way and cannot find its tracks yet with an odd strength which, once emerged from the thicket of his bewilderment, could be formidable.

I watched his face lying on the pillow, his eyelids fluttering as he dreamed, his slender hands resting at his side. Joe is beautiful.

I can't pinpoint the exact moment when I knew I loved him. It stole on me and took over my heart. But my mind remains clear. This is a love that is impossible.

He longed to take her in his arms but her look, complex and frightening, made him draw back. And he was glad for he needed time to explore his feelings, needed to understand the seismic change that was taking place, he needed to absorb the complex vistas it revealed.

They walked back on the hard frosty ground, not touching though Joe felt her burning presence at his side. As they approached the house she turned to him and lightly brushed his cheeks with her lips.

Inside, Otto looked at them briefly. Later Randolph came in.

'You realise what's happening?'

'Yes.'

'We have to stop them, before it's too late.'

'It already is,' Otto said.

Joe could not catch up with his feelings, his intellect unable to absorb what his joyful heart told him. Since uttering the three magic words, 'I love you,' he found himself inhabiting an enchanted world, a place where every particle, every blade reflected joy unbounded. He spoke to the trees, to the sky ecstatically of his love, he spread it across the universe, shouted it into the ether; this was to be alive, this was the elixir, the glorious zenith of existence. And from its height he perceived, as though a gauze curtain had been lifted, Otto, Randolph, Meredith, Belinda, with new lucidity. He saw them without awe, without fear, he ached to reach out and touch them and say, 'Whatever is the mystery of your lives, the secret heart of your existence, I am a part of it, a brother in your plight.'

A perverse fate, or was it a deliberate pause, a still moment before passion overwhelmed them, kept him and Kathryn apart during the next days. Meetings were brief, eyes averted. Joe's elation was punctuated by moments of stark desolation. Was she avoiding him? Was his declaration repugnant to her? He looked for a sign, some indication other than the light kiss she had given him, that she reciprocated his feelings. For days that stretched to eternity Joe waited in an agony of suspense and unrequited love.

I can't sustain this much longer, have tried to deny my feelings, tried to avoid the vortex I know is lying in wait. And as though my own confusion were not enough Randolph cornered me and warned me not to proceed with a relationship with Joe. He spelled out all its inherent dangers, as though I didn't know them already. He almost commanded me to deny my feelings.

The longing in my body gives me a different message.

It's the way Joe looks at me, the promise in his eyes. A world apart is pulling me inexorably into its orbit.

One morning, as Kathryn and Joe were tending a sick calf, their hands touched. She did not take hers away and looked him full in the face. There was no mistaking the message. Joe knew that the uncertainty and the suspense were over. He walked on air the remainder of the day, almost faint with anticipated joy.

After dark had fallen and the house was still, he waited by his door and when he heard her padded footsteps approach he leapt to open it and wrap her in his arms. That night, and every other night that was to come, Joe learned the transcendental power of love and Kathryn an ecstasy beyond the imagined possible.

The others were wary at first in their acceptance of this new development. It altered the pattern of long-established relationships. To Meredith, lost as he always was in his thoughts, it appeared to make scant difference though secretly he harboured his own form of love for Kathryn. Although it neither demanded nor required her response he could not avoid a twinge of envy, swiftly repressed, at Joe's good fortune. Belinda felt a cold draught of loneliness. As Kathryn and Joe spent more and more time together the confidences she had always shared with Kathryn became less frequent and less intimate. Randolph watched developments with a wary but not necessarily unsympathetic eye. He was no stranger to the joys and pangs of love but feared for Joe and Kathryn, two beings whose roots lay in lands far apart. Only Otto remained subtly aloof, implying silently that their liaison was folly. This Joe swept aside, treating it as an intrusion. Kathryn was more circumspect. She knew well enough the reasons for Otto's unease but she was not yet ready to share them with Joe. Joe did not press her, knowing that the situation was not as straightforward as it seemed. He was content with present joys.

Happiness is infectious and it spread through the group. Their serious attitude to life was now frequently punctuated with laughter, silence broken with talk. Joe felt he was at last among friends. Even the dread of an attack in the oncoming winter was diminished. But the threat was no less real for that and watch had still to be kept night and day. A changeover took place at midnight based on a rota system which allowed Joe and Kathryn limited nights together.

One night Joe was on duty for the first watch, to be replaced by Kathryn for the second. He heard her climb the tree and, when her head appeared over the edge of the platform, hauled her to her feet. They sat together for a while, contemplating the dark.

'Aren't you going?' she asked eventually. 'You need some sleep.'

'Why now? Haven't had any for the last few weeks.'

They stayed together until morning.

From then on they did duty together, but every second or third night both were free for long ecstatic explorations of surpassing tenderness and passion that left them limp with happiness. They walked in glory.

The weather grew more severe, the temperature dropped below freezing, maintaining its icy grip even at midday. The house was cold, only the kitchen offered a welcome warmth. One night, dark lowering clouds filled the sky.

An unaccustomed silence, a shift in the light, luminous and soft as it filtered through frosted windows, roused Kathryn and Joe early next morning. They beheld a world of snow, blinding in the reflection of the rising sun, the branches of trees raising white arms to a clear sky. Only the paw marks of wild predators disturbed the virgin surface of the ground.

They ran out and, arms spread, threw themselves into banks of snow piled against the house, one impression after another, a row of shining snow angels burnished by light; they kicked up minuscule snowstorms, they pelted each other with snowballs and made a slide along the frozen pond. Kathryn broke a section of ice at its edge and, turning it over, revealed its intricate, crystalline patterns. Joe wished they could be preserved forever.

They made a snowman from two huge rolled snowballs and dressed him in a hat and scarf. The traditional carrot served as his nose, his smiling mouth was formed by pebbles; they pulled a heavy wooden sledge, normally used to haul wood and cattle feed, out of a shed and set it on the crest of the hill. Joe had a sudden vision of his mother taking him to London to buy him a toboggan for Christmas. They had gone to Hamley's, for an expensive, barely affordable, slatted affair. He wished he had it now as they spun down on an erratic course, arriving in a heap beside a pair of astonished oxen. Up the slope, down, again and again in wild exhilaration, sometimes on their backs watching the sky revolve, then face down, the earth speeding past. Joe clasped Kathryn in a tight, close embrace.

'I'll never let you go,' he said.

At night the moon lit snow reflecting fields and trees, it shone through windows into the house. They left the shutters open while they ate their meals, lights doused. But their vigilance tightened as the danger increased with every wintry day. Joe was taken to a previously unexplored armoury deep in the bowels of the house. Long arrays of axes, swords, scabbards and sharp bladed knives adorned the walls. He was initiated into their use in attack and self defence. He learned to be nimble and sure-footed but regarded with awe and some fear the possibility that he would be expected to kill another human being, an eventuality that had never occurred to him, not even in his wildest imaginings; but with every practice his confidence grew and he learned to handle his weapons with a skill he found exhilarating.

'We can never quite tell, ' Randolph said, ' but usually they come in carts, six or seven of them.'

'How do they get over the cliffs - they're much too steep for oxen?'

'Further east the land is lower.'

'What weapons do they use?'

'Swords, knives, axes.'

'Sounds bloody.'

'It is, though they're usually satisfied with one death for each raid, two at the most. Then they leave.'

'Why?'

'Hard to tell.'

But Randolph knew.

There was a limit to what could be done on the farm. It remained only to feed, bed and water the animals twice a day. Neither goats nor cows yielded well and the hens ceased laying altogether. After a time, animal feed ran low and had to be rationed to a daily minimum. Inside, the community was increasingly reliant on its stores.

But the winter provided an unexpected benefit for Kathryn and Joe. Freed from the constant demands of work outside, they revelled in each extra minute spent together. Both knew that what the gods have granted they can take away.

*

The sewers underlie the town in a complicated network, culminating in four different sumps in which, filtered by gates, solid detritus remains. This the children have to empty into wheelbarrows and push up a tunnel. The gradient is steep. At the far end a grill is opened and other, older prisoners take over and wheel the sludge away. It is terrible work. The citizens living their lives above, deposit not only human waste but all decomposing matter. It piles up in great heaps. As soon as they have cleared a sump, it fills almost instantaneously. At least the waste gives off a modicum of warmth but the stench is unendurable. Some get accustomed to it, others die after a few days.

Susie suffers it as best she can. She is greatly sustained by her friendship with Ian and by her indomitable spirit. They are both determined to survive.

*

For all their love and passion Joe was acutely aware of a barrier between himself and Kathryn, inevitable he supposed, with so little of a past to share. He wanted to draw her in, to tell her about his life as it had been up to that moment, his previous hopes, ambitions, fears. He had no desire to return, he repeatedly assured her, but he wanted her to understand the world that had shaped him. He would begin by telling her about school, his mother, his father's desertion, the kind of life he used to lead. Though she listened with attention he could sense resistance. Puzzled at first and hurt he gradually realised that it was not for lack of interest in what he had to say, but fear - fear that he regretted being with her and would try to return to his world. So he desisted and spoke only of the present.

I wish I didn't know what he's keeping back - his longing for his former life, I see the regret in his eyes when he talks about it. Sometimes, when he's morose and silent, he's off and away on another planet where I can't reach him.

I have my own secret, don't I; I prevaricate when he asks me about my past. I can only tell him so much, piecemeal bits of information so that he doesn't guess the rest. This is not the way to conduct a loving relationship and I hate myself for my cowardice. It's fear of losing him that is holding me back. I know already that Joe is my destiny, the most passionate love of my life, yet we neither of us can offer the other the confidences natural to lovers, we circle round the dangerous areas, ignore the pools of silence. My fear is that we'll drown in them in the end. Somehow, sometime, I will have to take the risk. I will have to break the deadlock. But not yet, not yet.

—

Chapter Eight

JOE'S expectations of a loving relationship were, like Kathryn's, high, his desire to share, to confide, to be honest about who he was and who he aspired to be, part of a romantic ideal that he had acquired, perhaps from television and films, perhaps from books; certainly not from his parents who, before they separated, lived in an atmosphere of barely suppressed aggression and of intense disappointment. This was a situation Joe did not want repeated. He wanted to hold nothing back from Kathryn and Kathryn to hold nothing back from him. Yet he had already been forced into a position in which he was reluctant to talk about his past. So was Kathryn. He could not imagine why. That their lack of openness would affect their intense love was his greatest fear. Their bodies were totally committed to one another, but their minds remained closed.

This studied non-communication extended to the others. Joe suspected them of conspiring with Kathryn to keep him ignorant of the reasons for their precarious situation. They in turn took Joe's compliance for granted. He sensed also that they kept from him other, deeper truths.

His attempts at questions wavered from straightforward to subtle. These were met with skilfully balanced and firmly ambivalent replies. His only remaining option was to force the issue and break the silence but he was reluctant to implicate Kathryn, fearing the harm it might do to their relationship. He did not want to challenge her.

Opportunity presented itself one night when Belinda was on watch duty and everyone else in the kitchen holding a council of war about the possibility of an attack. Joe was unable to contain himself any longer and broke into the discussion with a demand that they be more specific about the reasons for the guerilla war being threatened.

'Do they attack every winter?' he asked

'No, only sometimes.'

'It's time you let me in. I want to know what's going on. I belong here now.'

They were silent at first, each one waiting for the other to speak. Otto, as always, took the lead.

'Not ultimately. You can't banish your roots and nor can we.'

'It's what you feel that matters, not what you are,' Joe said.

'It matters in the long run,' Randolph said.

'You don't understand.'

'I wish we didn't.'

There was a sadness in Otto's voice that silenced Joe.

Later Randolph took Kathryn aside.

'We won't be able to hold back much longer. He'll have to be told.'

'Be patient,' she later begged Joe, 'there are things about us you don't yet know. We'll tell you. Just give us a little more time.'

Time for what? he wondered. But he respected her wish and said no more.

The sun ceased to shine. The air, grey, frozen and still, concealed the world like a shroud. Sheep had to be dug out of snowdrifts and brought in, water carried daily from the well, for the stream had frozen, and precious hay and straw, normally rationed, provided in greater quantity. It was too cold to milk the cows in the mornings so they confined milking to midday until eventually the yield dropped to nothing. A continuation of the cold would force slaughtering them. This Joe dreaded, knowing it would be hard for Kathryn to bear.

Watch duty was confined to three hours at a stretch. Climbing up the frozen slippery trunk of the pine required thick boots and sheepskin clothing, making the ascent ever more hazardous. Otto offered to take his turn.

'No,' Randolph said, 'we need you in the house, you know that.'

Otto acquiesced. He provided constant hot food and heated bricks inside hay sacks for the watchers to take.

'It's for your hands and feet. If you're too cold you won't be able to climb down.'

The oxen were brought in. Wild deer grew tame and in desperation for food tried poaching hay. Birds died, petrified with the cold. Joe watched a wood pigeon slide off an ice laden roof and land with a thud at his feet. Its glazed eyes were open and stared at him helplessly. It was already stiff. In the night, the howl of wolves circling the animals kept them awake. The pack was hungry and dangerous, bold enough to appear during the day uncomfortably close to the house. Sheds had to be made wolf-proof. One night Joe dreamed that their faces were pressed against his window, seeking entry.

He remembered with a shiver his previous encounter in the woods. His cries woke Kathryn.

'What is it?'

He had scrupulously heeded her request to let matters lie and this, he had concluded, meant respecting also her reluctance to be drawn into his story; but now he forced her to listen as he traced his gradual metamorphosis from innocent boy to young man. He wanted her to understand the terror the wolves had inspired, not from their physical threat but through dark Stygian forces lying in his unconscious.

*

It is cold in the dungeon and the temperature is still dropping fast. Susie does not know how much longer she is going to last. The children are severely undernourished and several have died and been dragged away without ceremony.

Although talk is not allowed and any child caught speaking is punished by being deprived of their meagre ration of water and gruel, Ian and Susie talk at night. There is no guard on duty because none is prepared to spend even an hour in the dungeon. These precious hours are their salvation. Though they are half-dead with fatigue they tell each other everything; and they plot to escape despite the slim chances of success. The only visible way out is through the grill to which the wheelbarrows are taken but this is heavily guarded and the children are hit by batons if there is any misdemeanour, imagined or real. The guards are not frightened to batter the children to death. They are destined to die because they are illegal. Children are not supposed to exist.

Susie asks if anyone has seen a girl called Rose but no one has.

*

A blizzard hit some ten days after the first snow. To keep watch was impossible, the likelihood of the townspeople appearing remote. The wind roared through the trees, it beat great flurries of snow into the air and built up deep drifts. It howled round the buildings, sought every cranny, an evil spirit trying to gain entry. The house creaked and groaned in the onslaught and at the far end, as walls crumbled, wind and snow blasted their way inside. A section of the roof caved in. They repaired the damage as best they could but as often as not new reparations had to be made the next morning. It was war, the humans against the elements.

The animals, dispirited, retreated into a state of semi-hibernation, huddling together to keep warm. Feeding them once a day, buffeted by wind and snow, became a hazardous expedition. The goats and poultry were brought into a section of the house. The goats' yields rose a little in the warmer atmosphere and kept the community supplied with small quantities milk but the chickens, heads lowered, feathers ruffled, refused to lay.

The humans spent their spare time in the kitchen next to a blazing fire generously fed by the logs they had sawn and saved. While Randolph shut out the wind's howls with haunting melodies on the flute they busied themselves with a variety of odd jobs. Sometimes Kathryn sang.

One evening Joe had found in the carving shed a variety of soft woods piled in a corner. He had learned enough by then to recognise them as among the varieties used to make musical instruments. He had himself, when his mother was too hard up to buy him one, set out to make a guitar and had littered the garden shed with pieces of wood picked up from skips and waste grounds. He and Martin had studied the relevant manuals but after a first burst of enthusiasm were forced to give up. It was too difficult. His grandparents, in one of their few generous gestures, had eventually bought him one.

Now, as he listened to Randolph, he longed to play again. He missed his music.

'I don't suppose,' he said, 'it would be possible to make a guitar.'

They looked puzzled. He explained.

Randolph sprang up and moments later came back with a six stringed, violin shaped instrument, similar to a viola. Its top was made from spruce, the body from rosewood. Though it had a patina to protect it, it was not highly polished like those at home but when Joe held it against his chest and strummed it gently he coaxed from it a mellow, dark sound that pleased him. The strings were made from gut. These were difficult to tune but he managed after a time to bring the instrument close to a D major scale. It had clearly not been played for some time.

He tentatively played the songs he knew best, singing along and gaining confidence as he familiarised himself with the instrument. The Red Hot Chilli Peppers, Van Morrison, any song he could remember even if only in phrases, poured from his fingers. To Joe's astonishment Randolph quickly joined in, picking up refrains as he went along. With a purely oral tradition behind him, Randolph was adept at doing this. It made Joe wonder whether at home they had, despite all their carefully acquired literacy and notations, lost a true feeling for making music.

After several evenings of playing together they were able to regale their entranced listeners with songs by Aretha Franklin, Sting, Dido, Bob Dylan, the soul music of James Brown. It was a bizarre development, popular music from Joe's times transferred to this empty wilderness for people who had never heard an electronic instrument, never mind CD's or tapes, and who had certainly never been to a gig. But, once accustomed to the new sound, they revelled in it and would sing along with words to which they could not always relate but which they liked.

Some nights they told stories. These were extraordinary, unlike any Joe had ever heard, tales that travelled into realms undreamed of and unknown. One person would begin, someone else take up the tale then another and another in a round robin that could last all night. Joe was spellbound, drowned in a collective unconscious that reached into time immemorial.

At the onset of the cold weather Joe and Randolph had transferred the contents of the carving shed into a spare room in the house. Sometimes Joe brought his work into the kitchen and as he listened the enchantment of the words manifested itself in the creatures that crawled out of the wood. What nature killed outside he re-created. His first, an otter, long, lithe and delicate, crouched in the grass he gave to Belinda who had been coveting it with her eyes. Next came a fox for Randolph, bushy tail trailing as he had seen it on the night watches across the frozen fields. Otto, picking it up, said,

'You're very talented, like my father.'

'Your father? Was he a wood carver?'

'Yes, he carved all the wood in this house.'

'Even the mantelpiece in the long room?'

'Especially the mantelpiece in the long room.'

'Am I using his tools?'

'Yes.'

They contained his magic, of this Joe was convinced. He could feel it through his fingertips.

One evening Joe launched into 'When I'm Sixty Four'. It was the first time he had sung them a Beatles song and they were enchanted by it and hummed along with him but when he got to 'sixty four' he caught a conspiratorial look between Kathryn and Randolph. It made him angry and resentful. He was still excluded from the group's most intimate secrets, and it hurt. He stopped playing

'What was all that about?' he asked later when he and Kathryn were alone.

'What was what about?'

'You and Randolph exchanging significant looks when I sang the Beatles song.'

'Joe,' she said, 'I asked you to wait.'

'I've waited. You still don't trust me!'

'It's nothing to do with trust.'

'What then?'

She turned away.

It was the closest they had come to an argument. He did not sing 'When I get older' again but he was puzzled. Of the many songs in his repertoire, this was the least controversial. It was about love, nothing else. He could not imagine why it should have been singled out for special consideration but supposed he would eventually be told. The group would have finally to reveal this great secret of theirs.

He thought he might ask Randolph during the many hours they worked together at their carvings but never quite dared. It felt too much like going behind Kathryn's back. So he kept quiet. He was, in any case, often alone in the shed which, in many ways, he preferred. As he cut, gouged and sculpted, drawing from the wood the life it yielded, the power of creation absorbed him utterly.

Better able now to appreciate the technical skill that had gone into the making of the mantelpiece in the long room, he returned one morning to look at it again. The murky light obscured the finer points of the carving so Joe, ignoring the snow and wind outside, forced open a shutter. He studied the masterly handiwork, as intricate in its own way as the patterned ice Kathryn had presented to him the first morning it froze. Kneeling on the floor he passed his hands over the shining wood and as he bent down to take a closer look at the protruding head of a snake he noticed that one of the wooden panels on the wall concealed a door. Curious, he pulled on a small flat handle cunningly made almost invisible and was astonished to find, in this bookless house, two thick leather-bound volumes, dry and dusty with age. He gently pulled one out and opened it at random to reveal a cursive hand-written script on thick paper, the edges rough as he had seen them on old manuscripts. The text was difficult though not impossible to decipher. The title page, written in a bold dark blue, bore the legend, The History of My People.

As if by some prearranged signal, Randolph walked in. Joe started guiltily as though caught in an illicit act but Randolph nodded approvingly and said,

'You'd better read those.'

Joe took away the first volume.

Written in the form of a story, it related the history of a people that had lived in England long ago; no dates were specified but the analysis of the society it depicted was detailed and exact, enumerating the many villages - there was no mention of towns or larger conurbations - spread over the country. These enjoyed a peaceful existence without precedent in Joe's knowledge of history, an Arcadia without wars, battles, kings, queens or prelates. People lived simply, apparently with few laws and little necessity to enforce them

Each village, surrounded by an ample acreage of pasture and arable land and in some places by mineral deposits like coal and iron ore, was self sufficient in its most basic needs and could survive if necessary as an independent entity. Trading existed, conducted without money on an ancient and unchanging barter system. Travellers journeyed from village to village in the spring and summer months, bringing goods and produce from all over the country, their arrival the occasion for elaborate celebrations. There was no discernible class system. The villages were run on a democratic rather than a hierarchical structure. Every villager had the same status regardless of function, whether he cleaned sewers or arbitrated disputes. Women were considered equal to men, held the same rights and were eligible in a universal franchise in the election of leader, a post held for five years.

There were other details but Joe skated over them and other pages that, like the Egyptian hieroglyphs, detailed the individual worth of animals and produce, balancing one against the other. Joe learned that one cow was the value of four sheep, certain ornaments for women were worth two chickens, dried salt cod was weighed against eggs, on and on for many pages. What emerged clearly was that the system was stable and could be maintained despite seasonal variations of supply. The mantra of constant economic growth did not apply.

Nature was nourished, sustained and worshipped in a pragmatic way, with festivals and celebrations as the year turned. Plant and animal breeding was sophisticated though for goals different from those in Joe's world. Instead of heavy high yielders, animals were bred for hardiness. Cattle and sheep stayed outdoors all the year round unless conditions were severe.

Schools were rare, though not unknown. Generally it was the task of parents to teach their children the rudiments of literacy and to put them through an apprenticeship whether for farming or a specialised skill like carpentry or mining. Most children entered the same sphere of work as their parents, acquiring experience as they grew up.

The villagers appeared to be satisfied with their lives and were neither constantly striving for more than they had nor jostling for position, for none had cause to feel oppressed. The book was a paean of praise for what Joe perceived as a primitive, pastoral society, an idealised, stable version of an England without conflict or expansion, picturesque but unattainable. With his twenty-first century cynicism Joe suspected a far rougher reality. Diplomatically, for he sensed he was treading on sensitive ground, he allowed some of his scepticism to show through.

'Are these legends?' he asked the assembled company one evening.

'No.'

'True?'

'All of it.'

'It's so perfect. Not a bit like now.'

'You'll see in the next volume. It didn't last. Not forever.'

'We acquired too much knowledge,' Otto said

'Too much knowledge?'

'Yes.'

Of what? They knew nothing compared even to an eighteen year old like himself - no maths, no physics, no electronics and no science. These people were in the Dark Ages. He could help them, teach them whatever science and medicine he knew. He would transform their mode of living, offer them at least some of the benefits of his own century. He saw himself no longer as an intruder but as a saviour and later eagerly told Kathryn all he had planned. He was surprised at her lack of enthusiasm but assumed it was impossible for her to understand the benefits he was offering.

*

Susie is convinced that her parents are dead but she is mistaken. They are still alive, shut up in solitary, windowless cells.

They are interrogated relentlessly about the boy in the park, sometimes together, sometimes apart. The junta think that he is the leader of a plot to overthrow the government and are trying to make Susie's parents give them information about him but this Susie's parents cannot do for they did not see him. At first they proclaim their innocence but soon realise that as long as the interrogators believe that they have more information to give they will be kept alive.

Although it is difficult to be consistent as often one does not know what the other has said, they succeed in fooling their interrogators for a while. They make up stories about Joe, giving out spurious pieces of information one at a time. They claim that he has come from far away but they do not know from where. They say that they have never met him and only heard about him but this earns them a beating because they were seen coming with him from the park. They then pretend that they tried to get information from him but he refused to give any but they did discover that he came from the far north and spoke with a strange accent that was difficult to understand. Finally, they make up a weird tale that he has come from another land, another planet. This is too much even for the credulous chiefs.

The interrogations stop and they are left in prison, sustained only by a minimum of food and water and hope, the hope that they will once again see their daughter.

*

Blizzards and snowstorms succeeded one another in a relentless cycle. The animals suffered most. One morning Kathryn found one of the heifers lying on her side, unable to rise. Another stood with her head down, eyes half shut, ribs sticking out. In normal times these would have been nursed back to health but the intense cold combined with a shortage of fodder left no choice. The heifers were slaughtered. So as not to attract the wolves with the smell, the blood was gathered in buckets to be emptied far away. Meredith took them on the sledge and was gone all day. The carcasses were cut up for meat, some of which was salted and hung to dry, some placed in ice wells for future use.

Two heifers gone, one year's breeding cycle lost. Joe admired Kathryn's stoicism for nothing showed on her face; nor did she comment later. It was only when Joe asked what her feelings were that she said,

'Life sustaining. It's part of the cycle.'

Her sense of reality was far greater than his; but he was learning. Life at this basic level did not allow for sentimentality or illusion.

One night, as they sat quietly round the fire, the dropping snow blanketing all sounds from outside, Joe brought in a block from the oak Randolph had kept for him. He held it in his hands, weighing it, feeling the texture, uncertain what he should create. He studied the grain and as he cut into it, he let his fingers make decisions. Gradually, over many days, a deer emerged, standing delicately, its head raised, large pointed ears pricked forward, its eyes sad, aware, capturing the innocence of the moment before Joe had slain it. It was his best work yet.

He gave it to Kathryn.

Next day the wind dropped. All was still.

They hurried out to the farm. Meredith showed Joe tracks made by wolves.

'See how close they've come.'

Joe shivered.

The days were spent in a frenzy of repair on farm and house. The three hour rota on the pine was resumed. No one went out alone and no one went unarmed. An attack was expected daily.

—

Chapter Nine

Here with a loaf of bread beneath the bough,
A flask of wine, a book of verse - and Thou
Beside me singing in the wilderness-
And wilderness is paradise enow.

The voice and music were unmistakably Joe's.
Kathryn, only half awake in the vacated bed, lay quietly
and listened.

'Ah, my beloved, fill the cup that clears
To-day of past regrets and future fears;
Tomorrow! – Why tomorrow I may be
Myself with yesterday's seven thousand years.

She ran to the window and, in an unconsciously
classical pose, leaned out.
'What are you doing?'
'Serenading you. I love you!'
She was enchanted. She was always enchanted these
days. Joe was a phenomenon in her life, astonishing and
delighting her at every turn. And passionate, with a kind
of carelessness as though the largesse of life was so
abundant he could scatter it heedlessly. She and the
others were parsimonious with food, objects of desire,
frivolity, even with love, but Joe had taught her that the
world is full of riches, nature careless in her prodigality.
She learned that she was allowed the same luxury.

Kathryn's life had become, if not carefree, at least as light as the wind.

'I'm going to call you Juliet,' he called up to her.

'Who she? An old girl friend?'

'Sort of. A character out of a story. I've always been a little in love with her.'

'Come up and tell me.'

She loved his stories, strange revealing tales that allowed her small glimpses into his world.

'I ought to climb up, really. You need a balcony.'

'Haven't got one. Try the stairs.'

He lay down beside her and she put her head on his shoulder.

'Juliet is a beautiful young girl, like you.' He kissed her, 'and she falls in love with Romeo, a beautiful young man, like me. But...'

'I knew there'd be a but. There always is!'

'Wouldn't be a story otherwise. Don't interrupt. It would all have been fine if it weren't for the fact that their families have been deadly enemies for generations. Juliet's father won't let her meet Romeo or marry him, which she is determined to do. Fortunately Juliet has a nurse and she protects the lovers. They spend enchanted nights together...'

'Like us.'

'Don't interrupt. They marry in secret and plan to run away but the stern father wants Juliet to marry someone else. He locks her up. Romeo doesn't help matters by killing someone in a fight. He has to flee the city. So... Juliet takes a special potion.'

'So you have them in your world?'

'This is a story, not reality. The scheme is that the potion induces a deathlike trance and she will appear to be dead, but she won't be, merely asleep. Romeo is to be told and to be ready to run away with her once she has woken but...'

'Another but...'

'Romeo hears that Juliet is dead. He is distraught with grief and vows to end his life. He gets a poisonous drink and finds what he thinks is her corpse lying by the family tomb, waiting for burial. The man Juliet's father wanted her to marry is also there. Romeo fights and kills him and then he swallows the poison and lies down beside her. Juliet regains consciousness and, seeing Romeo dead, kills herself with his dagger.'

'How sad! But all your stories are.'

'Only some - but yours are no different.'

'I suppose you're right.'

She paused.

'I hope nothing like that ever happens to us.'

'We're not star-crossed lovers,' he said.

Spring slowly announced itself and the danger of attack receded. The snow melted, crystals to water, leaving the earth sodden; but by early April wind and sun had done their work. The winter corn lost its bedraggled look and threw up fresh green shoots. Meredith and Randolph turned furrows of glistening soil and sowed spring oats. The surviving animals, scraggy, weak and underfed, were let out. The pungent scent of renewal went to their heads and sent them running round the fields as though the winter had never been. Day watches were discontinued. It seemed to Joe and

Kathryn that their cup of happiness was full. They danced their ecstasy to the music of the fresh spring wind.

Joe had resumed his reading during the winter months. Volume Two of The History of My People painted a very different picture from the first, one that Joe recognised, for its depiction of brutality and lust for power echoed the history of his own world. He was not surprised to learn that the peaceful idyll that had been so long maintained by the village states erupted with terrifying speed, the passive acceptance of the status quo blown apart. Its catalyst was a rumour that spread from village to village concerning a herbal potion concocted by two wise men living in the mountains to the west - Wales. Wise men were important members of each community. Doctors, herbalists and spiritualists, they held a position similar to that of the Celtic Druids but acted with greater benevolence. Their most important skill lay in their knowledge of the healing power of plants. They were able to ease pain and cure certain maladies but were unable to prolong life. A natural equilibrium was thus maintained. Birth and death balanced each other in equal measure.

But now these wise men claimed that they had made a herbal mixture from rare plants which arrested the process of ageing for an indefinite period from the moment the drug was taken though it did not confer immortality. Death from disease or by another's hand was still possible. The ingredients of this potent mix they had kept secret for one hundred and fifty years, the age they said they now were, still fit and young and with no sign of the years they carried. It was difficult to believe. People scoffed, asking for proof. Anyone, they said, could pretend to be any age they liked. Some adventurous souls made the long journey to Wales to see for themselves. They returned convinced. Old people who had known the wise men all their lives, who had been told about them by their fathers and their grandfathers, attested to the wise men's age.

Joe shared the scepticism of the villagers. It was inconceivable that a society as primitive as the one described should have arrived at a stage more advanced in prolonging the human life span than his own.

He read on.

Rumour of the drug's efficacy spread, particularly among the young who, with this new wave of possibility, saw their lives take a different shape from that of their forefathers. The drug's potency was exaggerated with every telling. It was now believed that it made those who took it immortal, that nothing could kill them. This caught the popular imagination like a fever. The populace grew restive. Everyone wanted to take the drug while others, more enterprising, sought to learn how to mix it and hold its power in their hands. A stampede began. All over England groups of young people defied their village elders and travelled west to benefit from this miracle.

With this Joe could identify. The older generation seemed always to want to maintain the old order, could never be convinced that innovation was not synonymous with decadence; but the young were anxious to forge ahead. In this case, though, the results were rather different. Long held traditions were cast aside but there was no new radical movement to take their place.

Instead, the younger generation moved west in search of the drug. Villages were depleted, harvests lost and livestock neglected. In the south, a village chief killed two boys in an attempt to prevent them leaving.

Such wholesale desertion had never happened before. An outraged populace, clinging to the old ways, rose in rebellion and fought the young vanguards of change. Within a short time stable communities had disintegrated. The young fought the old, family fought against family. Anarchy reigned and civil war escalated with frightening speed. After generations of peaceful living, the society was in turmoil. The two wise men were horrified at the disintegration they had unleashed but powerless to halt it. They went into hiding and, after many days' deliberation, agreed that the only hope of restoring order was to destroy the drug and all knowledge of it. As they were the only people who knew what its ingredients were, they would have to put themselves beyond reach. They made a suicide pact and withdrew in the hope that, after their deaths, life would eventually resume its normal pattern.

One of the wise men was the writer of the chronicle.

On the last page of Volume Two he had written:

'I Julian, attest to the truth of all I have written which was experienced by me. These are my last words. Tomorrow is the day of our death.'

That was all.

Joe put the volume back in its place beside the carved mantelpiece and pondered. Civil war was not an unfamiliar phenomenon, it was similar to the history of his own world but the context here was the stuff of legend and mythology. He found it hard to credit as literal history.

Randolph however clearly considered it important, for he had urged him to read it. Did this mean that the history had an immediate bearing on the present situation, that it was something he needed to know? He speculated on connections and assumed that this community was the remnant of a fleeing populace.

The time sequence was difficult to disentangle. Otto, the repository of all knowledge, could probably tell him more.

He found him slumped by the kitchen stove, head bent. Thinking he was asleep, Joe tiptoed by but Otto raised his head. Joe was shocked by what he saw. Otto's face had lost its youthful look. His eyes were sunken and his skin grey and wrinkled. He looked like an old man. Joe crept out and found Randolph repairing an implement.

'Otto is ill.'

He described what he had seen.

'He's not ill,' Randolph said. 'He's showing his real age. It happens sometimes.'

'What do you mean?'

Randolph gave him a long hard look.

'Tonight. We'll have a meeting tonight.'

*

Although severely debilitated, Susie and Ian have succeeded in surviving the winter, partly by supporting each other, partly because now and then a more kindly guard smuggles them extra blankets and food. There are more of such guards than they could have anticipated and it makes them hopeful that one day the populace will rise against the tyrant. Nevertheless, many have died and the two friends have watched with sadness the bodies being carted away and new children pushed into the dungeon.

Susie's parents are still in prison but barely alive. Each is alone in a cold empty cell without contact with other people, a cruel punishment, designed to dehumanise the prisoners. At first they find the strength to rebel against their isolation and fight the despair it causes but cold and hunger soon take over. They can think of little else except the next thin meal, the next glimpse of a guard. Hope that their child has survived keeps them doggedly alive. Like many another prisoner, they have devised small stratagems for survival. Signals through the walls keep them in contact with the people in the neighbouring cells. There is a network of communication that goes right through the prison and everyone is kept abreast of events.

The prisoners are, like the children, sometimes fortunate enough to have guards on duty who try to ease their lot whenever they can. And as the weather improves they are allowed out into a yard for limited exercise.

They assume this is allowed because they will be useful for work. In this they are not mistaken.

*

They sat round the table once their meal was over, the windows open to the invigorating scent of the spring air. To Joe's relief, Otto had recovered, his features once again normal.

Joe pressed Kathryn's hand but she, looking both apprehensive and defiant, removed it.

'What's' wrong?' he asked her quietly, but she deliberately turned to Belinda. She too seemed ill at ease.

Kathryn's rejection was unexpected and, as far as Joe could make out, without foundation. No quarrel had taken place, no cross word passed between them, not at any time; nor could he think of anything in his behaviour that could have offended her. Angry and hurt, he looked round the table and was astonished at the unease on every face. He was clearly once again in the dock and waited apprehensively for whatever storm was about to break over his head, remembering how the last time such a gathering had taken place the same heavy air of expectancy had preceded the Star Chamber interrogation. Once again, the unpredictability of these young people had taken him by surprise and brought hurtling back his previous sense of alienation. With it came the bitter knowledge that when the chips were down he was still alone, without Kathryn's support. This tasted of betrayal and plunged him into an abyss of despair.

The meeting proceeded and Joe felt relieved that the community appeared to have nothing more dramatic in mind than to continue explaining their history at the point it had left off in Volume Two. What then was wrong with Kathryn? He tried to concentrate on the matter in hand.

'If the two wise men died and knowledge of the drug with them, did the rebellions cease and the villagers return to their homes?' he now asked.

'Far from it. And the two wise men didn't die. Only one. My grandfather, the author of the history.'

'That,' Joe thought, 'explains a lot about this strange young man.'

'When did all this happen?' he asked.

'Over three hundred years ago.'

He saw a look exchanged between the two girls but, too preoccupied with the conclusion that he was beginning to formulate, took little notice. If the events described had occurred three hundred years ago, Otto's grandfather could not have taken part in the related history for there would have to be several generations between then and now; the so-called 'grandfather' would be several 'greats'. The mathematics did not add up.

He asked them.

'No, that's correct. Otto's grandfather.'

'Three hundred years ago?'

No one replied.

The other possibility was that the drug had worked and the normal span of one generation been stretched to unimaginable lengths; but history was a fairy tale, concocted in times past by unsophisticated people. He must not be drawn into a whirlpool of ancient superstitions. He said so.

'But it's true. The drug exists and it works. It prolongs life if not forever, almost indefinitely.'

Looking at their intelligent faces, Joe reminded himself that these were people without the advantages of a scientific education, that one could not expect sophistication equivalent to his own. He could not help a slight lift of superiority but was immediately ashamed. People in his world were no different, fought and died for outmoded beliefs, divided into warring sects, worshipped primitive symbols that, on a rational basis, were unsustainable.

'Helmuth, my grandfather's partner,' Otto continued, 'saw his opportunity for absolute power. He pretended to go along with the planned suicide but did not take his own life. He watched my grandfather die and announced that he had suddenly fallen ill. He ordered a ceremonious burial and pretended to be deeply grieved.'

As soon it was over and the traditional period of mourning observed, Helmuth put carefully laid plans into action. Together with other conspirators he formed an army with rigorous admission rules, creating a top class of chiefs who had to be between thirty and forty years old. These were allowed to take the drug. They were all-powerful and, roaming the countryside with their armies, subjugated each community as they came to it. Many of their chiefs fell in the battlefield against groups of strong young men who opposed them but these, year by year, were eliminated and thousands of people assassinated until Helmuth and his junta reigned supreme over a decimated population.

'No young people escaped?'

Otto paused.

'Some did and went into hiding.'

'You,' Joe said.

Otto nodded.

'All of you here?'

'Yes.'

'Helmuth is still in charge?'

The portrait in Fairfax Road. Joe recalled it with terrifying clarity.

'Yes. He and his chiefs separated into smaller townships, like the one in Bantage, though we think it's now the only one that survives.

'What happened to the others?'

'No one really knows. Perhaps the chiefs weren't strong enough without Helmuth. He wields a terrifying power. The junta he gathered round him imposes a strict regime. One of the laws forbids people to have children.'

Joe looked incredulous.

'For those who have taken the drug, children get in the way. Immortal, or at least such long lived parents don't need to continue the family. They are the family. Some killed their children. Youth became an unnecessary burden and a threat.'

'Does no one die?'

'Yes, disease has not been eradicated but it is rare. And accidents occur, and murders; and at some point old age takes over but it takes a long, long time. Citizens are replaced only when numbers are dwindling. This is done by designated families who are given permission to have children. These are taken away at three months and brought up by the state, indoctrinated and taught to obey orders. At the required age, forty or so, they are given the drug. You can imagine the kind of people they

159

become, servants who perpetuate the tyrant state. That way Helmuth and his cronies stay in power forever. Some parents have been known to hide their children and bring them up secretly but they are usually caught and used as slave labour until they die of exhaustion - which is not long. Certainly none have reached here.'

The girl skipping in the night, the image of perilous innocence, a child hidden from the townspeople. Joe now understood the significance of what he had seen in his headlong flight and his heart went out in pity. He prayed fervently that she was still alive.

The pieces of the puzzle were coming together. Joe with his youthful looks had been a maverick, a threat appearing out of nowhere.

'Why do they want to kill you? Out here in the wilderness you pose no challenge.'

'But we do. They are attached to us as surely as if we were calling them. I hear their longing.'

'Longing to kill you?'

'People often kill the thing they love.'

Joe had heard this said before, back in his world, but now it seemed to him obscene. He could not imagine a situation in which he was even remotely involved with harming Kathryn, never mind being in any way responsible for her death.

'It's a universal truth. They love us because we are their youth, we hold ideals they once had, a purpose in life they have lost. They hate us savagely because they can never quite erase the memory of what they once held sacred.'

'Which is?'

'A belief in the dignity of man, his right to bring up his own children, live in a decent society, the right if you like of happiness, as it used to be, before we lost our innocence.'

'Innocence?'

'We did not know that so much evil was stalking us; that people who had lived in perfect harmony could kill one another. Murderous instinct, lust for power, ruthlessness, all these must have always been part of our society, but hidden. It needed the right circumstances for man's inhumanity to emerge.'

'You wouldn't think it surprising if you lived in my world,' Joe thought. Evil was an accepted fact, evident in every aspect of his civilisation. Wars, unrest and murder were everyday occurrences. The greed for money and for power was relentless. Indeed, it was considered normal, even desirable. People died as a result, thousands, millions. Against such numbers, the demise of these young people and indeed of himself was insignificant, a mere statistic in the vast panorama of the dead.

'That's how the world has always been,' he said.

'Not for us.'

'Cast out of Paradise,' Joe murmured

'What's that?'

'It's a myth we have about a man and a woman who had the chance to live without evil, who sacrificed their innocence for knowledge.'

He explained briefly.

'Yes,' Otto said. 'We've eaten the apple and it tastes bitter.'

As he said this Otto's face was transformed. Was this an illusion, a trick of the eye? The old, ancient Otto was looking at him again, his face wrinkled and grey, his eyes heavy with a world of experience.

'You've all taken the drug, haven't you?' Joe said, but he was looking straight at Kathryn. 'You're not really young people at all.'

'We're as young as the day we took it,' she said, and there was defiance in her voice. 'That's the magic of it. We don't change.'

'But Otto….'

'Otto's different,' Randolph cut in, 'Otto is the grandson of a sage.'

But Joe was not interested in Otto. He was thinking only of Kathryn, trying to absorb knowledge he had probably known in the innermost recesses of his mind but had rejected. And rejected still. It was impossible to think of Kathryn as old as Otto now looked, his beautiful, graceful love. But incredulity was swiftly replaced by bitterness. This was the great secret they had concealed, which Kathryn had entreated him to ignore, this was the essence of their existence, the reason for their enigmatic silences which had haunted and puzzled him. No wonder that an unfathomable abyss had lain, no matter how intimate or passionate their love, between them. She was not who he had thought she was. She had deceived him.

He felt as though the earth had opened and he was slipping into its dark core.

'I have to go away for a while,' he said.

No one tried to prevent him and he left the room. They looked after him, resigned and sad.

Kathryn did not come to him that night and the next day he left.

*

The dungeon door is thrown open and a new girl flung down the steps. Her name is Margaret. She has only just been caught, a girl of twelve with fair hair and dark brown eyes. Very pretty but the other children know this will not last. She will soon look like all the rest, ghosts that once were children.

Margaret's parents have been accused of plotting to overthrow the chief, Helmuth, and she is certain they have been killed. But, she says, there are others who want to topple the regime. She knows some of them. But the state is vigilant. People live in terror. Neighbours inform on neighbours, there are spies everywhere.

Susie and Ian tell Margaret that they are devising ways of escape though so far no opportunity has presented itself. And Susie, who has been imprisoned longer than her friends, is growing weak. She urgently needs help.

For once luck is with them.

One of Margaret's relatives is occasionally on guard duty. She is too frightened to be an outright rebel but is prepared to smuggle extra food and clothing for the children when she can. This she whispers to Margaret as she is brought in. Her hope is that she is given the duty of fetching the children for work in the mornings or when they return at night. That way, she can leave food behind with less danger of discovery.

The children plan and plot their escape. Perhaps through Margaret's relative they may be able to make contact with the undrugged children who are still at liberty.

*

Under Otto's watchful eye Joe took essential supplies and stuffed them into a rucksack, enough to last him the long walk to the cave.

'Are you intending to come back?' Otto asked.

'Why didn't you tell me earlier?' Joe countered.

'There's a right time and place for everything.'

Otto's usual gnomic reply. Joe slammed out.

Dawn was breaking as he trekked through the woods, oblivious to the rising mist, to the sun tipped leaves, to the sky embracing the growing light. He made for the river and walked along its bank, spent one night in the open, another in his old bivouac, sadly reduced by time and weather. By midday he was standing approximately opposite the cliff that contained his cave. All markers to it had vanished and he despaired of finding it. One or two climbs up the rock face brought nothing but weariness and frustration, adding to the warring emotions threatening to explode inside his head. He desperately needed, for reasons he could not explain, to be back in that dark womb in which he had learned to survive, through will power, through the insistent demands of life - he knew not what - independent and free. Perhaps the cave's healing powers would work their magic again; or so he hoped.

It was almost dark when, torn and bleeding, he found himself astonishingly on his platform. The tree had grown, the thrush still happily making it its home. The water, after the heavy snows, ran more fiercely from the rock face but inside the cave nothing had changed. He crawled into it with a sense of release and collapsed on his old bracken bedding, dried out and pricking against his skin, but his own, familiar nesting place. He lit the lamp he had brought and in its small encircling light crept apprehensively to the back to find, to his immeasurable relief, his possessions still intact, his watch, a talisman from a life left behind, still going, impassively informing him that almost a year had passed since he had been expelled from home. He thought ruefully of the hapless and innocent boy he had then been, a schoolboy, callow, uncaring, with scant regard for life outside immediate preoccupations. He marvelled now at what these had been, school, friends, television, video games, music, alcohol, drugs. They were more than a lifetime away, they belonged to another world both metaphorical and actual. He wanted no more to do with them.

He sat throughout the night, as he had so often done, watching the play of ghostly light on the land, listening to the night noises of birds and small prey, their cries of distress echoing his own intense confusion.

Kathryn's betrayal tasted like gall. She had lied to him by default, failed to tell him the truth. They had all failed to tell him the truth, content to let him go about his daily business in a cloud of delusion. All were guilty but none more so than Kathryn to whom he had given his great and only gift, his trust, his passion and his love.

It had never occurred to him to question her age. With hindsight this appeared naive. He had read the history and had learned that the drug conferred long life. He had found it difficult, despite the community's assurances to the contrary, to accept this as anything other than a myth, reshaped in the telling. She had traded on that, had done nothing to disillusion him. He was not her first love, probably the successor to countless older loves going back he did not know how many years. He tried to banish images of other men who must have touched her, kissed her, loved her. He had not been exploring new territory but ploughing old furrows and he remembered now with pain how more experienced in the game of love she was, guiding him early on through the strange and intricate country of their passion. He relived every detail, every nuance, their vows of love, the joy of their consummation. He had, he thought bitterly, found the ultimate elixir, the reason for being alive; but it was all illusion, a wayward, taunting ghost. The world was dross, a tableau of mirages evaporating as you approached. Who had her lovers been? Older men, young boys like himself, ancient men who remained forever young? How great was her love for them? Did she caress them, did she use the same endearments on them as she had when she caressed him? She must have offered for their delectation her ineffably beautiful body, her soft lips, her warm, translucent skin. He pictured her nestling in someone else's embrace, in that same house, perhaps in the same bed. It drove him to the point of madness, rage and jealousy.

He looked for the nearest object on which to wreak his vengeance. He seized the ash growing out of the sparse soil and shook it until its roots groaned. The thrush, disturbed in its nest, flew with surprised cries into the night. Joe collapsed on the ground and wept.

The confines of the small platform and the cave could no longer contain him. He hurriedly stuffed his meagre possessions into the rucksack and in the lightening dark climbed down the cliff, determined on escape, across the river, to face dangers unknown. His survival was of scant importance.

He travelled through the night, using the stars to guide him, and by early afternoon of the next day was standing on the river's bank. He had wrapped his coins, all those months ago when they seemed to matter, in the Andrew WK page of 'The Face' and now he spread it out. The text, 'The most passionate emotions are happiness, love, hate and just fucking killing,' struck him as obscene and he tore it into small pieces and let them float away, wondering how he could have even read about so savage a philosophy. He pulled his watch out of his pocket and studied the second hand moving in its tight circle, pitilessly advancing time. The smooth, cool metal against his skin brought back painful memories he preferred to forget, his deliberately offhand acceptance of a gift valued only as a status symbol with which to impress his friends, his mother's rebuffed withdrawal. He had rejected her love and now he was rejecting another. But Kathryn deserves it, he told himself fiercely, and with pent-up rage hurled the watch into the fast flowing current. It sank out of sight to be carried away to the distant ocean. Joe felt his past life go with it.

He stripped and, holding his possessions aloft, prepared to swim across the turbulent water.

—

Chapter Ten

SUSIE'S mother and father are growing weaker. One day the guards order them out of their cells and herd them into a yard crowded with other prisoners. Susie's parents are happy to see each other even though they are scarcely recognisable, so devastating have been the privations to which they have been subjected. But they succeed in smiling and in touching before they are shackled and tied to a cart and with other prisoners driven like donkeys out of the town. Susie's parents succeed in staying close to one another and that gives them strength but others are beaten as they falter. Dogs harass them. Two die on the way, their bodies thrown unceremoniously into bushes for animals to devour. The prisoners are dragged along all that day, and the next and the next until they come to a hillside that, in other circumstances, they would have regarded as beautiful. Now all they can see is a dark door leading into a tunnel into which they are forced, pick axes pushed into their hands.

They are in the salt mines, the grave of countless others.

*

The black greedy mouth of the mine stands open, a scar in the side of a green valley whose smooth grass is an invitation to roll down as we did as children, how long ago, tumbling round and round until the world was spinning and you couldn't stand for dizziness; or cart-wheeling until you dropped, oh so many years back when the world and I were still innocent and young.

We set out five days ago, Randolph and I, to the salt mine, a hard and hazardous journey on a track long out of use, blocked by storm-felled trees, rocks, stones and heady new growth. We're remaking the track as we go along, ready for the return journey and its heavy load; the return journey? I can't think an hour ahead, not a day, not a night, I lie on the cart, helpless, impotent. Randolph is labouring alone, says he doesn't mind, but I mind, I can't move, my mind is numb, my body frozen, seized up like a dead thing. I'm unable to lift the smallest stone, there is too heavy a load in my heart. Joe has gone, his going sudden, our life torn apart in as long as it takes to say ten words, in a moment of time faster than a darting lizard's tongue. One minute he was there, my love, my life, and the next he was gone.

We stop at dusk every night and Randolph lights a fire to keep away the wolves and keep us warm but I'm cold, my body trembling, uncontrolled and uncontrol-lable, no longer mine. I crawl under the cart, don't want to see the stars, prefer the blackness to the open sky.

I can't blame Joe for going, I should have known that a new-born couldn't inhabit our skin and know what it means to live so many years, watching the past mist over as though wrapped in veils. We carry youth and the shadow of a no longer existing old age in our minds and bodies, looking and feeling oh so young, for the experience and wisdom accumulated over the years dies away. Only Otto holds on to it. He's altogether different, like his grandfather, a terrifying figure when we were children and adults too, his utterances like orders proclaimed by an all-powerful spirit; not that Otto is terrifying, far from it, he's tender and vulnerable because he knows...what does he know? He won't tell and we don't ask, perhaps because we don't want to learn what's going to happen before it's happened. He alone is burdened with the future, helpless to alter it, able only to guide; people will do what they will do, their fate is in the stars and in their characters. Otto is not a divine meddler, only an observer. Did he observe Joe's coming, did he know that this stranger would drop out of nowhere and change my life, our lives forever, and could he see the ripples of his alien presence and how it would touch us all?

All the years, have they changed me? I feel no different, I don't think I do but how can one tell, how hold in the memory how one was, what one thought at any past moment? We alter every second, every minute. There is no present, time moves inexorably forward, even for us, it's the equation that's different, one hour a miniscule fraction of my life while each hour and day brings Joe significantly closer to death. I now remember what I had long forgotten, the urgent desire to take the drug, the power of it driving us crazy, the beckoning chimera of indefinite life, of out-staring death.

We boasted we had found the unfathomable elixir; but we didn't know the price we'd have to pay. We didn't realise we'd made a bargain with evil. We posture and exhibit our young minds and bodies but maybe we are deluded like my poor mother gazing into the glass and putting her fingers to the creases in her face saying, 'It's odd, I feel like I did when I was in my twenties,

171

thirties.' But she wasn't a young woman any more, the years had changed her imperceptibly, crept up on her, stealing time. We're done with all that, but the truth we have to recognise is that however much events from the past are lost from memory they have occurred, small layers of experience are added, subtly changing minds and perceptions. I failed to take this into account in my relationship with Joe. Or did I understand it only too well, deliberately not telling him the truth because I feared the thing that has now happened? I allowed one mystification to lead to another, gave permission to our relationship to be normal, that of two ordinary people who happened to fall in love and would spend the rest of their lives together. It was a lie, a deliberate obfuscation, Joe convincing himself that he was with us forever when we both knew he could disappear without warning. Oh yes, we discussed it as a possibility but never truly believed it would happen; and I willingly played 'the teenager' because I thought that was what he wanted me to be. I was so confident that our love, our passion could make the differences drop away like chaff.

I was wrong, should have known that in the throes of first love an ideal is formed, a crystal tower that seems impregnable but shatters if the smallest crack appears. Though I have loved before, I have never loved like this. Joe is my destiny.

We should have lived with the truth, but the truth was too painful.

The mine is the closest source of salt both to us and to the townspeople and we've tried to avoid using it but the alternative is to travel to the coast in the spring, dig salt pans within reach of the tide and return in the autumn to collect the deposit. It's two long journeys for two people during spring sowing and during harvest, absences we could afford in the past when there were many of us, but not now. So we have to come here for our salt, despite the risk of confrontation.

We approach the mine with caution, not really believing that fate could be malign enough to bring us face to face with the townspeople but our belief was misplaced. We draw back in shock.

Skeletal figures unrecognisable as humans are moving blindly in and out of the mine, staggering with rocks too heavy to carry. It's a refined method of killing them, men and women turned to waste, kicked aside, dead or alive while others take their place. The green, grassy valley of death is bathed in sunshine as we watch guards drive the prisoners with whips and batons and harass them with dogs; yet they keep going, an inspiring example of man's determination to hang onto life at all costs. It's difficult to understand. Why don't they accept their fate? That's what I would like to do, to bring an end to my suffering. But there's no freedom for that decision. I and the others have voluntarily taken on the burden of years and responsibility towards one another for time everlasting. If I needed a reminder, it lies in the fate of the miserable wretches below who have brought me humbly to my knees, unlocked my heart in pity and, in the face of death, offered me the gift of life.

*

The prisoners are at the bottom of a dark shaft, hacking with the last of their strength at the unyielding rock face. They stand knee-deep in water, for the walls are dripping, and they are faint from the stench, so intense even the guards won't come inside, of damp, defecation and decay. The prisoners do not talk to one another, all their remaining energy goes into hewing the rock, knowing that unless they emerge with a burden of salt they will be instantly killed. It would be far easier to give up and die but life's spark rarely admits defeat. The prisoners hang onto the forlorn hope that they will be rescued at the last moment.

Susie's mother and father harbour no such illusions and can see little point in obeying the guards and even trying to hew the impregnable rock. Better to hold on to what little dignity remains and accept their fate for they cannot survive this ordeal. Instead, with one accord, they put down their tools and, holding hands, struggle up the tunnel and emerge defiant into the light.

*

One couple, a man and a woman, come out of the mine holding hands. It's clear they are defying the guards for they are not carrying rocks and I can see from the way they hold their heads high on their emaciated bodies that they are refusing to be cowed. The guards recognise their defiance and beat them ferociously on head and shoulders, the dogs attack them; I start to run down the slope but Randolph holds onto me and we huddle together, forced to watch, for I cannot turn my head away. I see how they remain upright until the last moment when their bodies give way and they fall, but this is more than I can bear and

Randolph signals that we should back away. In any case, the guards' dogs are sniffing in our direction. So we retreat and lead the oxen and cart across the stream to the other side of the hill where we cannot be seen and where the water has obliterated our scent.

We dare not light a fire in case its smoke and reflection on the clouds gives us away, so we huddle together beneath a tall ash and listen to the rustle of its leaves in the still night, disturbed only by the cry of dying prey, nature asserting itself in its timeless rhythm, one organism living off another. But surely none is as cruel as man, no animal is meeting its end like the unhappy creatures below.

I find myself getting up, stealing away from Randolph on a mad scheme of rescue. He is asleep and does not hear me go. I reach the crest of the hill and look down at the embers of fires in the encampment and I make a plan. If I only rescue one man, one woman, my life is justified. But now Randolph is at my side. He does not try to stop me going down to the encampment, does not take on responsibility for my life, leaves that to me; he just stands and watches me, a sad look on his face. It is enough to bring me back from the brink of making a useless sacrifice. I owe allegiance to him and to the others who still live, small band that we are; and to the memory of the many who lost their lives in our battles against Helmuth.

I think about how elated we all were, wild with hope and excitement, when the drug made its first appearance. There was nothing we couldn't do, no aim too high. For a time we lived in a state of exultation, even after the riots began. We were so confident they would die down and things settle; then Otto's grandfather died and Helmuth took over and the world turned black. Nothing would ever be the same again. Many of us escaped the fighting and made our way to the wild region that is now our home. We built our house, carrying bricks one by one from wrecked villages, we captured feral animals, we cultivated the ground, we made a pact that we would fight back, free the captives and restore peace; but an epidemic struck, many died, all the children and Otto's father. It was a sad, tragic time. We feared that fate was punishing us for defying it with the drug. But later hope revived, we rallied as one must and trained in warfare. A band of twenty left for Bantage one stormy autumn day, intent on organising the dissidents - we know there are some still in hiding though we don't know where - and instigating a rebellion to bring down Helmuth, a man we once revered, a saint turned devil. Was it power that corrupted him or evil hidden in his heart? Ten more of us were to follow after a smoke signal was sent up from the hills. It never came. A group went to the town and found it heavily fortified. There was no sign of our companions. We were forced to retreat to save the remnants of our community and have never learned what happened. They never came back though we hoped and waited. Later, the townspeople began attacking us at irregular intervals, though they never claim more than one life at a time. They want to wipe us out but they don't want us to disappear. Some remnant of the past binds us to them.

*

Ian has appointed himself the head of a committee and shares out extra food between the twenty or so children incarcerated in the dungeon. The group also devises means of escape and ways of contacting other children still in hiding. They all know how difficult this is going to be. Many people have been assassinated, killed by slave labour, tortured to death. Fear is the strongest element that holds the township together. But as there is nothing to lose they plot and plan.

There is no way out of the sewers that is not guarded day and night. They can't ask Margaret's relative to help them escape. They have to be careful not to expect too much from her. She is already frightened by the risks she is taking.

One day Susie tells them about the diary hidden in her old room. Ian and Margaret are amazed. They have never learned to read or write and want to know who taught her but Susie explains that no one did, she taught herself and has evolved writing and symbols of her own.

Ian sees this as their breakthrough and they try to make writing tools but for the moment do not know how to go about it. Susie shows them her letters and symbols by drawing on the wet floor with her foot but the imprint is quickly washed away by water.

*

We have watched the townspeople leave the valley, their oxen pulling the rock-laden carts while the prisoners, shackled and bound, walk behind, a pathetic sight that wrings my heart; but it has strengthened my resolve. I have put my selfish sorrows behind me and will hold onto my belief that we can keep our community alive and one day restore peace to the land. I have to keep faith.

The guards and prisoners were at last out of sight. When we ventured down the slope to the carnage below, we found five bodies lying round the mine's entrance in pools of blood. Two were that of the man and woman whom we saw being beaten to death, their arms stretched out to one another, fingers touching. Their upturned faces were bloody, their bodies black and blue. We loaded the corpses onto the cart and took them to the wood below and there, under the arching branches of the trees, we dug graves, three to hold single bodies, and one double for the couple who will now lie together for eternity. We erected a small cairn of stones to mark this small impromptu graveyard and I stood before it and fleetingly wished it were me and Joe, that here would stop our suffering - a thought to be banished.

I am turning my face towards the limitless future.

Too exhausted to start mining that day we waited until the next morning to go down into the earth's dark interior and hack the rock. But there was little to do. Some of the prisoners, unable to carry the weight, had left large rocks lying in the water, for the mine is still flooded from the winter rains and wet underfoot. We loaded as much as we thought the oxen could pull and were out of beautiful death valley by the third day and on our way home.

We had a slow return journey. It rained all of one day, leaving the track a sea of mud on which the oxen slipped and slithered with their heavy load. Wheels stuck fast and the cart was in frequent danger of overturning. These unforeseen delays eroded our supply of food and we lost further time hunting for game and allowing the exhausted oxen to rest and graze.

It was not until well after we were expected that we drew towards familiar landmarks. I was sure that the others, worried at the delay in our return, would be looking out for us. Sure enough, I could hear his approach, Meredith, good, steady Meredith who never falters, never lets one down.

But it was not Meredith who appeared. It was Joe.

—

Chapter Eleven

JOE swam across the river, holding his bundle of clothes aloft. It hampered his stroke and with the current flowing fast he needed all his strength to reach the far bank. He struggled out, exhausted, disturbing a pair of red crested ducks, the male resplendent in brown, black and white, rising swiftly with a loud kurr out of tall reeds.

The terrain this side of the river was wilder and more overgrown than Joe expected. He hacked his way through shrubs, saplings and thickets, cutting a zigzag path towards the hills which rose to unexpected heights, a forest of green broad-leaved trees. He walked mechanically, barely aware of what he was doing or where he was going; or indeed why. If there was a purpose that had brought him to this wild spot it was lost in the labyrinth of his unconscious; if there was feeling it had died. In its place lay a vacuum. This, he thought, is what it must be like to be a ghost, seeing everything but feeling nothing. His heart had turned to ice.

He reached the foothills on the third night and collapsed, haunted by hosts of strangers flitting in and out of his dreams. In the morning he found he had been sleeping on the edge of a ruined village.

Had he not come on it by chance he would not have found it. It lay hidden beneath a canopy of trees though here and there unshaded patches shimmered in stippled sunlight. In these exotic weeds flourished, festively decorating what had once been houses alive with men, women, children, dogs. Their noise and bustle had long since yielded to the silence of departed souls. But Joe felt their presence still dwelling in the abandoned stones, a village of the dead. He was treading on hallowed ground.

All day he wandered listlessly about the small settlement, picking up broken pieces of painted ceramics, inscribed seals and ornaments, the poignant detritus of former lives littering the ground. Dwellings, built from the same red bricks as The Manor, had been modest but not cramped and the ruins varied in size. Joe remembered from Volume One of the history that homes were interchangeable according to family circumstance. A wide street, now mud-caked but with stone slabs still solid underfoot, ran through the middle. This must have been the main thoroughfare. The foundations of stately buildings remained, centres no doubt for village elders and for meetings.

A stream beside the settlement fed the remains of a water mill. Joe crossed the rickety bridge over a ferocious mill race, into the roofless interior. One large millstone was still miraculously whole, the other lay in large, jagged pieces among the residue of the last milling, scattered on the ancient crumbling floor. Joe let the old, hard grains of corn fall through his fingers. Of the majestic waterwheel nothing remained but hub and spokes, the main shaft long since disintegrated. So much human effort gone to waste. He left it with a sickening sense of the futility of human endeavour.

He followed the stream a little way down to a cistern where water escaped over flattened walls, the wreckage of an impressive drainage system connected to small bath houses and latrines. Drains ran into covered sewers which disappeared into the earth, to feed into the river below.

Two gateways marked the entrance to the village, one either side of the main street but there was no sign of a surrounding defensive wall. This was not like the ruins in his world which indicated a constant threat from marauding enemies. Instead, Joe imagined the travellers who came regularly to exchange goods in the square, large enough to hold people, carts and horses. It was now almost entirely obscured by trees, shutting out sunlight that must have illuminated a lively scene. A well, handsomely faced off with knapped flints taken from the chalky hills opposite, stood in the middle. It contained water but too far down for Joe to reach. He found a cracked earthenware pot and lowered it on a rope of twisted grass. The water tasted sweet and cool. He wondered how long ago the last human had drunk it.

He found a wooden doll with only one arm and half a leg. It looked at him dully, long abandoned and unloved.

He felt woefully alone in this dead place that had once housed people.

On the outskirts were the remains of sheds and farm buildings. Joe settled there for the night.

In the morning, as he walked out into the dawn, mist rising at his feet, the sun sent a splinter of light against a wall. For no reason that later he could explain, Joe knelt beside it and dug away leaves and soil to reveal a flat, heavy object, some six centimetres long, encrusted with dirt. He sat in the warmth of the rising sun, scraping it clean, careful not to damage its hard shiny surface. Gradually a yellow gleam revealed a lustrous polished stone, triangular in shape with a small finely crafted silver ring at its apex, clearly a pendant to be worn round a woman's neck. He held it in his hand, an object that he could not doubt was fashioned as a love token, radiating the passion of its maker. What beautiful woman had it adorned? He could think only of one, whose tawny hair exactly matched the amber of the stone.

He could see now, painfully and in vivid detail, the desolation on Kathryn's face as he walked away, the utter loss of hope. His anger evaporated. Overcome with longing he could no longer recall why he had left. Was it because he felt betrayed? Had she betrayed him? She had not denied that the community had secrets that they were concealing and she had promised that when the time was right these would be revealed. She had asked him to wait. He knew now why. She had wanted to protect their love for reasons for which he had supplied ample justification. When told the truth he had fled because the truth was too painful to bear.

Who was he to act as judge on the way the community ran their lives? An inexperienced boy who had failed to grow up, who had made judgements on the assumption that the rules governing his world had validity in another. He had arrogantly taken it for granted that he could and would fashion events to suit his preconceived ideas, he had tried to impose his will where he should have, in all humility, accepted the principles by which the community lived and for which they were prepared to die. Kathryn was not the girl next door, she was not a teenage model. Kathryn was not like anyone he had known or dreamed of, she was herself, shaped by her circumstances and her years. If he could not accept her at her own value, he had no business in her life.

Even more shameful was the realisation that he had succumbed to jealousy, the green god had devoured him. That was the reason he was alone in this desolate spot, with only the memory of the woman he loved. He was shocked at himself. His liberal attitudes, always taken for granted were, after all, skin-deep. His unconscious wish, now bubbling to the surface, was that Kathryn had been a virgin when they first fell in love, that he was the sole possessor of her beautiful being. What was this? Some primitive male droit de seigneur? He was overcome with remorse, devastated that he might have destroyed the most precious thing in his life for reasons he now found untenable and degrading. He realised he must have hurt her profoundly.

He wrapped the amber pendant carefully in dry leaves, put it in his pocket and set off urgently downhill. He did not doubt that he could win Kathryn back and that he would once again hold her close.

*

The committee is still trying to devise ways of escaping but can find none. The children are weak, closely watched and all exits are guarded. The door into the dungeon is barred and locked and is well beyond their strength to break down. There are no windows and their only glimpse of the outside world is at the end of the tunnel, the point at which the laden wheelies are taken over by other prisoners to be emptied elsewhere.

One morning, they find one of the children lying on the floor, dead. This is no unusual occurrence. The body is put into a wheelie and taken away by a guard, up the sloping channel to the tunnel's mouth. Susie looks at the corpse with pity in her heart. So young a child to die. She will do anything to survive, to go on living, to get out of this hell. It is then that she realises that the means of escape is at hand but they have been too blind to see it. It is often the simplest solutions that are the best, as Susie is finding out.

She puts her plan to the committee. One of them will pretend to be dead. They will be wheeled out, into the precious open. She cannot of course tell what will happen next, but it is a risk worth taking. No risks, no freedom. They immediately agree to put her plan into action. Pretending to be dead will not need much subterfuge because they are hanging onto life only by a thread, helped by the food Margaret's relative still supplies whenever she can. Though they do not know where dead bodies are dumped they guess that, knowing how casual the guards are, it is possible that there will be time to make a getaway before they are buried. It is a dangerous plan. It could mean the end of them all. They wonder if they should put it to the other children whose lives they are risking but they decide against it. Most of them are too apathetic to care, many will die soon and the more people who know about the plan the less likely is it to succeed.

*

Joe stood on the track, nodding a greeting at Randolph but looking at me, questions and expectation in his eyes, his face taut, white lipped. I did not respond, though inside I was panic-stricken, unable to look at him or speak to him. Escape was the only option. I needed time to battle with the fact that he had come back, though for what I could not be sure. A reconciliation? Or did he want to taunt me? We stood there, the three of us, frozen, not knowing what to say. Randolph urged the oxen forward. He wanted to escape too or perhaps he thought he was doing us a favour by leaving us on our own. I put out a restraining arm to stop him leaving and in a futile attempt to break the silence made a foolish remark like 'I see you're back,' and fled, leaving Joe standing.

I found out later from Belinda that he had returned some five days previously, dishevelled and exhausted, had come straight round to the farm, looking for me but finding only her. She gave him short shrift. He seemed incredulous that Randolph and I had gone away, because of course no one ever leaves home except on the salt gathering expedition and he knew that we had no need of further supplies. The others had conspired to get me away and take my mind off what had happened. They succeeded though not in the way that was intended. No one could have anticipated the horrors we experienced though these at least put my unhappiness in perspective, made me come to terms with Joe leaving. Or so I thought. But no. One sight of him and I am in the same confusion, pain, anger and dismay as before.

186

It would have been better if he'd kept away. I'm suf-focating, feel his eyes on me all day, I sense his shadow wherever I go. There's no escape even though I turn away if I see him. I don't want to speak to him, don't want to hear what he has to say. I'm afraid, terrified his words will pierce my heart.

Yesterday I brought Randolph a message from Otto. I didn't realise Joe was working with him. I walked past, as though he wasn't there but I could see him looking at me, a mixture of sorrow and anger on his face.

We can't go on like this. Everyone is walking on tiptoe. We're living in a loud, echoing silence.

At night I creep upstairs, back to my and Belinda's room, blocking out the image of the sloping wooden roof that has seen so much, the sound of familiar creaking floorboards, the sun in the welcoming morn-ings, the love, the love. If only I could forget or pretend it never happened but my face is the mirror to my heart and while the others avoid looking at me, too painful for them, Otto watches me silently with his inscrutable, don't-come-too-near-me eyes. I wish he would say something, condolence, recrimination, anything, he's making it worse, unendurable.

We're going to crack, all of us, and I'm helpless to stop it. I'm caught in a vice. I can't get out. I love him still, of course I do, how could one root out so intense a passion but I'm terrified. Belinda says the time has come to solve things one way or another. It's all very well for her, no, that's not fair, it isn't at all, seeing me with a new love while her old one has gone stale. But I can't tell her what I hardly dare tell myself, it's this; I can forgive him for walking away, I understand why he did it and blame myself for not being more courageous early on. It's not that. Something else.

I keep looking at myself, am I old, am I old? I go constantly to the bedroom, strip bare, examine my body in the long mirror minutely inch by inch. I can find neither mark nor blemish on my skin, no telltale creases under my eyes or on my cheeks. My breasts are smooth and high and my thighs silky and soft. But what does Joe see now that he knows? An old woman, ravaged by time?

I would prefer to die.

'You're beautiful!'

He was standing in the doorway, looking at her looking at herself. She ran to the bed, pulled off a blanket and covered herself, crying and shouting, pushing him out of the door, beating him with her fists but he held her tight and would not let her go until her sobbing subsided and she lay with her head against him and he covered her with kisses.

Later, as they lay together, exhausted by love, he softly traced her face with his forefinger, then propped himself on his arms to look into her eyes.

'You must have thought me an intolerant pig,' he said.

She looked at him innocently.

'Me? Never!'

And later still.

'Do you think of me as old, Joe, do you?'

'I think of you as you are, beautiful, exotic. You're my exotic bird,' he said.

One morning a new child is pushed into the dungeon, a boy called Rob. He, like Susie, has been brought up in secret and discovered. He is older and bigger than the others and as yet not worn down by privation. They immediately make him a member of the committee and tell him of their escape plans.

Rob has seen that the dead are dumped in a large shed not far from the sewer's entrance. They are then pitched into a mass grave outside the town and covered with lime. He approves their plan to be wheeled out alongside a corpse. They can all escape that way so long as they do it one by one, at reasonable intervals of time. They won't be missed. The guards change constantly and do not know the prisoners individually. No one person is in charge. The guards dump the bodies and go away. Someone else buries them.

*

He gave her the amber stone and it hung from Kathryn's neck, finding its reflection in her hair just as Joe had imagined it would. Randolph, displaying his skill as a metal worker, forged a linked chain and threaded it through. The stone was Joe's and Kathryn's talisman, a flawless affirmation of their love, a link between the past whence it came and the present where it belonged.

Shocked by their recent separation, by their almost fatal parting, they jealously guarded every moment together. Work rotas were altered to accommodate their need, extending even to guard duty on the pine. The once hazardous ascent was now a joy to Joe, a favourite time for him and Kathryn. They were alone in a secret world, invisible from below and with only the stars and moon to see them from above. The quivering branches of the trees and the darkening panorama embraced them like a caress. They sat back to back, looking, watching, swivelling round to change perspective, the warmth of their bodies flowing one into the other. They talked until words ran out and away, and in the silence heard the song of their love.

'Will you tell me about other times?' Joe asked one night.

'You mean other lovers?'

'Well, yes.'

'I could but they really aren't important,' Kathryn said, 'I've been waiting for you, preparing for you.'

'How come?'

'I always knew there'd be a great love, someone special.'

'Precisely me, Joe? Tall, handsome, clever…. from another world?'

'Handsome certainly.'

'Up to expectations?'

'Almost!'

Supremely happy, Joe gazed at the silver river snaking into the distance, at the brimming sky, grasping at a moment when the conjunction of love, passion and the rapture of the surrounding beauty gathered into a boundless perfection.

'Look, there's Orion's belt,' he said, pointing to the sky.

'Is that what you call it?'

'Yes, and that we call the Great Bear.'

'And we call it The Four Wheel Cart.'

'Great Bear.'

'We've known it longer than you. We've known it since time immemorial.'

'So have we. The same stars in a different world. Unfathomable!'

Like their love.

*

There are long discussions as to who should risk themselves first by pretending to be dead. Susie, Margaret, Ian and Rob all volunteer but it is finally decided that the most appropriate person is Susie. She is thin and small and looks so white and drawn she could easily fool the guards.

If she succeeds in getting out of the shed, where should she go? For a child to move around in Bantage is inviting instant imprisonment and death. The many children in the dungeon are witness to how difficult it is to be concealed.

They know that there are several empty houses in the town because the population is dwindling and considerable numbers of people, deemed to be acting unlawfully, have been killed. Susie thinks that her house may be unoccupied but for her to go there is too risky. If the guards realise her corpse is missing they will know where to find her. Ian knows of another house that used to belong to a man accused of helping a teenage boy escape. Susie asks him to tell her more about the boy but Ian only knows of a rumour that he appeared out of nowhere, made no attempt to conceal himself and then somehow got away. The junta blamed the man at whose house he knocked, the house at twenty two Fairfax Road. They imprisoned and killed him.

That boy again. She tells them how Joe followed her and her parents after her skipping exercise in the park the night after the bells rang. She tells him that, though they never saw him, her parents were accused of helping him escape. She hopes he is still alive.

Ian thinks that the boy left the town and went into the wilderness. This is not an option for the children. Their plans are more ambitious than survival. They want to free all other children and somehow, though they have no idea how, rid the town of Helmuth and his henchmen. It is a lofty goal for a group of starved, dying children but this is what is keeping them alive, hope and determination in the face of all odds.

Twenty-two Fairfax Road is where Susie will go if she escapes. Ian is able to give her all the details she needs because he used to live nearby in Gipsy Lane and was allowed out at night.

Susie has somehow to let the committee know once she gets there. This is the next problem they have to solve.

*

A holiday mood prevailed. Like buds in warm sunshine the group opened their hearts to one another, revealing themselves in guises new to Joe. And for the first time since his arrival he felt the freedom to talk about himself. He told them about his world, so far from their experience that they refused at first to believe in the towns, cities, cars, aeroplanes and trains he did his best to describe. He told them of shops, supermarkets, television, telephones, books, magazines, newspapers, of schools and universities, computers, technology and medical advance, of Dolly the sheep and the potential of cloning humans. He explained the structure of democracy and its opposing forces, he told them of wars and terrorists, of ethnic cleansing and famines. They listened with awe and wonder and dismay.

Joe sometimes found himself remembering wistfully the easy life he had left behind, half longing for computers, the fun to be had on the internet, for video games, for films, for shops which provided food and clothes, for all the comforts and the pleasures; for time, for fun, a word no longer part of his vocabulary. Despite himself he was conscious of the occasional note of regret straying into his voice, aware that Kathryn heard it too.

'Do you think I would like your world?' she asked one day.

'You'd like some of it,' he said thoughtfully, 'but not all.'

He could not picture Kathryn at home, could find no place where she would fit. He tried to imagine her at number twenty-two. How would she view his materially driven technological world? With disdain. He could see her at peace rallies, leading a non violent animal rights movement, destroying motor cars, protecting the countryside. What would his friends make of her? She had none of the experiences or interests of her peer group - though what her peer group would be was difficult to gauge. She would undoubtedly feel as strange in his world as he had first felt in hers. He was shocked to discover that the idea of Kathryn at home was an impossible concept. Did it mean that he did not want her there, that his love for her was confined to this world and that, if ever he returned, it would slip from him like a discarded cloak? Were the two worlds waging war against one another in his unconscious?

Such moments of self-doubt filled him with guilt and alarm, shocked by the possibility that an unspoken, transitory wish could catapult him back.

These were his thoughts one evening as he sat in the kitchen playing idly with his calculator which still miraculously worked. He felt a presence at his shoulder. Looking up he saw Meredith.

'What's that?' Meredith asked.

'A calculator.'

'What does it do?'

'Calculates.'

'Numbers?'

'Yes.'

'Can I have a look?'

'Sure.'

Joe handed it over. Meredith took it with shaking fingers, a strange excitement in his eyes.

'How does it work?'

'Takes energy from sunlight, stores and uses it as electrical impulses. You can't leave it long in the dark or it will stop working. It took me ages to get it going again after I rescued it from the cave. Look, this is what you do.'

Joe demonstrated a random sum going into eight figures. Meredith could not believe what he was seeing and tried sums of his own. Entranced, he asked to borrow it.

'You can have it.'

'Have it?'

Meredith could not believe that Joe would give away so wondrous a thing.

'Sure.'

It pleased Joe to see this icon of the modern world in Meredith's hands, making its calculations in this strange, wild place.

Meredith was besotted with his new toy. Dawn would frequently find him in the kitchen, pale, bleary-eyed, pushing number after number into the machine, triumphant at problems solved, frustrated if the calculator had failed him or, as he put it, he had failed it. Meredith drove it in a way Joe could not match and he regarded him with envy and awe, embarrassed because in his world calculators were two a penny and neither he nor his friends had ever bothered to find out how to use them to full effect. But Meredith, as time went on and he became more familiar with the instrument's potential, used it for complex calculations that were far beyond Joe's range of knowledge. Meredith was a better mathematician from a standing start than anyone Joe had ever met. He would thrive back home, probably get a Nobel prize for some achievement or other.

'Let's look at the stars together tonight,' Meredith said one evening. 'It's getting near the longest day and there are no clouds.'

They climbed the hill and gazed at the sky.

'There's a comet due in five years. It comes every seventy six,' Meredith said. Halley's Comet. How many times had Meredith seen it? In Joe's world many people never did. How privileged in this respect Meredith was. Joe listened spellbound as he talked on, for each and every circling star and planet was his friend, each constellation his familiar. Meredith gave a long and detailed account of what he knew of the moon. He had charted its movement, had calculated the size of its craters and its effect on the tides. Joe made a point of not telling him about the moon landing. He knew the community held the moon sacred and spun myths round it. After harvest each year its reflection was crowned in the well with a garland of herbs. He had been ill during the previous ceremony but had been told about it. He did not savour telling Meredith that their holy symbol was nothing more than a dead, airless, silent world strewn with rocks and that its surface sported the Stars and Stripes. But Meredith, with uncanny instinct, asked him outright if humans from his technologically canny world had ever landed on its surface.

'Yes,' Joe said, and forestalled the next question.

'We built a rocket with a capsule…'

'Rocket?'

'A machine that is propelled into the sky by using special fuel. Very powerful. We called the rocket Apollo 11 and sent it up with three astronauts inside.'

'Astronauts?'

'People trained to travel in space. They lived in a small capsule and circled round the moon. Then an even smaller capsule detached itself from the rocket and two men landed.'

'They actually landed?'

It was hard for him to visualise.

'Yes, and left footsteps. Should you go to the moon in ten million years time you'll still be able to see them.'

'Not even I will be alive that long.'

'A lot longer than me.'

Meredith looked at him thoughtfully, faced with their essential difference.

Meredith plied Joe with questions, pushing him to the limits of his knowledge and beyond, unwittingly making him once again feel ashamed because information infinitely precious to Meredith was commonplace at home, readily available and largely ignored. Later, Meredith told Joe that it was his dream to soar into the sky, how he had tried to copy the birds and build wings. The flight to the moon symbolised all his dreams, the ultimate poetry of man's earth-bound existence.

'The possibility of flight has been my only reason for staying alive indefinitely.'

'The only reason?'

'Yes, and you've told me what I always suspected, that the impossible is possible. It needs only time and knowledge.'

Knowledge clearly was valued in inverse proportion to its availability, the largesse of technical and scientific advance in Joe's world as pearls strewn before swine.

But in similar circumstances would it in the long run be any different here? He had acquired enough cynicism to doubt it.

It was Meredith who, on one of their nocturnal walks, suggested that Joe might be a traveller from another phase in time. This had occurred to Joe but he had dismissed it as improbable, a piece of science fiction. He had seen plenty of SF films, had read SF books but to apply to himself the deliberate improbabilities of such stories Joe scorned. But now with the suggestion coming from Meredith, who had seen neither films nor read novels, he was forced to reconsider the idea more seriously and together they examined it from every angle. They came to no satisfactory conclusion. If time traveller he was, why had he not appeared in a different period in his own world? The one he was in fitted nowhere in English history despite the similarities of country and of language. Time travel left too many questions unanswered.

Joe no longer attached any importance to such speculations. Neither why nor how he had arrived signified, only how to prevent being snatched away.

When the rest of the group learned about space flight, they regarded Joe with awe as though he were personally responsible. He hastened to disabuse them. He explained that scientific experts sent shuttles into space, exploring deeper and deeper into the universe, how landing craft sent data back to Earth; he tried to explain, though he was on uncertain ground, the correlation between time and space, a concept only grasped by Meredith.

'You mean if you travel far enough into space, the time you're in the shuttle is different from the time passing on earth, that you could come back after an hour and find a century had passed?'

Joe looked at him in wonder.

'If you go far enough, for long enough, yes.'

He told them that there could be life on Mars, which they called The Red Planet, that bacteria had been found in one of its rock deposits, and possibly signs of water. He told them as much as he understood about Einstein's theory; he told them about nuclear fusion and the hope and power it brought, and the despair. He told them about Chernobyl and Hiroshima, about the conflict with Iraq; he explained the destructive capacity of the latest nuclear devices.

'Do you realise,' Joe said, 'that with all our wonderful achievements and our scientific discoveries, we haven't even begun to tackle death? We're as far from conquering it as our primitive forefathers were. Yet you have a drug that prolongs life indefinitely.'

Randolph merely shrugged.

'We've travelled along different paths, your civilisation and ours, but it seems to me we've arrived at the same point. Man's destruction of man. We're all the same.'

Joe did not then attach any significance to Randolph's remark, offered without emphasis and with a dismissive shrug.

Joe had always taken life for granted. The limited world of home, school, family and friends had absorbed him and, while he had some personal problems, they were not major threats to his well-being. The all-

199

inclusive term 'adolescent', like some label at the supermarket, reduced them to an apparently common denominator. He would mysteriously grow out of his difficulties. This, at least, was the myth but as he approached the end of his teens he could see no reduction in the weight of inner conflicts. If anything, they increased and he was exponentially less able to deal with them.

The wider world, the one outside his private exist-ence, he left to other people. He watched world events in an unfocussed kind of way, conscious of their poten-tial danger but not seriously disturbed by them. The words and works of politicians sounded like a howling gale on mountain ranges too high for him to hear. He had other things to think about.

Here, in this wilderness that offered no distractions but left each individual with a choice, fend for yourself or perish, the more fundamental issues of being human were thrown into relief. He pondered on what lay behind Randolph's remark.

He turned to Kathryn, breathing easily in her sleep, her face partially concealed by her fair hair. He gently pushed it aside and she opened her eyes to meet Joe's serious gaze.

'Is it time to get up?'

Dawn was breaking, promising a clear day. She half rose but he pushed her down.

'Not quite. I wanted to ask you something.'

'Yes?'

'Do you think people are inherently evil?'

'When they wake other people and face them first thing in the morning with deep philosophical questions, yes.'

'If they got you a hot drink?'

'Then I would think them very good indeed.'

Joe padded upstairs with two steaming mugs of a herbal tea that was the common beverage and returned to the attack.

'Well, do you?'

'I don't think I have a clear-cut answer. There are certainly plenty of wicked people about. We've got Helmuth and, by the sound of it, you've got more than your fair share of tyrants and dictators.'

'What makes them behave as they do? What's in it for them?'

'Power,' she said. 'It corrupts people. Look at Helmuth! He was a good man until power was put in his hands.'

He supposed she was right. In the history of his world there was one common factor - domination. Whatever the stated aims of imperialist countries, the outcome was the same. Give any set of people a means to hold sway over the rest of humanity and they would use it without mercy. Long-life drugs, nuclear weapons. It came to the same thing.

He put his arms round her. Had they got time?

—

'YOU don't seriously believe in a superhuman being called God who alone created the universe?' Otto asked. His tone was incredulous.

Joe's had been a conventional protestant upbringing; he had been christened and had an elaborately illustrated card of Jesus surrounded by angels to prove it, and he and his mother went to church at Christmas with his grandparents, sometimes at Easter. It had always seemed a meaningless and formal affair to Joe whose mind was on other things less spiritual. He was constantly amazed at the fervour with which people prayed to a God who remained stubbornly invisible. He had tried the odd bit of prayer himself, once when a particularly fierce row was in progress in the bedroom next door. He asked God to put a stop to it, to have his father stay with them forever and ever, and he made a deal. If God left a leaf on his bed during the night he, Joe, would believe in Him. It seemed a fair bargain as God was always asking mankind for one's soul. But there was no leaf in the morning and his father left home shortly after.

That settled the matter. God did not exist, not at least in his, Joe's orbit and when, at age thirteen, the question of his confirmation came up he refused to countenance it. His grandfather, who lived in a thirties middle England long extinct, was outraged. When threats failed to work he tried bribing Joe with the promise of a gold watch, the last thing Joe wanted. Mrs

Harding, who was indifferent to the outcome, was surprised by Joe's intransigence, the first manifestation of a character trait she was to encounter with more serious consequences at a later date.

But God was clearly a presence for other people. When a fight broke out at school between a Catholic boy and a Protestant from Belfast, it gave Joe pause and instituted a school debate to which he listened with attention, concluding that hard economics was the major motivating force on both sides. The different religious interpretations he viewed with superior disdain. Later, comparative religious studies at school gave him a wider breadth of understanding while Ground Zero, Afghanistan, Northern Ireland and the Middle East conflicts left little room for ignorance to even the most disinterested.

The group listened intently to Joe's description of the major religions. These were so far removed from their beliefs and experiences that Joe despaired of making them understand the complexities of the various dogma. But he had once again under estimated their grasp of essentials.

'All your religions,' Otto, who had questioned him closely, now said, 'they may have different names but they're really all the same. Monotheistic. Mere superstition. We left that behind generations ago.'

This assumption of superiority nettled Joe. Feeling he owed a debt of loyalty to his own world, he put up a defensive argument.

'I didn't say God was superhuman. The belief is that He has no body, He is an incorporeal spirit and it is part of that spirit that He has bequeathed to us - the divine spark. We're not like animals. God has raised us above them.'

Joe was glad Kathryn was busy elsewhere. She would most certainly have protested.

'We appreciate beauty,' he continued, 'we can read, write, we can think abstract thoughts. We believe in the spirit, we believe in an afterlife. Well, some people do.'

'What kind of afterlife?'

'When you die God or his son Jesus Christ…'

'Son?'

'Yes, God sent to earth His only son to save mankind.'

'Doesn't seem to have made too good a job of it.'

Joe ignored this and continued, 'God judges whether you have led a good life and followed the Ten Commandments.'

'Which are?'

'Ten exact instructions on how to live. Thou shalt not kill. Thou shalt not steal. Thou shalt not commit adultery. Thou shalt honour thy father and mother. They're are about the only ones I can remember.'

'Seem eminently sensible to me. How can He tell whether you have followed them?'

'The eye of God is always on you.'

'So, if God approves of your conduct…. '

'Come Judgement Day….'

'What's that?"

'That's when God decides where all the dead spirits go. If you have led a good life you'll be resurrected and reside in heaven for eternity.'

'And if you haven't obeyed the commandments?'

'You stay dead. Forever. You are sent to hell, to the devil.'

'The devil?'

'He's the evil spirit. He tempts us to sin.'

Otto looked at him in amazement.

'One personification for good and one for evil. Interesting, but a bit simplistic, don't you think? All this sophistication you've been telling us about, all the scientific and medical marvels and advances. We're just primitive people, aren't we, but…'

'I never said that!'

'No, but you thought it.'

Joe looked abashed.

'…but at least we don't have to invent and dress up a couple of beings and pretend they stand in for good and evil.'

'As I explained, there are lots of religions.'

'Do they all promise life after death?'

'As far as I know, yes.'

'That at least I can understand. People hanker after some kind of personal survival, like to pretend they never die.'

'Which you don't believe?'

'Yes and no.'

'What does that mean?''

'It means first of all that we haven't divided the afterworld into hierarchies with one lot of people going to heaven and another lot to hell; secondly, we don't have a god. No one hands out goodies or bribes us to behave.'

'That would explain Helmuth and his crowd!'

'You mean that because of your religions everyone in your world is good? Doesn't sound like it from what you've told us, sounds as though people use their religion as an excuse for intolerance.'

'That's partially true.'

'So it doesn't make any difference either way. The logical conclusion is that man is inherently evil no matter who or where he is.'

'Then what Otto, according to you, is the alternative? What's your recipe? Your philosophy hasn't worked any better than ours.'

'That's true. But it once did and perhaps will again. And whatever we do, it doesn't stop the world existing.'

Did it not? Otto was referring to the world as he knew it; but what, in Joe's world, of the apocalyptic prophecies of the end of civilisation? They had become almost commonplace but were ignored except by odd individuals, like his geography teacher, who lectured on Gaia and gave humanity only one hundred years more existence, a mere blink of the eye to these people. Should he tell them? He thought not. It would open the floodgates to speculations impossible to satisfy. The similarities and differences between the two worlds were irreconcilable. Same heavens, same vegetation, same towns, even same names, presumably same earth but the two worlds at variance with one another. He could not understand how, under such circumstances, the atmosphere above this world remained unpolluted while back in his the ozone layer had a hole, ever getting wider. What had prevented the pollutants leaking into this atmosphere? And if there were nuclear meltdown back home would this world be affected? Probably not.

It was impossible to devise a logical structure to this conundrum and he did not try. It would remain as puzzling as his sudden arrival.

'Just look around you,' Otto continued, more animated than Joe had ever seen him, 'there's a divine element in everything, animals, fish, plants, even stones and rocks. There's absolutely no need to invent gods.'

Joe pointed to the kitchen flagstones.

'Even in these? Or the erratic in Bantage?'

'Yes, why not? Stones and rocks have been shaped by the elements for millions of years, by water and ice and weather. They're our time clocks. Their span is merely different from ours and of course much, much longer.'

'What about man? How does he fit in?'

'Perhaps due to a cosmic accident, Man has been given the capacity to perceive divinity. I don't know if animals or plants do. They may. We have no means of knowing but what is sure is that we have the privilege of being able to perceive the mystery of Being and to believe in a nature that is numinous. And that places a great responsibility on us.'

'Does that apply to the townspeople?'

'They no longer recognise it, discarded it long ago. Don't you know that people with only power as their goal lose all sense of perspective, all spirituality, all humility in the face of creation? It enables them to perpetrate the most terrible atrocities.'

Flashes of past and potential history confirmed every word Otto was saying. It made Joe shiver with apprehension for his civilisation, made him realise to what extent he and his contemporaries had turned away from facing basic issues. And there was little time.

'Isn't this true of all the tyrants in your world? I'd be surprised if it wasn't. You see there's a basic flaw in your argument. If your God is all powerful and good why doesn't he stop evil?'

'Free will,' Joe replied.

That's what he'd been told anyway.

'Sounds like a good excuse for God's lack of power to fulfil His most basic function,' Otto said.

Joe found this difficult to deny. He changed tack.

'OK, so you believe in divinity. In which case, what happens to you when you die?'

'You lie in the ground and decompose.'

'Well, that's cheering. Not much divinity in that.'

'But there is. Our bodies decompose and feed the earth, they are part of the material universe. They die and revitalise. That's an afterlife.'

'According to your philosophy a person just disappears as though they'd never been. They're nothing but food for worms.'

'There's nothing wrong with worms. And a person doesn't just disappear. Their good deeds live after them. The greater the deeds, the longer they're remembered and the resonance of what they achieved continued. And don't forget, they leave possessions and works of art. What about my father's carving that you value so greatly? What about the animals you've made since you've been here? They won't disappear, even if you do. We'll always treasure them.'

This sounded like an obituary. Did Otto, with his uncanny prescience, know something Joe did not? Joe was not prepared to pursue the possibility.

Otto continued.

'These are real forms of afterlife and add up to the kind of survival that we at least find satisfying. What's more, our version stimulates great kindness and consideration, better efforts to improve the world, it gives people a sense of responsibility. And as I said, we don't have to be bribed with some fairy tale vision. I think that's important.'

'People in my world don't look at them as fairy tales. They believe they're real. They believe that God in heaven is looking after them all through their lives and afterwards. That's comforting.'

'It's not comfort we're after, but the truth. That's all you've got to live by. The truth.'

'Truth is what you believe. What's more, our god helps us by giving absolution, divine forgiveness for our wickedness on Earth. In the Christian religions anyway. He forgives before we die. He'll even forgive someone evil like Helmuth.'

'He may, but posterity won't. I want no truck with your nebulous deity if he hands out pardons to all and sundry, regardless of what kind of lives they have led.

'So what do you want to do? Get your revenge on Helmuth? Kill him if you can?'

Understanding that Joe had laid a trap and could easily gain the moral high ground Otto hesitated, but honesty compelled him to say,

'Yes, and all the tyrants. Think of how many people they have killed!'

'An eye for an eye, a tooth for a tooth.'

'You mean revenge? If you like.'

'We at least have got beyond that. We at least give people the right to defend themselves, to state their case. However evil, they're still humans! In our society everyone has the right to justice.'

'Do they always get it?'

'No. But the principle remains.'

*

The committee is unable to devise a way in which Susie can let them know that she is safe once she has escaped. She cannot predict where she will be nor how she can get in touch. There are too many factors to be taken into consideration, too many unforeseen events. As no one else can leave until they get the go-ahead from Susie, the children are once again faced with an intractable problem.

The most expedient method would be to use Margaret's relative to pass a message, but it means that Susie has to get back to the dungeon's entrance without being seen. Fairfax Road is a long way away and the children are, in any case, anxious not to implicate their ally.

They conclude that Susie should devise her own method of getting in contact once she knows how the land lies. They will be on the lookout for anything unusual.

'Your writing,' Ian says 'perhaps we can use it now.'

'How?' Susie asks.

'I'm not sure. Perhaps you can scratch an agreed letter on the sides of the empty wheelies before they're brought back for filling up; or drop a message inside one. Or something,' he adds lamely.

It is very difficult to come up with an answer. Susie will have to use her ingenuity.

*

As Joe and the community tried to come to terms with each other's worlds, these intense debates, sometimes reaching long into the night, became a regular feature of their lives. Similarities and differences were evaluated and compared, discussed and analysed. Joe was at an advantage for he lived in their world and had lived in his own. Because their experience was one-sided they were frequently unable to grasp the foreign concepts which he tried to describe.

This in particular was the case with money.

'Why would goods have a value other than their own?' Randolph asked.

It was not an easy question to answer. As Joe's knowledge of the workings of international trade was at best limited, he concentrated on explaining supply and demand.

'Necessities, food, clothes, don't change their worth,' Randolph pointed out.

'They do if a lot of people want them, and there is a shortage, or even a glut.'

'A meal is a meal, a loaf of bread a loaf of bread. Once you start equating them with something

211

meaningless like your coins,' Randolph said, 'they are degraded.'

'Or upgraded. Say you were short of corn one year and everybody wanted some. That would alter the value and in our world the price. While you express it in, say, the number of goats per ton of oats we use coins. But the principle remains. The list of the barter value of goods in Volume One states the price of goods quite clearly.'

'It doesn't change. It stays the same summer and winter, good years and bad. What's more, we can see what we've bought. It's tangible. And it is, or at least was, common to the whole country. Everyone knows what everything is worth and when there's a shortage, say due to a severe winter, we share.'

'And if there's a glut?'

'Doesn't make any difference.'

It was impossible to explain world trade, different currencies, companies, corporations, stocks and shares, free trade, the fluctuations of global markets. Joe did not even try. He could hardly understand them himself. As it was the group listened with growing bewilderment to his description of the urban sprawl that left England without wild beasts, forests or space.

'The world population is growing. By the end of this century there will be seven hundred billion people on Earth.'

'Seven hundred billion!'

They tried to comprehend such numbers of human beings.

'What happens when the world is overrun?

'Time will tell but it may never happen. People die of diseases. Even with modern medicine these have not been eliminated. As soon as we cure one, another springs up. Nature used to maintain a balance though it's losing the battle now. And we have our own method of keeping the numbers down. Organised slaughter. In polite circles we call it war. It has all kinds of benefits attached to it, bringing advances in medicine and in science. It even has its own rules, like a game. And we've invented something called ethnic cleansing. This is quite simple - you kill anyone who is not of your colour or creed.'

'We know something about that. It's been happening to us for several hundred years.'

'So you say. But how do you know? It's all hearsay, nothing is recorded. How are future generations ever going to believe you?'

'What future generations? We are the future generations.'

This brought Joe to a momentary halt.

'All the same, I bet you never tell the same tale twice, I bet it gets changed over the years so that in the end it has probably been altered beyond recognition. We write our history down. You gave up writing it. Why?'

'We prefer to preserve our history by word of mouth,' Randolph said.

'Doesn't it change with every storyteller?'

'Of course. What do you think history is?'

'The recording of facts from the past so that they can be passed accurately to the future.'

'Accurately,' Kathryn said, 'that's an illusion. Events are accurate to one person alone.'

'Who?'

'The person who experiences them. For each individual the so-called accuracy is different. Accuracy does not exist, it's a disembodied concept.'

'What about the facts?'

'There are hundreds of facts for each event. If you went round this table and asked each person to give an exact account of their experiences, few facts would be the same; like Otto's grandfather taking his life.'

'That's a fact, isn't it?

'Possible but uncertain,' Otto said, ' maybe his partner killed him. I have no means of telling. I've tried to get at the truth and I've talked about it to many people but each one gave a different version. Maybe none is true. Who can tell?'

'But we have hundreds of people doing research, writing books, striving to present history as it was.'

Joe remembered ruefully the long hours of frustration he had spent at school trying to bring alive the history being taught. Much of it had seemed flat and boring, bearing little relation to people alive or dead. Was it possible that events died when imprisoned inside the covers of a book, that they could only fly and soar when related to individuals who had lived them, as had the people round this table? We have none of these advantages, he thought, we cannot talk to people who experienced events countless years ago.

'At least we have first hand accounts written down. That's almost the same.'

Joe was being forced into an analysis of his complex world. He had never questioned its values and had always taken for granted all the luxury, comfort and benefits it offered. But these, he saw, ran alongside the more sinister aspects of modern life, normally buried in the pleasure-seeking ethos of his generation. This last he now viewed with a sense of unease, not unmixed with longing. Self-indulgent their lives might be but they were easy and pleasurable. Here life was hard, dangerous and uncomfortable. Principles were maintained at a high price.

In some respects the two worlds were mirror images of each other. Power was equated with evil and imperialism while a minority of liberal people tried to maintain their humanity. It was the scale that was dif-ferent and the means.

I've listened and listened and I've learned that I would never fit into Joe's world. Even if I could reach it I'd be a lost soul, a burden and an embarrassment. There's no place for me there. He knows that though he won't admit it, but there's anyway no chance. I'm excluded, cut off from Joe's real life. Once he goes I'll vanish as though I'd never been, and when I said this to him in a despairing moment he denied it vehemently. He believes he'll love me forever and perhaps he may, perhaps our destinies are intertwined no matter where we are, in two worlds or in one; but I'm still afraid, he could disappear suddenly, without warning, without wanting to. We're puppets, we have no control, we're worked at the end of someone else's string, manipulated perhaps by this god of Joe's who's decided to mix our worlds, allowed us to taste the nectar of our love only to torture us by taking it away.

I live in ecstasy and in fear.

*

The committee has not abandoned its aim to free all the children in the dungeon, as well as all who are prisoners in the town. They plan to find the children kept in hiding by their parents and rescue those snatched by the State. They discuss the possibilities night after night, making plans that are unrealistic and overly ambitious, though of this they are unaware. For the time being they must concentrate their efforts on escaping and reaching the outside world. Only then they can decide on their next step.

'Fairfax Road is the agreed meeting place,' Ian says.

'What happens if it is occupied, if I can't use it?' Susie asks.

'We'll have Jarvis Road as the next port of call.'

'And if that doesn't work?'

Ian shrugs.

'It's impossible to plan for everything.'

*

'This house is rather sad,' Joe said one day, 'most of it is empty, echoing with lives that no longer exist.'

He wondered if he had been tactless and hurt Kathryn but he had come to love the house in a way he had never loved his own. It held a mysterious familiarity as though he had always belonged to it and it had been waiting for him. He felt the welcome in its rooms and rambling corridors, silent guardians of a thousand secrets whispered inside walls in which sometimes, if he listened attentively, he could faintly discern the long low murmur of dead souls. They spoke to him and recognised him as one of their own. This was home; he wanted to open all its windows and let in light and love. He wanted to wake it from its sleep.

'Yes, that's why I never go into the empty rooms.'

'Perhaps we can heal their souls,' Joe said. 'I can think of a way.

'Can you now?'

The next night she appeared with pillows and a feather duvet.

'This way.'

She led Joe into the long room and they threw open the shutters and let in the night air. They could feel the room breathe with joy as, beneath the benign eye of the carving, they made love the night through.

'In memory,' Kathryn said.

'In love.'

He felt as though he had sealed a bargain.

'Not only in here.'

'No.'

They visited every room in turn and if the others knew or heard they did not comment. Perhaps they heard the murmurs too.

—

ENJOYMENT was low on the list of the group's priorities, leisure almost unknown, work constant, the underlying dread of an attack sapping energy. To this was added, in Joe's case, the unrelenting travails of the last year. Too much to absorb, too much to understand. Exhausted, mind and spirit weary, he needed space in which to do nothing and to dream.

It was not politic to ask outright for days off. The community was in need and unused to easing their vigilance but Joe succeeded in introducing the concept of holidays or days off by subtle insinuation. Not in vain. A meeting was held and, with the surprising support of Otto, it was decided that, so long as no immediate danger threatened, everyone was allowed one day free every two weeks. A meagre allowance Joe thought, but better than nothing.

Meredith seized the chance to absorb himself further in his abstract calculations concerning the heavens and beyond. From time to time he tried explaining some of this to Joe, whose interest was genuine but comprehension limited. Meredith spoke in tongues, in his case a mathematical language he had invented for himself. Joe understood in principle but could not follow in detail.

Randolph used his spare days to disappear alone into the wilderness, laying traps, returning with rabbit or game. His intimacy with nature and its extravagant growth, its burgeoning life and rhythm, gave him a singular individuality. Some evenings he spent in the carving shed where Joe often joined him. They worked quietly together, absorbed in their separate tasks. Randolph made furniture, decorating it with elaborate patterns while Joe, having with surprising speed graduated from small animals, created larger objects, some representational, others abstract. The latter were regarded with curiosity but not without interest. One wooden sculpture, a long smooth burnished curve tapering towards the sky like an ascending bird, was given place of honour in the centre of the kitchen table, a symbol of the community's hopes.

These odd days of leisure failed to satisfy Joe. He needed longer, a time for consideration and consolidation, away from the constant company of the group and the unrelenting work ethic. And he wanted to be alone with Kathryn. A pointedly casual question to Meredith about the time it would take to reach the coast bore fruit. It was suggested that Joe and Kathryn, ostensibly to obliterate her experiences at the salt mine, go for sea salt; or at least dig pans for collecting crystals in early autumn.

They set off on foot one morning as the dew was lifting. It was the fecund period before high summer. The trees were in full bloom, flowers tumbled out of hedgerows and spread with abandonment at their feet. They headed west on an overgrown track, one of the many, Kathryn explained, crossing the country in an intricate network. These had been used in the old days by travellers as they traded from village to village. Most were now reclaimed by the wilderness but some were still serviceable.

Joe was not unfamiliar with the route they were taking, not unfamiliar that is with the route as he had known it in his world; but here it was without roads, buildings or signs. There was nothing to guide them but the sun setting in the west and the planets travelling over the night sky. They passed ruined villages and land that bore the marks of having once been cultivated, field boundaries still plain to see, patches of wild corn and oats self-seeded, keeping to the rhythm of their year.

It took them several leisurely days to reach the western scarp where the land fell sharply. Joe pointed to the Welsh mountains shadowed in the distance, the cradle of the drug that had destroyed the old life. It was here that they came across a path, clearly in use, the ground flattened, free of intruding growth. They followed it cautiously, curious to see where it led.

'Another township?" Joe suggested.

Kathryn shook her head and led him on, as far as a high brick wall heavily defended by jagged glass. Keeping close they reached a spiked, wrought iron gate which revealed an extensive, rough grassy area and a tall four-storied building almost obscured by trees. Its facade was as grim as a prison's. In the distance a group of what were clearly young people were doing exercises in perfect unison, 'arms up, down to the sides, jog on your toes, one, two, three.'

Kathryn pulled him away.

'What is it?' Joe found the house threatening and without goodwill.

'It's where the state brings up children, turns them step by step into dangerous people, spies and informers.

I've always wondered where it was. Let's get away. I feel infected.'

Even when they had put considerable distance between themselves and the house its grim presence haunted them. But the day was glorious and their absorption in each other absolute. They spent the night under a hedge and looked at the stars.

They travelled next day under a blue sky and reached the heights above the river Severn snaking between the hills. No path led down to the valley floor but they scrambled down, through thickets of bramble and hawthorn, startling red squirrels, foxes, feral goats who scuttled out of the way, disturbed by these unusual visitors. Large tracts of marsh, wet and impassable, sent them back to the hill track and on to Bristol which, once a settlement of some size, was now a heap of ruins. Joe remembered the visit he had so recently made in his own world prospecting a place at the university. He had loved the hills, the buildings, the river busy with the traffic of boats and ships, he sensed that this was a town where things happened. He wanted to be part of it and wistfully hoped to take up the offer of a place if he got the right grades and could manage the finance.

Now it was nothing but a sad memorial. He led Kathryn to where he thought the Clifton Suspension Bridge crossed the river, over what in this world was a wild, untamed and noisy torrent between the cliffs. Standing among the wooded wilderness in which fallen trees festooned with moss, honeysuckle and ivy grew as far as the cliff edge and cascaded down, made it difficult to describe nature built on and subdued.

He had a vivid memory of standing when very young in the middle of the bridge and peering down into the gorge, wondering how it was possible to build at this height without the support of pillars. He was nervous of the swaying motion, hoping the bridge would not give way. He walked backwards and forwards until his mother tiredly coaxed him away but the wonder of it never left him.

They once again made the descent to the river and were able to cross on a perilous, half-submerged causeway. Mud banks either side housed feeding flocks of waders, a bird-watcher's paradise. Turning south they found themselves in kinder country, travelling through Glastonbury, Yeovil, Dorchester, names Joe knew well; but the ruins they passed bore no relation to the places he had known. It was as though that world were layered on this, possible to touch if only he knew how. Could he put his hand out and find it? Was it tangible? Did it inhabit the same space in the universe, part of the ground he was treading ? The wild possibilities yielded no answer.

The forested country opening before them looked impenetrable but they found a route amid well spaced trees, over territory that had suffered forest fires and was sprouting new brambles and purple flowers. This was wolf country. They heard packs baying in the distance and at night slept by a fire. One morning they came on a herd of short, shaggy ponies.

'Why do you never use horses?' Joe asked

'We used to but now we don't go anywhere. And they need fodder in the winter.'

From high hills they saw the beckoning sea between green downs, in the distance flecks of moving white.

'Swans,' Kathryn said. 'Abbotsbury,' Joe thought.

They waded across marshland and reached the sea as the sun was setting. This was their goal and their nirvana. They made camp on the beach in the shelter of the western cliffs, they lived in the open, on sand dunes Joe had known, in the generous bay familiar from childhood holidays but now untrammelled, ringed with sea, sky and the folding hills. And peace, utter peace. They spent their days swimming, fishing, building sandcastles swept away daily by the tide; they collected shells among the rocks, they walked to Lulworth Cove over the downs, they bathed in its narrow creek, they explored Chesil Bay and the causeway to Portland Bill. They were children, they were adults. They sang sad and happy songs, they made love with only the birds and burrowing creatures to watch them.

*

The days go by. The usual drudgery and privations prevail. The committee confides its plans to no one. They are waiting, waiting for another child to die so that Susie can be carried out without being detected. It is a gruesome situation but they steel themselves against it in the knowledge that their actions will in the end provide liberty for all. That at least is the hope. It is all they have to keep them going.

One member of the committee is always on duty in the early hours to see if anyone has died, thus giving Susie time to prepare herself. One morning the expected

223

happens. A girl of about Susie's age who has not been long in the dungeon dies in the night. Susie looks at her poor emaciated body which from the first had no hope of survival. Before the guards come in to order the gangs to work, Susie slumps on the ground in the position of a corpse, a spectacle to which she is no stranger.

Seeing two bodies the guards shout to someone outside. By and by another guard comes in with an empty wheelie and throws in the two corpses. Susie is underneath, shuddering at the proximity of death. Her heart is beating so loudly she fears it will give her away. She is both frightened and elated.

The wheelie is pushed up the steep tunnel and through the entrance into the sunlight which penetrates Susie's closed eyelids even as she lies below the corpse. The fresh air hits her like a revivifying spirit, making her head reel.

The wheelie is pushed for some distance. It is then put down, a door is opened. Voices, two sets of arms pick up first the dead girl and then Susie. They are throw onto a hard brick floor. The dead girl's body breaks Susie's fall. The door is shut, the voices fade. It has not, as far as Susie can tell, been locked.

*

They took no count of the days but knew when the time had come to leave their paradise. As they trudged back in the direction of The Manor, sun-soaked and drenched with happiness, the last days on their own, Joe braced himself for opening a subject that had been much on is mind.

'You're so beautiful,' he told her for the hundredth time.

'And you're so handsome,' she teased.

'How much longer do you think I'll stay that way?'

'Oh, a day or two.'

'A year or two, perhaps three, perhaps five, even ten. What then?'

She knew what he was driving at and remained silent.

'I'm going to get older every year while you stay young.'

Coming from a culture of youth, Joe was accustomed to being pampered and regarded as the inheritor of the earth, a valiant hope for the future; but under the rules imposed by the drug, this situation was reversed. Young people who had not taken the drug had no future; not in the same terms as those whose active lives had been prolonged indefinitely. The terrible truth was that he would grow old while the others remained young. He imagined how he would be with the passing years, hair turning grey, his skin that now glowed becoming pockmarked, leathery, dry, his taut stomach bulging over his knees. He'd seen enough old men, the crotches of their trousers stained, life leaking stealthily away, sans teeth, sans eyes, sans everything. And Kathryn, forever young, beautiful, vibrant, would be forced to watch him crumble into his dotage. His and Kathryn's life span ran according to different clocks. The years would tear them apart.

The time would come when she could no longer love him, only pity him.

'How would it be if I took the drug?' he asked diffidently, his casual air belying the importance he attached to the question. It did not deceive Kathryn.

'It would be as bad for you, as it's been bad for us. It corrupts people, it's skewed our lives. Don't you see Joe, everything that's gone wrong is to do with the drug.'

'That's because of Helmuth. Without a tyrant your lives would be untroubled and full of opportunity.'

'If there's power available, there's a tyrant. They go hand in hand. And I told you, Helmuth used to be a good man. He used to be a priest, dispensing justice and helping and advising people. Power changed him. It can change anyone.'

'You're not suggesting I could become like him?'

'Of course not. But Helmuth is not an exception. We all have the potential to become despots, you, me, Otto, anyone.'

She started crying and he comforted her, feeling guilty at her unhappiness. He could not deny the truth of what she was saying, knew too well from his own world how corrupt apparently civilised people could become. Nevertheless, if his and Kathryn's future was to be assured, they had no alternative but to confront the reality of the situation. In that sense, the drug indeed skewed their lives.

But he was not prepared for the vehemence of her feelings.

'It's not as wonderful as you imagine, living so long,' she said accusingly.

'You've forgotten what it's like not to, don't know how lucky you are.'

'Don't I? I wonder. Remember the time you and Otto were left alone and you didn't know where we were?'

'Yes.'

'Have you never wondered about it?'

'I thought perhaps you hibernated. '

'No. We don't hibernate. We become apathetic. A deadening apathy takes hold and we can do nothing, not even speak. It's the weight of all those years, on and on. The reason goes out of being alive, the colour out of the sky, the world looks grey, dull and stale, survival becomes worthless and one almost hopes that the townspeople will put an end to it. Time is a burden.'

'Is it the same for the townspeople?'

'Yes. Their longevity makes them apathetic much of the time, they can't be bothered to finish things off. They could have killed us all by now, but they haven't. I expect it's the same in the town. Nothing is done properly. Even so, it doesn't stop their world functioning, like it does here because there's more of them, they can stand in for each other. And because they are not faced with constant danger they don't have to be on the defensive.

Cat Walk. Joe suddenly remembered his surprise at not being followed into the waste ground and finished off.

Kathryn went on.

227

'Sometimes these phases are so long that when we wake up the farm animals are either dead or have strayed and we have to start all over again.'

'But Otto stays awake.'

'He has a stronger spirit than us. But even he is overcome sometimes. I think it's only the danger from the townspeople that's kept us going all these years. They pose a challenge.'

'You haven't had one of your sleeping spells again.'

She looked at him strangely.

'Because of you.'

'Me?'

'Your youth. It's revivified us; but that would stop if you took the drug. You'd be like us and....'

She hesitated.

'And what?'

'It's difficult to love forever.'

'Not for me it isn't.'

'You don't know. Time wears you away. Randolph and Belinda....'

'Yes?'

'They were lovers, together for a long, long time, oh I don't know how many years. Then their love faded, bit by bit, I saw it wasting away until nothing remained but its shreds.'

'You mean I'll grow tired of you?'

'Perhaps. Probably.'

He laughed at her.

'Anyway, we don't have the drug. They'll kill you if you try to get it. Life without you....'

Her words trailed off into desolation.

It was difficult to prevail against her impassioned plea.

*

Susie lies in the shed all day. Other bodies are brought and thrown in. The smell of unwashed corpses waiting to be buried is overpowering. Susie has to hold herself back not to rush out when evening falls but she waits until the middle of the night and there is no sound of movement outside.

The door is on a latch. Susie opens it bit by bit and looks out. She can see no one. Fearfully, quietly, she slips out. She closes the door softly behind her, as though not to disturb the sleeping bodies inside.

She is not certain where she is for this is a part of Bantage she has not been in before. She is not in open country near the farms nor in the town centre but somewhere on the immediate outskirts. As her eyes adjust she can see a concentration of roofs ahead and she tentatively moves towards them, pausing every few minutes to make sure she is alone. The night is silent and she gains in confidence and hastens her steps until she finds herself in a set of roads that look familiar. Soon she is at the back of the park.

It is tempting to take the route to her house - perhaps her parents are there - but she resists it. Later. For the time being she must stick to the plan and investigate the possibilities of twenty two Fairfax Road. While she is not entirely certain where it is, she has a rough idea and goes in the direction Ian has described, skirting the park's perimeter. She looks apprehensively at the bells but their clappers are still. The silence is absolute.

She is hungry and thirsty but these are minor considerations. She must first find shelter.

After some trial and error she sees the welcome sign, Fairfax Road. It is very frightening moving along inhabited streets. Every moment Susie expects a door or window to open and the bells to ring; but it does not happen. She appears to be invisible.

She slides along the street until she reaches number twenty two. Then she stops. The house, like all the others, is silent and still. Is it empty? Susie does not know how to find out. All she can do is rely on Ian's account.

She opens the gate and creeps along the side of the house, avoiding the front door. The garden door is forbiddingly closed and when she applies gentle pressure remains firmly locked. She cannot and dare not break it down.

Tears of frustration fall down her cheeks but she brushes them away and follows Ian's alternative instructions to go round to the back and slip in through the garden. He has described this minutely. She follows the same path that Joe took so long ago and is at last standing before the garden shed, gazing with fear at the dark and impenetrable doors and windows at the back of the house. If there is anyone inside there is no sign of them.

Susie tries the shed door. To her infinite relief it is unlocked. It is dark inside and she is scared of bumping into something and making a noise. And she is very, very tired. She can feel rough cloth underfoot. Hoping that this is sacks, she lies down, covers herself and goes to sleep.

*

They were almost home, only two nights away. A fine drizzle had sent them into the shelter of an abandoned building and they lay on the ground, wrapped in one another's arms.

'You think we can attain perfect happiness,' Kathryn whispered

'We already have,' he said but knew he was playing with the truth.

'We can't, not even us with our long lives.'

'Why not?' he turned to her, his mouth against her hair.

'We're not immortal. Life isn't infinite.'

'But long, much longer than I can hope for! I don't want us to be confined to my puny years.'

But they might be all they had. Kathryn was alarmed to find that she could discern no future for Joe and her, only a terrifying blankness. Time was passing. She had no faith in the future Joe so confidently predicted.

She saw too that Joe's desire to obtain the drug was not confined to his fears about ageing; she had already warned him of the power of the drug itself, its insidious temptations undiminished. They too had thought that to live countless years was to experience bliss, to have penetrated nature's holiest secret a triumph; but they had been credulous. Failing to see the consequences of their arrogance, they had unknowingly made a pact with evil. Now they were paying the price, Nature's revenge for defying her, frustrating her infinite rhythm of death and regeneration. Even her womb, Kathryn reflected bitterly, failed to bear life, her precious seeds gone to waste. It filled her with shame but on this point at least Joe was able to comfort her for he had never contemplated the possibility of having children. In many respects he was still a child himself. Although it poured balm on her hurt, his response was of a piece with their doomed but determined effort to bring their diverse lives into alignment, to iron out differences and create a reality that did not exist.

When first settled at the house, the community had relied on having children, on restoring to a new generation the principles of liberty on which they themselves had been raised; but the years passed without new life, a loss that affected the relationship between couples who, without the next generation to nurture, gave way to a sense of hopelessness. Various herbal remedies were tried to induce conception, the cycles of the moon brought into play. Without success. Plans for the future of the community had to be readjusted. It was a severe blow. Nor could they understand the reasons. If the drug were responsible the townspeople would be infertile. They were not. They concluded that either a hidden, inner safety mechanism was at work, for without the drug parents with an indefinite life span would be forced to see their children die, or the stress of their lives made childbearing impossible.

Susie sleeps all that night and most of the next day for it is the first time since her incarceration that she is able to breathe without the overpowering stench of decay and can rest in darkness and in quiet. It is a glorious feeling and when, towards evening, she rouses herself, she can feel life returning to her wasted limbs. But she needs food.

Susie knows the way of the townspeople. Each house has a cellar in which provisions are stored, the amount varying according to what goods individuals have to barter. A shoemaker for instance would do well, or a weaver or tailor for they supply objects that are essential. She wonders what the captured man used to do and if his store is full. She also knows that garden sheds are sometimes used for keeping vegetables§ but they also often house man-catching nets. In the dim light coming through the cracks of the door she sees two leaning threateningly against the back wall. She tries to ignore them. In a wooden box filled with sand she finds carrots and potatoes. She bites into them hungrily. They have gone soft and taste bitter but it is the first fresh food she has eaten since she was taken from her home. Even the raw potatoes taste like manna from heaven. She eats as much as she can but she is still thirsty. Despite this, she lies down and goes to sleep again, hoping against hope that no one will discover her.

She sleeps until just before dawn the next morning. Her stomach feels distended and sore and her need for water has become urgent. She slowly opens the shed door. There is, as yet, no one awake but there is dew on the grass. She picks handfuls and sucks them dry. There are also rows of vegetables in the garden, some gone to seed, others overgrown with weeds. This matters little to Susie. Once it is dark she can steal out and pick them. She can also see, up against the house, a water barrel into which a pipe empties rainwater from the roof but she dare not cross the garden in daylight. She waits in the shed, listening to the sound of a waking town, windows opening and closing, doors banging, people talking. No one disturbs her and from time to time she falls asleep, wakes, then falls asleep again. It is a glorious luxury and she wishes all the children were there to share it; but she must not indulge herself, forget the purpose for which she is there.

Only when it is dark does she peer out. She can see lights seeping out of shutters from rooms either side of number twenty-two. The house itself remains in darkness. She thinks and hopes it is empty. She waits until all the neighbours' lamps have been extinguished and then, using trees and the many overgrown bushes as camouflage, creeps to the house. First she drinks out of the barrel and splashes refreshing water on her face. Then she tries the backdoor. It is locked. Braver now, she tries to open a window. This too fails to yield.

She does not know that the man living in number twenty is standing by his partially opened shutters. He watches Susie's movements with interest.

She is dismayed because she cannot get into the house. She dare not break a window pane. She is uncertain what to do and goes back into the shed to work out a plan.

The man at number twenty closes his shutters.

Susie has to get a signal to the others. This means returning to the sewer entrance, the other side of the town. She now realises that they have made an arrangement that she does not know how to fulfil. She spends another day and another night in the shed. She learns not to eat too much at a time and begins to feel

234

stronger and more confident. Certain now that the house is empty, she comes to the conclusion that, rather than risk being caught in the shed where she feels vulnerable, she should gain entry. Perhaps when she is used to being free she will find a way of sending her signal. For the time being it is more important to establish a base.

—

THE man at number twenty is keeping a close eye on Susie. This he cannot do during the day because he works as a minor official for the junta but he watches her movements in the evenings and at night.

He knows he should be reporting her presence but he decides to hold back for the time being. He persuades himself that he is waiting for her to lead him to other children. That way he will be able to prove his loyalty to the state.

Although Susie does not know that she is under surveillance, she is only too well aware that her situation is precarious and that she is in constant danger of discovery. She dare not leave the shed during daylight hours but by looking through a knot-hole in the shed's walls she has learned that a man and wife live at number twenty four and, as far as she can tell, only a man at number twenty. All leave for work in the morning and come back in the evening. They do not go out again. The town at night settles into silence as though it were uninhabited with only the occasional footsteps echoing down the streets. These usually mean guards are patrolling.

So far Susie has been lucky. Nothing disturbs her except wild animals, foxes who come nosing round the shed, rabbits nibbling at the vegetation, a veritable wildlife park, a fascinating novelty to Susie who has spent all her life indoors. It is a great thrill for her.

Susie soon adapts to her new conditions and keeps herself alive by pulling vegetables from the garden at night and drinking water from the rain tub.

The days are frustrating, lonely and boring. Susie makes another doll with a stick and a piece of sacking. She calls her Susie Three. She is not as satisfying as Susie Two because there is no flat surface on which to draw a face but Susie imagines Susie Three's different expressions. These vary from day to day. Sometimes Susie Three cries and Susie has to comfort her and wipe away her tears, but she is told quite firmly that crying does no good.

*

'What if you'd taken the drug and your world took you back? You'd be the only one to stay young...'

Kathryn and Joe were inside the cascading wall of a willow tree. It was the last night of their holiday.

'Methuselah.'

'Who's that?'

'An old, old man, He's supposed to have lived until he was nine hundred and sixty nine.'

'Quite young really,' she teased.

'But even if the drug worked in my world, I wouldn't be old, would I, not so that anybody would notice. Not for a time, anyway.'

But it was a daunting prospect that had not occurred to him. As his friends and contemporaries grew older, as they died, he'd still be there, forever young. He would be looked on as a freak. He held her in a tight grip.

'It's not going to happen anyway. I'm here for good, d'you understand!'

But he knew, as Kathryn knew, that he was trying to fool them both, clinging to a hope that had no basis. He could at any moment be pulled back to a life he no longer wished to own. His present happiness plummeted at this untimely reminder of the fragility of their situation. No matter how often he said that he loved her forever, that his life was linked to hers for all eternity, the same question hovered in the shadows. Eternity in whose time, his or hers? They were aeons apart, two minuscule dots who, due to a cosmic accident, had touched and were clinging to a permanent state in the monstrous panorama of impermanence.

'Maybe that's our fate.'

'Being parted?'

'Yes.'

He looked at her with incredulity and some anger, vehemently seizing both her shoulders.

'How can you say such a thing?'

'You'll know one day.'

She would say no more, could say no more for the words had come out of nowhere, from a dark place she did not want to visit.

He was helpless against her implacable refusal to explain.

*

Susie is having a nightmare. She can't breathe. She is suffocating. She struggles to wake and barely stops

238

herself from screaming with terror. There is an animal at her throat. As she flails her arms to push it off sharp claws dig into her neck. Susie cries out in pain, sits up with a start and dislodges a large and indignant cat which springs to the ground and looks at her accusingly. Relieved, Susie puts her hand out to stroke it. The cat approaches cautiously, sniffs her fingers and purrs. Susie lies down again and the cat climbs on her and once again curls itself round her neck. They go to sleep together. In the morning Susie sees a large tabby with a white throat and four white feet. She cannot imagine how it got in because the door is always tightly shut but the cat springs up onto a beam and slips outside through a small hole between the roof and beams Susie has not noticed before. Tabby, as Susie calls her, is back that evening and every other evening, sometimes early, sometimes late. Susie has a nightly companion. This is of great comfort to her.

*

A feast was laid on to celebrate their return, news exchanged, a report on the state of ruined villages carefully listened to. With the exception of the children's penitentiary, they had seen no sign of other inhabitants and this was important, for the community never knew if there were other groups, either hostile or friendly, who would move south, disturbing the balance of forces. But as they ate and drank Kathryn and Joe noted other significant changes, a shift in the relationships among them.

The group, before Joe's coming, had consisted of individuals bonded by a long, common history, constant danger and need. Relationships had formed and re-formed over the years; a friendship so close had developed between the two girls that the sharing of confidences, of solace and mutual support, had become an essential ingredient in the lives of both. But if Joe's presence did little initially to alter the status quo, his growing love affair with Kathryn disturbed the balance, imperceptibly at first, but with greater force as their intimacy grew. When Kathryn finally moved out of the bedroom she shared with Belinda in order to live in Joe's, Belinda could not prevent feeling a profound sense of loss. She was in mourning for a person with whom she was in daily contact but seemed untouchable. And, though she would never have admitted it even to herself, she found Joe powerfully attractive.

Kathryn had initially taken it for granted that the flow of openness between them would continue unbroken but as time went on she found it more and more difficult to maintain. Joe absorbed all her love and passion, all her interest. He drew her into a whirlpool, into profound depths. He held her in thrall. She tried explaining this to Belinda but it was impossible and she would end by helplessly exclaiming, 'That's how it is.' Belinda, for powerful reasons of her own, had no real wish to understand. It was too painful. Gradually, without either of them wishing it, they drifted apart.

Though Belinda used her every emotional resource to rejoice on Kathryn's behalf she could not wholly silence her jealousy. She loved them both. When they disappeared for what felt like days without end, an unheard of absence, she felt bereft, perilously close to being unwilling to go on. This she revealed to no one and in an effort to control her feelings of rejection and isolation, she would wander off on her own, frequently to the graveyard which was peaceful and restorative, to cry unseen.

It was there, under a beech guarding one of their dead companions, that Randolph, returning from a hunting expedition, found her early one evening. She had no need to explain the reasons for her misery for he too had suffered from the unconscious and unintended selfishness of the lovers. Everyone felt excluded, apart from Meredith who was not a person who relied for his welfare on relationships.

Now Randolph sat down beside Belinda and took her hand in his and they sat quietly together, saying little but bound by their mutual sense of loss and memories of their past relationship. After a time in which silent communication flowed between them, they left the cemetery, arms round one another, not quite ready to resume where they had left off but with the nascent promise of rekindled love. This gradually revived in the reflected glow of Joe's and Kathryn's passion; and with the increase of Belinda's happiness a closer relationship, untainted by jealousy, once again flowed between the two girls. The group's dynamics had altered like the coloured pieces of a shaken kaleidoscope.

*

Having the cat around makes Susie a little stronger in herself. She starts exploring the vicinity at night, going further afield as her confidence grows. Tabby follows her. Susie is afraid she will give her away but the cat, as though aware of the lurking dangers, is entirely discreet. Together they slink along hedges, learn the geography of the streets and discover the movements and habits of neighbours.

William, for that is the name of the man at number twenty, sees Susie's forays into the town. Sometimes he follows her for a short distance. He has never had any contact with children and is intrigued by the independence and courage of this little girl, alone in a hostile environment.

One night Susie gets as far as the park. It is silent and deserted. She slips into The Field but no one is skipping there now. She is very near Jarvis Road. The temptation is great. Looking carefully in every direction she crosses the familiar streets and hides behind trees opposite her erstwhile home.

It is dark and shuttered. Susie knows that it is unlikely that her parents have been released and that they are inside and indeed, though she stays well over an hour, there is no sign of life. This makes her feel even more desolate and alone and she returns to the shed and cries for her poor parents who tried so hard to give her a normal life. She misses them and dare not imagine what has happened to them. She returns to her house the next night and the next but there is no one inside.

At dusk the following evening, she hears the man from number twenty going to the bottom of his garden. He stays there for a long time while Susie shivers in her hiding place. He finally goes inside but Susie feels she has had a narrow escape. She knows it is only a matter of time before he sees that his neighbour's vegetables have been uprooted, discovers her and reports her to the junta. Not to report anyone or anything suspicious is a crime punishable by death; most people will lie and betray to save their skins or to curry favour. Susie knows spying is rife. Some days before they were arrested she saw her neighbour's twitching curtain but she was too frightened to tell her parents. She wishes she had. She is certain that the neighbour is responsible for reporting them.

She has not even guessed how closely the man next door is monitoring her, nor that he is gradually becoming involved with her life. William tries to imagine how Susie comes to be in the shed, what her background is and what her aims. That she has recently been imprisoned is clear from her wasted frame and sunken cheeks. How did she manage to escape? William intends to find out.

After all the lamps have been extinguished Susie makes an attempt to reach the sewers and on an impulse again stops by Jarvis Road. She stays for about an hour, watching and waiting for she knows not what. She is about to leave when, to her amazement, she sees a sliver of light escaping the edges of the shutters. She is mesmerised. It soon disappears and though she waits a long time, it does not reappear. Susie does not know what to do. Someone is after all in the house and does not want it known. Could it be another fugitive like herself; could it be, hope against hope, her parents ? She cannot be sure and she dare not go in alone to find out.

Susie returns to the shed. She wishes very much that there was someone she could talk to. Susie Three listens to her whispers but cannot advise her and the cat is only concerned with her own affairs.

Susie's wish is soon to be fulfilled because the situation in the dungeon has become so desperate the committee does not think it can afford to wait any longer for a signal from Susie before taking further action. Margaret's relative has disappeared, another guard taken her place. Food rations have been reduced. If they do not soon escape they will perish. They draw lots and it falls to Ian to be the next one out. Their hope is that he will be able to make contact with other dissidents and organise a revolt that will bring Helmuth down and free them all. This is far beyond their resources but because they are young and inexperienced they do not know how perilous it is going to be. It would not, in any case, deter them. Nothing could be more hopeless than the situation they are in. Ian arranges with the committee members left behind that they should not wait for a signal from him once he has gone but should pursue any plans for escape that they can make.

Ian does not expect to see Susie, so certain are they that she has been recaptured and put to labour elsewhere; or that she is dead.

It is not long before the next child dies. Ian acts dead just as Susie did. The same routine is followed and by nightfall Ian is free. He is weak and has difficulty walking any distance but though it takes him most of the night he gradually makes his way to number twenty two Fairfax Road. He goes round to the back, watches the house and listens for sounds from the garden shed. Susie may be inside but he cannot tell. In any case he is too tired for any other action. He must first rest. He gently opens the shed door. It is empty though it is clear, when he goes in, that this is where Susie has been living. Susie Three is tucked up in the sacks that serve as bedding, and there is order everywhere. He waits a long while but at last gives up his lingering hope that Susie is still alive. If she has been taken from the shed, he will have to move before it is light; but now he is too exhausted. He lies down and tries to figure out what to do next. The cat, who has had a late night out hunting, comes in and, delighted to find another human, settles on Ian. Ian strokes her absent-mindedly.

He is so deep in thought that he does not hear the sound of movement. Susie has returned from her vigil outside her house and is about to slip into the shed when she hears a noise coming from inside. She is very frightened and creeps into the hedge. Who has discovered her? She dare not remain in the garden, but she has nowhere to go. This is Susie's most desperate moment. She crouches in long grass. Soft fur brushes against her legs. The cat has heard her. She pushes it aside. She cannot look after the cat in these circumstances. She does not see that Ian following, is standing in the moonlit shadow of the shed. But Ian has seen her. He does not call out straightaway because he does not want to frighten her further. He waits until Susie stands in readiness to flee and gives a low whistle. Susie stops and Ian softly calls her name. Susie can hardly believe what she is hearing. A moment later they are in each other's arms, sobbing with relief.

William is amazed to see another child join Susie.

*

245

Despite the heavier burden of work caused by their absence, Meredith had been much occupied on his own account while Joe and Kathryn were away. The calculator had transformed his life, every spare moment and most nights spent on its wondrous possibilities. Now he was reaping the reward. For years he had followed the movement of stars and planets in their band of sky, observing the moon in all its manifestations, calculating distances with what primitive tools were at hand. He had never been certain whether, when natural phenomena arrived at the predicted time, he had been merely lucky or fiendishly clever. But now he had, at last, incontrovertible proof. The calculator had provided it and he was planning to demonstrate its efficacy with the coming solar eclipse. He summoned the group to gather before noon on the crest of the hill.

They did as Meredith asked. An eclipse was a phenomenon familiar enough to the others, though not to Joe. Eclipses there had been but he had never bothered to follow them and after a first cursory glance had carried on his daily life. But now it assumed different proportions and he listened with growing fascination as Meredith explained that, just today, just here, the moon was so small compared with the earth it would fit over the sun like a lid on a pot. That at least would be the illusion from their vantage point.

Never before had they been able to anticipate an eclipse to the exact minute and second that Meredith now counted down. It reminded Joe of the elaborate gadgetry, the banks of computers, the rows of experts that heralded a rocket launch. Here, there was nothing but one man whose commands nature obeyed. Meredith stood outlined against the sky like a god.

'Five, four, three, two, one, zero.'

Mystic bands of grey rippled across the ground and, like a magic lantern show, metamorphosed into minute spots of light, then multiplied into a myriad images of the sun's crescent. This was a fireworks show beyond compare. It faded away as daylight gave way to a transparent ghostly grey, an evil penumbra in which dead bodies rose from their graves, shadows died and living creatures, birds, animals and the group of waiting humans fell silent, overcome with awe. Only the insects buzzed in the still air. The world held its breath.

A single fierce gust of wind and a sudden drop in temperature left them shivering. Then a sparking necklace of brilliant lights circled the moon, the final signal before the earth was plunged into a spectral dark, leaving only a faint glimmer on the far horizon.

A scream, low, primitive and wild, rent the world, echoing through hills and valleys, a sound no human could make. Joe looked for its source. On the ground Kathryn was writhing in a paroxysm of terror, her face distorted, eyes staring, hands clutching her head. She was screaming with wild abandon. Joe knelt beside her and took her in his arms.

They carried her into the house and laid her down, Joe beside her, murmuring endearments, keeping her close.

Hemmed in on every side I'm swept along by the deafening roar of the crowd, demented, unrestrained, wildly brandishing weapons, axes, knives, batons, bricks, stones; adults, children as young as five or six, one small boy wielding a heavy spade against an older man, others fighting fiercely side by side in a frenzied turmoil, citizen against citizen. It's the uprising that we've hoped and prayed for, the death of the hated tyrant, the people's revenge for misery and suffering, at last, at last; but we're paying the price, there's carnage all around. As I'm carried by the crowd into Weymouth Square I fall over corpses. Blood is everywhere and it's infecting me, going to my head like champagne. I pick up a dropped knife and plunge it into the back of a man attacking a young girl. He falls dead at my feet and I exult. I'm a warrior, intent on killing, and I lash out in all directions. Now there's cheering from the far side of the Square, near the Meeting House, getting louder and closer as an even greater press of people mills round a young man holding a prisoner. I can't believe what I'm seeing. It is Meredith, he's captured Helmuth, the hated face, unchanged from when I last saw it so many years ago, distorted with pain and anger, the people falling on him. Meredith tries to protect him but Helmuth is hacked to pieces. One man picks up his severed head, pierces a rod through the neck and holds it up to the crowd, a bloody symbol of repression. The hated tyrant is dead, his followers mown down. A woman close by me sinks her teeth into an officer's neck. Blood spurts into her face. 'That's for my son!' she screams. Corpses litter the ground. I should be horrified but we're all intoxicated. Tears pour down my cheeks. We are witnesses to the beginning of the world.

It is then I see Joe, placed on a wall, a jubilant crowd at his feet, cheering him, touching him as though he were a lodestone. He is looking triumphant and, bizarrely, clutching a bunch of red roses. I push forward to join him but people block my way, I climb up on the erratic that stands in Weymouth Square and wave to Joe, why isn't he by my side? 'Joe, Joe, I'm here, I'm here,' I shout. I see him looking round for me and for one magic moment our eyes meet. His face lights up and he makes a move towards me. Then, from my elevated vantage point, I see behind him a burly man preparing to strike him with a heavy baton. Before I can even cry out the man brings it down on the back of Joe's head and he falls.

Joe is lying on the ground in a pool of his own blood, the flowers blood- soaked beside him. He does not move.

This is what I saw during the darkness of the eclipse.

*

Ian devises a plan for entry into number twenty-two. It is similar to that worked out previously by Joe - he will find a stone, wrap it in a piece of sacking and break a windowpane. He will climb through and let Susie in. This has to be done at the back, in the early hours while it is still dark, before anyone wakes.

It is surprisingly easy. He and Susie creep out of the shed over the dewy grass and across the vegetable garden. Ian is holding a piece of sacking. Inside it is a chisel they have found in the shed. Susie keeps watch while Ian tries to break the window panes; but they are made of tough glass and it is not as easy as they had hoped. They are frightened of making too much noise yet without a forceful blow they will not get inside. After an unsuccessful hour they withdraw into the shed.

The only other ploy Ian can think of is to try and pick the lock in the backdoor, but he is no practised thief and this too fails. Another night has been wasted.

The following night they grow bolder. They find a jagged stone and Ian smashes it into a small window below ground level. The pane shatters, shards of glass fall to the ground with what seems to them a noise like thunder; but no one stirs, no one has heard. Or this at least is what they hope. Ian covers his arm with the sack and puts it through the hole he has made. His fingers find the latch inside, he pulls it down, releases the catch and the window is open. They climb in, into a dank scullery and sink to the floor in relief.

William observes the children's entry into the house. Tomorrow he will report them.

*

For the first time Joe felt helpless without medical advice to refer to. As she slowly recovered over the following days his concern at Kathryn's fit manifested itself in questioning her closely, trying to discover the cause. He feared her paroxysm might be the sign of an illness or more permanent disturbance; but she was able to reassure him, dismissing it firmly as a side effect, a mere physical reaction to the changing light; and as Joe also had found the eclipse eerie and a little frightening, he believed her. Nevertheless, sensitive to her every mood, he discerned a restlessness beneath her painfully strenuous attempts to appear normal. He suspected that she was holding something back, that she had had an experience she was unwilling to share.

Not wanting to be importunate he let the matter drop; but it remained an uneasy murmur in his mind.

He was, in any case, harbouring his own secret and, honest enough not to indulge in double standards, could not blame Kathryn for keeping hers. Yet he was hurt by her lack of confidence and bitterly aware that fate had once again manoeuvred them into something akin to mutual distrust.

The idea of going into the town and finding the long life drug, despite Kathryn's fearful arguments against it, had taken hold and, try as he might, he could not dislodge it. Arguments within himself in which he decided that Kathryn was right in thinking it folly to go to Bantage were soon dispelled by the inevitability of growing old and seeing pity replace love. It was a prospect more abhorrent than any danger. There was also, he could not deny, an element of revenge in his plan, of hurt personal pride. His defeat, his ignominious flight from the town, had lowered his estimation of himself. Though no more than a schoolboy, helpless against overwhelming odds, it rankled. He felt that now, tall, strong and with a beautiful girl in love with him he had, like some latter day St George, to prove his valour. He did not contemplate immediate action. The right moment to fight the dragon would announce itself.

He dismissed the possibility that he might be defeated and not return.

*

William goes to work in the morning, intent on giving the children away. But he does not do it. Something is holding him back. Instead, he continues to watch whenever they venture outside and to listen to their movements through the dividing wall between their houses.

Susie and Ian have established themselves in Fairfax Road. They share a bedroom for they are too frightened to sleep on their own but revel in having the run of the house. They have removed all portraits of the hated tyrant, except those visible from the street, but left everything else untouched. There is a sufficient supply of preserved food, strips of dried meat hanging on hooks, a barrel of salted meat and dried salt cod. The remains of last year's harvest of apples and pears, ranged on slatted shelves, fill the cellar with their pungent aroma. Someone very careful has been living here. They cannot believe their good fortune. But they are not careless. No lamps are lit at night and they only go out into the back garden when necessary.

Susie has told Ian about the light she saw in Jarvis Road and her faint hope that her parents might be hiding there. One night they leave when all outside is still and make their silent way to the house. There too absolute quiet reigns. They wait and watch but see nothing, neither light nor movement. Susie would like to know whether the house is empty. She knows a secret way to open the back door but to their amazement it is unlocked. They go in. No one disturbs them. They move quietly through the downstairs rooms, a kitchen, scullery, passageway and front and back rooms which, as far as they can see from the light of their small and shaded lamp, are empty. But once they are on the first floor Susie suddenly grasps Ian's arm and they stand absolutely still. At first they hear nothing but then a thin wailing cry, quickly subdued, breaks the silence. They wait but nothing happens until they hear a shuffling sound and see a door slowly opening.

'Come back in here,' a young voice whispers from inside the room.

Susie and Ian can just make out a small figure. They wait, breathless.

'It's nothing,' the voice says.

The door is shut.

It is clear from what they have seen and heard that there are young fugitive children hiding in the house. The danger is that they may not be alone, that some adult who would resent Susie's and Ian's presence, is lurking. And even if they are alone, they represent a huge problem. Small children is the last thing Ian and Susie need, a liability and responsibility for which they do not have the resources. They will be of no help, will have to be fed, looked after and, above all, kept silent. Susie and Ian withdraw to the kitchen and confer in low whispers. The alternative, to steal away and leave them to their fate, occurs to both and is at once dismissed by both. They must add this burden to all the others. They will work something out. They return upstairs. For the moment their most pressing problem is how to reveal themselves without creating a disturbance and frightening the children.

Susie goes forward and knocks gently on the door. There is a terrified silence.

She knocks again.

'We're friends,' she whispers urgently.

There is still no response.

'We're children, come to help you. Let us in.'

The young voice they heard before replies,

'How do I know that?'

'We'd have come and seized you if we weren't. There's only two of us. Come and look.'

Hesitation, then padding feet; two heads appear in the doorway, one above the other. Ian lights the lamp and puts it in the hands of the elder child, a boy who gravely lets it travel over their faces.

With odd formality he says,

'My name is John and this is my sister Issie.'

They shake hands. John is seven years old, they learn, and his sister Issie four. John is tall for his age but both are painfully thin and have the ravaged look that spells deprivation.

The children sit down together and in low whispers get to know one another. Their histories are similar but John and Issie have had a particularly hard time. The children of a farming couple on the outskirts of the town, they were successfully hidden at the insistence of their mother. The father, a rough and brutal man, ill-treated them and resented the danger they represented. One day, despite their mother's pitiful protests, he pulled them from their hiding place and kicked them out of the house, telling them they would have to fend for themselves. They have been on the run ever since, hiding at night, foraging where they could, their only respite when discovered by a woman who gave them food and shelter for a few days but was too frightened to keep them longer. Everyone is frightened, John tells Susie and Ian, no one feels safe.

'How did you know that this house was empty?'

'We kept a watch on it.'

'And the neighbour next door? Did you see him?' Susie asks anxiously.

'No, we have seen no one; but we haven't been here very long.'

They now have to decide which house to stay in, this one or Fairfax Road. They weigh the pros and cons and calculate that the risks of discovery are probably less in Fairfax Road; and it holds a greater store of food. John and Issie are down to the last few potatoes and have been forced to steal from neighbours' gardens. This is really dangerous and Ian curses inwardly at the aggravated risk. There is no help for it. They must move on. But first Susie asks them to wait. She climbs upstairs with painful familiarity until she reaches the attic. Here everything is untouched as though she and her parents had only just left. She pushes the cupboard aside and crawls into her little room. It looks smaller and more cramped than it did before. It too has been left undisturbed. Susie Two is lying on the bed, looking at her miserably. Susie picks her up and cradles her in her arms. Then she removes the brick from the wall under her bed and extracts her diary and her writing materials.

She takes them downstairs. Issie has never had a doll and can't take covetous eyes off Susie Two. Susie places the doll in Issie's arms. At first Issie's large lustrous eyes glow with joy but when she looks more closely at Susie Two tears course down her cheeks.

'What's wrong?' Susie asks.

Issie does not reply. Issie is a beautiful child. She has abundant, dark, curly hair, pale skin that is now taut on her face but does not spoil her extraordinary ethereal quality. As Susie waits for Issie's answer her heart goes out to her.

'She doesn't speak,' John says.

'What d'you mean, she doesn't speak?' Ian asks.

'What I say. She doesn't utter a word but she understands everything.'

Susie kneels down and takes Issie in her arms. She wipes away her tears and takes Susie Two back. She rubs out Susie Two's down-turned mouth and sad eyes and with her newly acquired charcoal stick draws a happy face.

Issie's face lights up. This is all the thanks Susie needs.

They make a plan. Ian and Issie are to leave the house first. They gather up some tattered clothing and go into the night. Issie is clutching the doll. Despite Ian's worries he finds she is well versed in the need to move silently. The streets are quiet and she follows him submissively to number twenty-two. Ian breathes a sigh of relief once they are safely inside.

Susie and John wait a while and then they too make their way. But their journey is not uneventful. As they come out of the house Susie sees her hated neighbour slink out of his front door. He looks around suspiciously but after a few moments goes in again. The children, who have shrunk into the shadows against a wall, do not think he saw or heard them but they cannot be certain.

Susie takes a long way round to Fairfax Road, stopping regularly to make sure they are not being followed. But another shock awaits them. As they are about to turn into their road they hear footsteps. Four men march into sight, clad in the familiar long black coats. Two of them are carrying nets. They look purposeful and the children cannot doubt that they are on their way to make an arrest.

Petrified, they wait for the patrol to turn into number twenty-two but to their profound relief it marches on. Their hearts go out in pity to the next victim to be caught.

They wait a long time and eventually join Ian and Issie who have been anxious about them. This is a state of mind they are used to. Anxiety and fear are their constant companions and would overwhelm them if they knew that William is biding his time before he acts.

—

Chapter Fifteen

JUST as Kathryn had long ago foreseen a great passion, so now she had no reason to doubt that she had caught a glimpse of the future. That it spelled part calamity, part good fortune, left her shocked and confused, her thoughts spinning round the violent and apocalyptic events to which she had been an unwilling witness.

One night the vision replayed in full. She again saw Joe being killed, saw him lying bloodied and dead. She screamed and woke to find she was safely in bed, Joe holding her close, his arms tightly round her, comforting her.

'It's all right,' he murmured, 'it's only a nightmare.'

She did not contradict him but moved close against the warmth of his body. She thought about death.

'Tell me about it,' he urged, 'it'll make it go away.'

She dug her face into the nape of his neck until her trembling subsided.

"My love, my love,' he murmured and caressed her and they made love while the tears streamed down her cheeks and her ecstatic cries broke into sobs.

He asked her again the next morning.

'One of those awful nightmares,' she said, 'can't remember it all.'

He did not wholly believe her but not wishing to force her reply let the matter rest. He knew that, before discussing them, Kathryn often found it necessary to work problems out for herself. He would wait, as he had

258

so often waited, until she was ready and in this his instinct and his intimate knowledge of her was right. She did indeed feel the necessity to assimilate and to analyse her experience.

The pigs, small, long legged and razor backed, their skins a ruddy brown, were kept outside during the summer months though they posed constant problems. The carefully layered hedges failed to keep them enclosed and palisades alongside were frequently brought down. But sometimes they were let loose in the wood that lay the other side of the stream for they dug for roots and acorns and efficiently cleared the ground. After a time they were herded together and brought in, an exasperating task that occupied at least three people.

This had to be done the morning after Kathryn's nightmare. Weary and bleary eyed she, Meredith and Joe plunged into the wood to bring the pigs, four sows, two gilts and a young boar, to the farm. Scattered under the trees the pigs showed unwilling to co-operate and two of the gilts, thoroughly enjoying their unlimited freedom, made up their minds to stay in their acorn strewn paradise. Their technique was simple but effective. They ran side by side in one direction, usually through a thicket, the humans coming at them in a pincer movement from opposite ends; but pigs are smart and before they could be cajoled into turning round one went one way, the other in the opposite direction, screaming in triumph. Joe was escorting the main herd across the stream and left Kathryn and Meredith to deal with the two runaways. After their fifth attempt to turn them round, muddy and out of breath, their exasperation turned to laughter. They sat on a tree stump holding their stomachs in an effort to contain their mirth, tears pouring down their faces; but Kathryn suddenly found herself crying and hoped that Meredith had not noticed. But he had.

'Darling, what's wrong?'

She needed support but could not turn to the one person who could give it. Dared she unload her anxieties and fears on Meredith? His logical turn of mind would evaluate them objectively and she could trust him for they had known each other for countless years and had shared tribulation and terror. Kathryn knew that his feelings for her went beyond friendship but he demanded nothing. That was Meredith. She feared now she might be trading on his emotions by burdening him with her vision; but her need was great.

'You remember what happened to me during the eclipse?'

'Of course.'

'It's like this Meredith. I had a terrifying, grotesque vision as the light was fading.'

She told him, down to the last detail, and he listened with the acute attention normal to Meredith. He remained silent for a while.

'How do you know it was a vision?' he asked. 'Sounds more like a nightmare to me.'

She took him by the shoulders.

'You've got to believe me. I had it again last night. I was seeing into the future.'

'Kathryn, be realistic. What would Joe, never mind me, be doing in Bantage, heading a revolution entirely on our own?'

'He hasn't told you?'

'Told me what?'

'He wants to go and get the drug. He wants to take it.'

He shook his head, surprised. Joe frequently confided in him. But not this time.

'In heaven's name why? He'd never succeed. And hasn't it brought enough misery on everyone?'

'He doesn't see it like that. He sees that as things stand he will age and I won't. Don't you see, I can't contradict him because it's true.'

Meredith considered and looked at her with pity.

'Kathryn, he's from another world. That's the price you're paying, you're bound to pay. Hoping your love will last forever is simply not realistic.'

He paused.

'Anyway, how can you believe that Joe and I, single handed, will succeed where so many of us have died and failed?'

He proceeded to list their names - Michael, Bronwyn, Roderick....Kathryn stopped him.

'I don't know, I don't know! All I can tell you is I saw it happening!'

'And what was your role? If Joe and I were there you must have been.'

'That was the strange thing,' she said. 'I was there and I wasn't. People ignored me as though I didn't exist, even while I was killing the guards... it wasn't until I saw Joe that I seemed to be taking part. I called out to him, you see...'

While not cynical, Meredith used logic as the basis for his existence. Mathematics, calculations and the unchanging, steady rhythm of the universe did not allow for metaphysical speculation. Phenomena were observable and real, they maintained an unchanging pattern and were worlds apart from the much fuzzier philosophy of his peers which fell between the spiritual, the pagan and the pragmatic. Meredith did not believe that Kathryn had seen a vision but that she had projected her fears about Joe's plan into her dream world. Her passionate conviction to the contrary made it impossible to tell her what he thought and he did not try.

'Have you told Otto?'

'No.'

'Why not?'

'I don't want to know what he knows.'

'Perhaps nothing.'

'Perhaps. But once he's told you your actions are in chains. You're left without free will, the fates have decreed and that's that.'

'He's never made predictions with that kind of assurance. And doesn't have them. He works by some strange, uncanny instinct and a wisdom peculiar to him alone. All he does is open up possibilities.'

'I don't need to know what they are. I know already.'

He waited.

'I know for sure that Joe is planning to go and that he won't tell me because he knows I'll try and stop him.'

'And will you?'

'If I can.'

'How? You can't physically restrain him. Can you talk him out of it?'

'No.'

'So what's your plan?'

'I don't know - yet.'

'Well, don't do anything too desperate. He may change his mind at the last minute.'

'Not Joe.'

As they moved back towards the farm Kathryn seized his arm.

'You won't tell him what I've told you?'

'Of course not.'

'You promise?'

'I promise.'

The pigs, bored by their own company, came back in the evening.

*

Susie, Ian and the two new children settle to a fugitive life. They have food and water and John and Issie lose their pallor and now and then even laugh and smile. Issie, growing ever more beautiful, proves to be gratifyingly tractable but as the children's health improves, so does their capacity to make a noise. Constant suppression is necessary and a moratorium on their going out at night beyond the water tub in the back garden is put in place; but the children are never bored. They play games of make-believe and dress up in the clothes they find in the wardrobe. This is a game neither Susie nor Ian have experienced and they join in enthusiastically. These small children are not, after all, the liability Susie and Ian feared. But they have to be careful that their games are quiet, especially when the neighbours are at home. They cannot afford one slip in their vigilance. They have two guard posts, one in the smaller front bedroom and one at the back. This gives an overview in all directions. If danger approaches they hide in the attic, in which they have built an improvised shelter behind some furniture. It is not satisfactory but is the best they can do. The chances of avoiding detection if a posse of guards comes to look for them are negligible but risk of discovery is so much part of their lives that it does not oppress them.

They have noted that the man from number twenty is constantly working in his garden and watching the back. This is a very worrying development and they discuss the possibility of moving but they have nowhere else to go. Jarvis Road also has a dangerous neighbour and they cannot wander around looking for an empty house. Four children in the streets would guarantee immediate discovery and they have, in any case, to remain at their rendezvous so that other children from the dungeon can find them. They cannot understand why more of the committee have not made their escape in the same way as they did and fear that some have died. It makes them very sad.

What Susie and Ian cannot realise is that the guards in the dungeon, for reasons the committee cannot discover, have become more vigilant. It is now their practice to pierce corpses through the heart before they are carried out. Pretending to be dead is no longer an option. They assume this means that Susie and Ian have been discovered. They lose hope.

The ultimate plan of bringing down Helmuth and his men has not been shelved. Susie and Ian have it constantly in mind and discuss it in detail. The first step, which they do not know how to take, is to make contact with other dissidents. They need Margaret to guide them for she knows some of the secret network and they hopefully wait for her to appear. If she does not, they will have to make other plans. They cannot stay in the house forever.

William, constantly watching, tries listening to their conversations but the walls are too thick. He has not yet reported the children. This surprises him. His long training under the junta should by now have conditioned him to being more vigilant and obeying the junta's rules. He is alarmed to find that these no longer hold sway and that other powerful forces are making him act in a way entirely foreign to him. His intellect is telling him to report the children, now before it is too late, but he has been unable to do it. Every day that he goes into work he decides that this is the day; but it never is. He cannot resolve his dilemma nor can he ignore the children's presence indefinitely. If they are discovered the neighbours either side of the house will carry the blame. The children must be taken away.

But now a new idea occurs to him. Perhaps he could get rid of them without anyone knowing. If he can't bring himself to report them he can at least remove them, though he is not quite sure how. He will decide later.

He goes into the back garden to wait for them to come outside for their rainwater. He has timed it well. Soon after he arrives the back door is quietly opened and first Issie and then Susie slip out. He moves forward.

*

Sleep became an impossible luxury. One night, leaving Joe alone in bed, Kathryn slipped quietly outside, past the house and down the slope to the farm where the quiet movement of animals accompanied her in a comforting murmur. Uncertain of her destination, she was surprised to find her steps leading her unerringly to the communal burial ground.

It was shaded by trees, silver birches, a weeping willow, oak, ash and beech recreating life in an eternal cycle. Long grasses encouraged to grow over the flattened graves whispered in the night breeze. A place of rest and renewal that was frequently used for contemplation, it held no terrors, but the comfort of friends long gone. Kathryn seated herself on a bench whose elaborate carvings proclaimed the master craftsman.

The vision had presented her with an irreconcilable dilemma. She had seen in that brief moment of future time that all the dreams of the community, of those long dead and those alive, would be fulfilled, peace and liberty restored. She had seen too that Meredith and Joe were leaders of the uprising, that they it was who harnessed the suppressed misery and rage of a subjugated people and gave them the freedom which they craved.

But it was Joe who was to pay the price.

Was this then the Faustian bargain she was forced to make, allowing Joe to go to his death in exchange for victory for her people? The warring emotions this produced was making her feel almost demented. She railed against the responsibility laid on her by a malign fate.

Her every instinct demanded that she save Joe. But quietly at first, then louder and louder, in the still night air, she could hear the dead clamouring justice for their sacrifice. She put her hands over her ears to block out their demands. She did not want to listen. The dead were dead and Joe was alive. She could not, would not, allow him to give his life for their sakes. Their ancient struggle was nothing to do with him, an innocent bystander, a young and vibrant man from another world. His death would taint them forever with his blood, the dragon's teeth would sprout, exact their revenge and bring further calamities to their lives.

And there was reason on her side. Kathryn knew too - who better? that while revolutions did not occur without leaders, neither were they initiated by them alone. They erupted on a tide of popular feeling, they broke out through the culmination of the people's will. No power on earth can halt an avalanche of humanity determined to get its way. The mass knows instinctively when the time to act is ripe. If her vision was to be believed Joe had happened to be present at this climactic moment, the wrong person in the right place.

To prevent his going was her duty, a decision she justified to herself and to her past companions lying in the ground. If forgiveness was what she needed, she asked them to forgive her.

Thus Kathryn used the imperious demands of her heart to silence her intellect; but Fate follows its own rules and sometimes we unwittingly deliver ourselves into her hands.

Joe sleepily put out an arm to find Kathryn but touched empty space. He wondered idly where she was but, occupied with his own thoughts, lost track of time. He was planning his trip to Bantage and intended to wait until autumn, before the hard winter set in, though he had only the vaguest plan of what he would do once there. His only potential contact was the skipping child and her parents. He remembered their house in Jarvis Road. It was certain that they were opponents to the regime for otherwise they would not have hidden the little girl. He could go to them for help, shelter and information. He needed to know where the drug was kept, what safeguards were employed, what alarm was in place, the routine of guards. His mission successfully completed he would leave, taking the girl with him. The parents would no doubt be glad to have her in a safe haven and it would add an extra member to the community.

His pride and sense of potential benefit to the others by bringing in a new life glossed over the most worrying aspect of his venture: the necessity of concealing it from Kathryn. No matter how obsessively he turned it over in his mind, he knew that once he had told her she would do everything in her power to stop him going. He would be helpless against her opposition and would, as time went by and he grew older, resent her for having prevented him from obtaining the drug and remaining vigorous and young. Unless he acquired it their future looked bleak.

There were other aspects to his quest of which Joe was not unaware, but he pushed them into the recesses of his mind: the attractions of the drug itself, the power over his own life that it would bestow, limitless opportunities for choices not available to people confined by a normal span. He had felt disadvantaged since he had learned of the drug's efficacy, an ordinary, puny human instead of the more Olympian figures of his companions.

He needed help. Meredith. He would seek his advice, ask him to tell Kathryn after he had left, protect her while he was away and above all stop her from following him. He felt no fear, confident that he was smarter than Helmuth and his henchmen and that he could infiltrate the town, steal the drug and come back safe and victorious. He pictured the hero's return and it filled him with exultation.

Kathryn did not return to bed and he rose, dressed and went into the kitchen but this too was empty. Outside, under the dim light of the stars, he followed her footsteps in the dewy grass, past the farm, down the hill and to the cemetery. He too had sometimes sat here, lost in thought, trying to reach the ghosts that had joined the festivities in the kitchen. It seemed long ago, in another era. He wished he could release them from their cold beds.

He saw her, sitting under the trees, in deep contemplation and gave a discreet cough. She turned in surprise and smiled at him. He sat down beside her and took her hand.

'What are you doing here?' he asked softly.

'Thinking.'

'About…?'

She turned towards him.

'If I hadn't been here or if we hadn't fallen in love would you have wanted to remain?'

He considered it with the care and honesty her question demanded and did not reply at once. He could no longer imagine life in this place without Kathryn. Heaven is here where Kathryn lives. He thought back on when he had first arrived, his sense of alienation and the trials he had had to endure before the community would or could accept him; he attempted to visualise what this new life would have been without the magic of his love affair - hard manual labour and commitment to a group of people from another world whose roots were far removed from his own. Yet he had grown to love and value them.

'I suppose, for a time. But not forever.'

'Would you have wanted to get back home? I mean, if given the opportunity?'

This was more difficult to gauge. He had long ago given up the possibility and indeed dreaded that it remained but he had not forgotten his pre-Kathryn longing to return to his old life.

'If given the opportunity, I suppose yes. But not now,' he added fiercely.

'You see, I was wondering,' she said quietly, 'if your love for me is keeping you here.'

'That's what I want more than anything in the world.'

They sat companionably in silence.

'What do you miss most?'

'My mother, friends, family, all the familiar things. And I worry about Mum, wonder what she thinks happened to me. Girls disappear often enough but boys of my age….I hope she doesn't think I've run away. It would kill her.'

'Gone to find your father perhaps. Would you?'

'Would have done eventually, yes. I need to know why he left. There's always that hidden feeling of guilt, was it something I did, was it my fault?'

She squeezed his hand.

'Perhaps he fell in love with someone else.'

It was what he had claimed.

'Did that kind of thing happen in your old world, I mean before the drug?'

'Yes and no. People married but on the whole they stayed together, certainly until their children grew up. Naturally, there were many infidelities but no one really cared. Didn't matter. People changed partners, we were all so close it didn't signify. There was no question of anyone disappearing. They might move on to another village but that was really it. The ties were strong.'

'Anyway it's all in the past,' he said, 'my father I mean.'

'The past has a way of catching up.'

They remained until the light crept forward on the far horizon and then, arms twined round one another, went to breakfast and their daily tasks.

*

Susie and Issie are washing in the tub when Susie feels a heavy hand on her shoulder. She turns with a streaming face and sees the neighbour from number twenty. Both she and Issie are paralysed with fear. Susie is not even able to call out and warn Ian and John.

They look at each other a long moment. Then William says,

'May I come inside?'

Susie does not know what to say. It is not a request to which she can agree but she has no means of stopping him. She watches with horror and amazement as he tries to take Issie's hand but Issie starts crying and shrinks into the wall. Susie hurries her inside.

'Don't be frightened,' William calls after the two girls.

He walks firmly behind them through the unlocked back door. Ian and John are speechless with terror but Ian stands bravely in front of the children, protecting them and facing the man even though he knows his stand is hopeless.

*

The essentially loaded question of how to stop Joe going to the town remained unresolved. Endless possibilities presented themselves, coercion, persuasion, explanation, even unashamed pleading. But in the final analysis these were, in the face of Joe's determination, weapons destined to fail. There was no alternative to Joe persuading himself to abandon his quest. It was the only way. How could this be achieved? A drastic event, perhaps, to induce a sense of reality about his venture; but no matter how hard Kathryn thought, she could not fathom what it could be.

The answer hit her early one morning as she lay in bed and watched the rising sunlight filter through the window, laying its complicated pattern on the floor. She sat up with a start, astonished that she had not thought of it before - but there it was, perfect in its symmetry, beautiful in its simplicity. She examined it from every angle, sought flaws and pitfalls but in this moment of overwhelming relief could find none. Arrived at by instinct, her new solution did not give way under logical scrutiny. It was simply this. Joe's motivation for risking his life was on their behalf, hers and Joe's. If she were absent, if she had gone, all reason for his journey would disappear and the fatal attractions of the drug would vanish. She needed to arrange her death.

She felt exultant and light-headed, as though all her past life was nothing other than a preparation for this moment. The years behind her seemed like an arduous mountain path which she had climbed with heavy burdens on her back. Now, at the summit, the world spread before her, she had given herself permission to shed them and lay herself to rest. For what, in the long run, had she to offer Joe? Childlessness and a lifestyle that was not his own, violence and fear. And love. She had to let him go.

It was the right decision. This she did not doubt, that it was achingly painful she could not deny; nor did she underestimate the grief that Joe would suffer if, when, she died. But he was young, adventurous, thirsty for a life still ahead. She had faith in his revivifying spirit. With time, he would adjust to her death and draw strength from their profound love. Love never ends, it continues beating its wings forever.

And what was the alternative to sacrificing herself? She weighed it with thoughtful care but the answer always came out the same. If she stayed alive and Joe was killed life would cease to have meaning. She would blame herself every minute of the night and day and would have no option but to die. The choices she had thought she had were no choices at all.

*

'Don't be frightened,' William says again. 'I've come to help you.'

The four children do not believe him. And indeed, William can hardly believe himself.

Ian steps forward.

'How can we be sure?' he asks.

'You can't,' the neighbour says, 'but time will tell.'

'What is your name?'

'William. I live next door at number twenty. I have been watching you for some time, first this little girl living in the garden shed,' he points at Susie, 'and then you. If I wanted to hand you in I would have done so by now.'

'And why haven't you?'

William is taken aback by this question for it is one he has asked himself time and time again. Now that he is face to face with the children he knows that his intended plan to get to know them in order to betray them is doomed to failure. He cannot bring himself to do it. He understands at last what has been preventing him. A part of him that has long lain dormant has resurfaced with sudden and frightening force, memories of his childhood and its lost innocence, of happiness and hope. These have confronted him daily in the form of these abandoned and persecuted children, they have opened his eyes to cruelties to which he has long been conditioned and which he has refused to countenance: even when they affected his very soul.

'Because I am against the regime,' he hears himself saying.

'Why? It's not you that suffers.'

William cannot bring himself to tell Ian his inner-most secret, long ago expunged from his memory.

He says nothing.

'Why?' Ian demands again.

His words speak themselves.

'Because they took my little girl. At least,' he says in shame and misery, 'I handed her over.'

It is the first time he has been faced so starkly with his guilt; and indeed the children's horrified expressions mirror what is in his heart.

'We were designated parents.'

'And you gave your child away?'

'Yes.'

There is a short silence.

'Where are these children kept?' Ian asks.

William does not know. Nobody knows. He explains that the children disappear as though they have never been and when they are returned as adults to the town they can no longer be identified. There has been one case when the mother thought she recognised her daughter. She was swiftly eliminated.

'Are you one of the people brought up by the state?'

'No, I am one of the original people to have taken the drug. I dimly remember the old life, before Helmuth turned into a tyrant.'

'So why did you do it?'

In a moment of acute pain and a dawning sense of release William replies,

'Because I was blind and foolish. Mary begged and begged me to keep our child hidden. No one had noticed her pregnancy and no one was present at the birth but I knew I would be putting our lives in danger if I did not report it. I was too frightened. I deeply regret it. I have lost my child and I lost Mary. She died of a broken heart. No long life drug could save her.'

The children listen silently to this tale. It is difficult not to believe, so stark is the man's grief.

'I will go now,' William says, 'but I will come back with food and things you need though I can't do so often. Someone will see me. Your neighbour at number twenty four is an informer. It was he who reported the man who owned this house.'

'What for?'

'A teenage boy came to him, perhaps for help and though he called the alarm it was thought he gave the boy a warning first. That is punishable by death.'

'Who was the boy?' Ian asks.

'We don't know. He disappeared.'

'I saw him too,' Susie says. This boy, she notes, seems constantly to show up. Everyone knows about him but no one knows who or where he is.

"The guards went after him,' William says, 'but failed to find him. They are making plans to go again.'

He rises to go.

'We will find a way of communicating more regularly. Once you trust me,' he says.

Two days later the children find a parcel tucked behind the water barrel. Inside are girls' clothes in all sizes, beautifully made. Susie and Issie gasp with joy. They have never seen such clothes. Their own have long been in tatters and they have never been decently dressed but Ian will not allow them to touch them.

*

The manner of her death was now Kathryn's sole preoccupation and she surprised herself by her dispassionate assessment of the alternatives. A straightforward suicide was the most obvious solution but this would pervert her purpose. Joe would guess the reason. It would leave him with an intolerable burden of guilt, a way of killing him by other means. No, her death had to be subtly engineered, made to look as though it was an accident.

A grisly parade of images floated before Kathryn's eyes. She could jump into the well as Joe had but they would find her body and know her death was not an accident; she could walk into the wilderness in the hope that the wolves would tear her apart but this was uncertain and she flinched from such an end. She did not, in any case, want to disappear. Her body had to be there, tangible. She needed something that would act invisibly and would make her death seem a natural event, to be mourned but inevitable, nature reclaiming its grip on mortality.

She had long been versed in the art of herbal remedies, was relied on to alleviate sickness and pain. She knew the potency of mushrooms. There was one, small, deadly and efficacious, that would perfectly answer her purpose.

She said nothing of this to Meredith but he felt a great sense of relief at seeing her return to cheerfulness and wondered whether Joe had changed his mind. Of this idea he was soon disabused. On a night walk observing the stars Joe appeared suddenly at his side and, after a decent interval, told him of his plan to go to Bantage, asking him to keep it to himself. Meredith's heart sank.

As the repository of both their confidences he was in the position of a spectator watching a tragedy unfold, helpless to change its course.

Thus all three, Kathryn, Meredith and Joe, were caught in the deadly grip of the drug.

—

SUNSHINE returned. A second cutting of the hay left long swathes of meadow grass lying in the fields, the air scented with thyme and clover. A period of comparative inactivity followed before the serious business of harvesting began.

The inner conflicts of the past weeks had subsided. Joe and Kathryn, having secretly made their respective decisions, were experiencing the tranquillity that comes after inner turmoil has occupied all one's waking moments. They both felt free, Joe delighting in what he took to be Kathryn's exuberant happiness, her joy in him, her intense pleasure in the shimmering countryside. They were at the zenith of their passion, every minute a world of experience. They took to wandering in the wild, making occasional forays to a deep pool below a waterfall, a green and silent place, the haunt of geese and ducks and, to their pleasure, swans.

'I wonder if they've come from Abbotsbury,' Joe said

'Where?'

'You remember the swans we saw outside Weymouth?'

She nodded.

'I didn't tell you at the time but in my world that's a swannery. Swans are bred and looked after there.'

'It's extraordinary,' Kathryn said, 'how everything is the same and everything is different. Do you think it's the same swans?'

'It's the same me.'

'But I'm not in your world.'

'No. I must have broken through, or something. It doesn't matter. I found you!'

They watched the swans, embellishments on the water.

'They're monogamous, you know, never change partners, even after one of them has died.'

He added, 'like us.'

The iridescent blue of a kingfisher flew past and disappeared into the river bank.

'If I died…' she began

'A likely chance!'

'Don't be so sure,' she said lightly.

'You're the one who is immortal.'

'No, long lived.'

The temptation to tell her his plan was great but caution prevailed.

'Joe, promise me one thing.'

'Anything!'

'Not to stay alone.'

'Alone?'

'If something happens to me.'

'Oh, I promise, I'll take four wives.'

He dived into the water and beckoned her to follow. He covered her face with kisses and they went under and emerged spluttering. But he was to remember her request and much later to understand its significance.

*

The children do not know what to make of their neighbour. Their habit is not to trust anyone but they are trapped.

Ian will not agree to the girls wearing the new clothes William has left them. They finger them with longing. The dresses and skirts are hand stitched, buttonholes exquisitely edged, pearl buttons exactly matched, embroidery decorating the skirts and sleeves. There is loving care in these clothes.

'If William and his wife had to give up their baby, how come he has clothes for five and twelve year olds?'

This is a question no one can answer. It increases their suspicion.

William does not reappear for some time and is not seen in his garden. The children fear that he too has been captured but one night they hear gentle knocking on the door. William has returned, explaining his long absence as caution.

Ian faces him with his doubts about the clothes.

'Mary made them after the baby had gone, clothes for every year of her age. She wouldn't believe Myra wasn't coming back. I couldn't stop her sewing. Her mind had given way.'

His distress is evident. None of the children can doubt its sincerity.

'I have a proposition to put to you,' William says. 'I cannot come to you through the garden. It's too dangerous. But we live next door to one another and…'

'We could open a connection between the two houses,' Susie puts in.

Ian, not so easily persuaded of William's trustworthiness, looks at her accusingly but Susie is putting her faith in her instinct about this man. She believes he will help them.

'Yes, that is what I wanted to propose. You can discuss it among yourselves and let me know whether you agree.'

He returns two days later but before committing them further, Ian has some questions for William. On his answers will depend their decision.

'You said you were one of the original people who took the drug.'

William concedes the point.

'Then why did you let Helmuth rule?' Ian asks. 'How could you allow things to get to this state, everyone living in terror? You've got a long life, but what's it for?'

This boy has the knack of asking uncomfortable, direct questions which put William in a place he does not want to be. He answers as best as he can but his memory of events leading to the present are confused.

'It's difficult for you to understand but at the beginning, after the drug was discovered, life was full of hope. We thought it would be wonderful to live forever and Helmuth promised so much!'

'How could you believe a man like that?'

'He used to be a sage, a wise man. There was no way of knowing he would turn into a tyrant. He said that anyone who followed him would have access to the drug, they would live in new towns and there'd be plenty and freedom. But things changed over the years, bit by bit.'

282

'You could have stopped it while it was happening!' Ian says.

"We didn't realise. You have no idea how gradual it was. Laws were passed, bit by bit. You don't notice the chains until they hold you helpless. Before we knew what had hit us we were nothing less than slaves.'

'And when they stopped you having children?'

'It was too late by then. And anyway, the junta made the argument sound logical, asked what did we need new generations for when the present one was still alive and wouldn't die? They'd be nothing but an economic burden, more and more people living for years on end. It made a sort of sense. We'd stopped thinking by then, though when there were some murmurs of protest Helmuth called a meeting and said we could vote on whether to pass the law or not.'

'But you did!' Susie says accusingly.

'There were secret spies all over the place. You didn't dare vote against a Helmuth decree. It meant certain death. We knew that.'

'Well, at least some parents defied the state. Like mine,' Susie says proudly.

'Yes, quite a lot have. But at what price!'

He has no need to elaborate. But then he asks them,

'Do you think they were right? Your parents I mean. Your lives….'

'Of course we do!' Susie feels she is speaking for them all. The children nod their agreement.

They sit in the cellar where they are less likely to be heard and talk well into the night. The children listen enthralled to a history the telling of which has been denied them. And in the end even Ian feels that he can trust this man and that he could be the key to the success of their grandiose hopes.

They agree to install a connecting door between the houses.

'I can come and go as we please though I won't intrude. We'll have an arranged signal. But,' he looks at them curiously, 'what do you want to do eventually? You can't stay here forever.'

'We know that.'

'There's a dissident community. I don't know where but somewhere in the wild.'

'No,' Ian says firmly, 'we have other plans.'

He explains that they are not leaving until they have brought down the regime and freed their friends and all other children.

William looks at them with incredulity.

'Have you any idea how? Have you got contacts in the town?'

'No, not yet,' Susie says. 'We're waiting for someone who has. Then we can make our plan.'

The four children pitted against Helmuth. William admires their foolhardy courage, possible only because they are innocent and inexperienced. He wonders for a moment whether he should back out. These children are dangerous. But he checks himself. He has determined to revenge his wife, his child and the hundreds of people who have cruelly suffered. He must hold firm.

'Now, what is the first thing I can do for you?'

'Contact the other children in the sewers,' Susie says, 'let them know we are safe.'

*

Kathryn made a careful reckoning of when she thought Joe would leave for Bantage. He was needed during harvest; cold, ice and snow would prevent a journey during winter. The likeliest time was late autumn and she prepared herself for the inevitability of events. But she remained unmoved in her resolve.

Joe too was making plans.

'When do you intend to go?' Meredith asked in one of his few references to Joe's foray into the town.

'Before the worst of the winter weather sets in.'

Meredith, who did not play to lose, made no attempt to dissuade him; but the knowledge weighed heavy. He had no power over what, from whichever angle he considered it, was the unfolding tragedy of two people whose passionate love for one another would destroy them. He had only once, many years ago, been deeply in love and that had ended in the death of his beloved, killed in battle by the townspeople. It was a long time ago but the hurt had left him unwilling to risk himself again. But now, against his every instinct and desire, he had been drawn into Kathryn's and Joe's heady relationship. Both had confided in him because both trusted him. He could not ignore their plight and indeed felt some lingering responsibility for it. Without his demonstration of the timing of the eclipse Kathryn might not have had her vision and the devastating train of events not occurred. Had his pride tempted fate and fate used him to its own ends? He feared this might be so. He had flown too high.

But what to do? He debated options through the long reaches of the night, methodically considering the merit of each. There were few available. Kathryn was like a closed book. Her evident happiness, an ecstatic almost unnatural joy, contrasted with brooding silences when she thought herself unobserved. It filled him with dread for he well knew the power of her will, her disregard for her own safety and her capacity for sacrifice. She had risked herself often to save friends; what would she now do to save her lover? Guarded questions met with evasion. As for Joe, he was as stubborn as she was and made it clear that his decision to go to the town was not negotiable. Meredith wearily decided that he could take responsibility for his own actions alone.

He could do little for Kathryn for he did not know her plan; but it seemed to him that the one in the greatest jeopardy was Joe. He needed protection and it followed that if he were saved Kathryn would not do whatever it was she had planned. In this way he might save them both.

The possibility of the townspeople claiming yet another of the people he loved filled Meredith with horror and with rage. He felt now that he had been passive too long, that he had not done enough against the enemy. He had, in any case, another reason for revenge, a personal vendetta against Helmuth which reached back to an earlier time when Helmuth's promises for a new society had seduced them all. Joe's foolhardiness might give him the opening to redress the balance. If Joe could not be prevented from going Meredith would go with him. One alone was doomed but with two people fighting, the possibility of success doubled. He would secretly follow Joe and reveal himself only when it was too late to turn back. But the central problem remained. Kathryn had to be pacified and held back after Joe and he had gone. His only recourse was to seek help from Randolph and Belinda and though he was reluctant to break a confidence, for he had promised not to tell, he felt the urgency of the situation demanded it.

These undercurrents did not go unnoticed by the others. Randolph and Belinda sensed and were mystified by the force of hidden emotion, while Otto, as always, kept his own counsel.

Randolph shrugged.

'Can't tell what's going on but I suppose we'll eventually find out.'

They were too involved in rediscovering one another to probe further.

But events were not to proceed as any one of them had anticipated.

*

'There's going to be an inspection of empty houses,' William tells the children one evening. 'You'll have to move, for a time at least.'

They are alarmed.

'Where to?'

'I think it best you come into my house. I'll hide you in the attic on the day.'

'What about the connecting door?' Ian asks.

'I'm going to brick it up with the old bricks. I've kept them.'

They spend the next two days removing every trace of their occupation, replacing objects as they had first found them. The house is cleaner than they would have liked but as the inspection is several days away the dust will settle and at least some of the musty smell return. There is, in any case, nothing else they can do.

Once settled in the more cramped quarters of William's attic they debate their future.

'We can't just hang around like this,' Susie says. 'We have to plan. We've got to get the others out and...'

'Bring the regime down,' Ian adds, not without irony.

Two days later they hear the guards go into number twenty two and noisily turn everything over. They sit shivering but after a time the front door bangs shut and steps in unison march down the street.

That evening, when he gets home, William allows the children downstairs.

'How did you know they were coming?' Susie asks.

'I work as a minor official,' he says. 'I'm in a good position to know what's going on.'

'We want to start planning. It's not enough to sit around, dependent on you, doing nothing,' Ian says, 'but we have to wait for Margaret's contacts.'

'Has it occurred to you that she may not have survived?' William asks.

There is a small silence.

'You realise what you are taking on? The chances of a pack of children bringing down Helmuth and the junta are practically nil.'

288

'We've nothing to lose.'

'Except your lives.'

'They're not much use until we do something,' Susie says, 'something worthwhile. We've all lost the people we love.'

She looks directly at William.

'We owe them.'

William's heart gives a lurch. These children know too much, have experienced too much. They are worldly wise and weary, grown up before their time. It tells on their pale, serious faces, even Issie's who, though not fully understanding what is at stake, is wide eyed with concern. He wants to pick her up and comfort her but such shows of affection would produce deep embarrassment. They are not used to demonstrative behaviour. Instead, he thinks of persuading them to leave the town, to go into the country, remove themselves from the horror of their future. But he understands from his own bitter experience that not to do what one thinks right, even in childhood or perhaps particularly then, can lead to guilt of the most brutal kind, more dangerous to the personality in its own way than physical assault. Nevertheless, he cannot allow them to throw their lives away.

Bringing the regime down has not been part of William's plan but now that the children have led him down the unexpected path of defying the junta he has been harbouring a dream. It is to return to the village where he grew up, to recapture the innocence of that time, to learn again what it means to live without fear, without terror stalking one's every moment. No matter if the village is in ruins, he will build it up again, he will smell the earth and regain some part of all that he has lost. He will take the children with him and teach them how to live. That way he may expiate his sins and give back to Mary what he took away.

But he cannot afford to be caught up in their mad fantasy and embark on a suicidal mission neither he nor they will survive. All hope will be lost. He will persuade them he is right and that they must abandon their ambition.

'We have to escape. As soon as possible,' he insists.

'No. We can't leave the others in the dungeon. It's what we promised and what we are determined to do.'

William wants to act for Mary, the children for their friends. Though locked into one another's fate they have diverging aims. This, William fears, is going to be their undoing. To gain time, he promises to try and rescue the prisoners from the dungeon and to find people who would join an uprising. It is highly improbable that he can. Movement and contacts are carefully monitored and regarded with deep suspicion. Meetings to get the necessary consensus and make a plan are essential to success but any assembly of people, no matter how discreetly conducted, is illegal and certain to be discovered.

'You'll have to let me think about it,' he says.

*

Early one morning, as everyone was leaving for their individual tasks, Belinda burst in from her night watch.

'They're coming,' she said. 'the townspeople.'

They gathered urgently in the kitchen.

'How far away?'

'About five hours I would say.'

'How many?'

'I haven't seen them yet.'

She had observed herds of animals moving swiftly away from the hills, had heard the warning squawk of alarmed birds in the distance. Their ears were finely tuned to the sound of danger.

'Go back up the pine,' Randolph said, 'report progress. Otto, if you stay below you can act as runner. You all know what to do?'

They nodded. They had practised hand to hand fighting with arms, knives, swords, axes and rehearsed numerous manoeuvres, learned the many tactics common to guerilla fighters. These were of a wide enough range to cover all possible emergencies. They had one great advantage - as a group they were flexible, able to react swiftly as necessity dictated whereas the townspeople followed a set routine, like programmed robots; or this in the past had always been the case.

It is almost impossible to tell how one will act when in danger, what inner impulse will take over, urging action which would previously have seemed impossible. This was going to be a new experience for Joe, the make believe turned into a bloody reality and he did not know, though his courage was high, if he would distinguish himself or fail miserably. He could feel himself tautening for the fight, his nerves stretched to breaking point. His first thought was to protect Kathryn. He moved instinctively towards her. Randolph saw.

'You have to remember that self defence and the death of the enemy is the first and foremost responsibility of each individual.'

He looked directly at Joe.

'If you don't trust your partner, if you look out for each other, the enemy will catch you off guard and you'll both be killed and leave the rest of us in even further danger. There's few enough of us as it is. In the past we were usually able to match numbers. That may not be the case today. Don't forget,' he added emphatically, 'it's each individual for himself in order to protect the others.'

Joe could not deny the logic of Randolph's statement and looked at Kathryn to see how she had reacted. She looked triumphant, the flush of victory on her face long before the battle had begun. She was, as he again reminded himself, a far more experienced fighter than he, well able to look after herself. He admired her more than ever at this moment, her courage, her indomitable spirit. That this magnificent woman loved him seemed to him a wonder and a miracle. He determined to prove himself to her. He would fight to the death. He felt strength flowing into his limbs.

Kathryn saw and understood. She had no doubts about Joe's prowess as a fighter, knew that his youthful vigour would compensate for his inexperience. He would survive.

But her own moment of truth, of epiphany had arrived, provided by the enemy. They had inadvertently come to her rescue, obviating the need to seek poisoned mushrooms, to deceive Joe and the others. Not an inglorious death but a glorious end awaited her.

Her plan was simple. Confident of her superior strength and skill she would first kill the enemy but leaving one alive, give him an opportunity to kill her, a stratagem that could not fail. The others would soon despatch him. Kathryn felt fear and ecstasy in equal measure, ecstasy at her impending end, fear for Joe at the grief he would feel. But not forever. His youth and the strength they had given each other through their love would sustain him. She quailed; but there was no turning back.

Her life with Joe replayed itself, all that he meant to her in the two years they had been together. She could barely recall a time before she knew him, years that trickled away like water into the earth; all that mattered was her love for this young man, a passion of an intensity that rolled all she ever felt, all past emotion, all present joy, into one ball. They had discovered love, they were the first lovers in the universe, the most astonished, the most passionate. So it had seemed at the beginning and so it seemed still. This message passed between them. Kathryn put her hand lightly on Joe's cheek and moved away, afraid that her sorrow would show.

They turned to the matter in hand.

'The plan is this,' Randolph said.

'We conceal ourselves at the edge of the wood - I'll give you your individual positions and we will then wait for the townspeople to approach. Usually they come by ox and cart and finally on foot but we can't be sure. But whatever their formation our biggest advantage is surprise. We have to remain hidden until the last moment and then spring on them. It's best that we gather at the edge of the tree line and use it as our point of attack. Belinda is going to climb a tree near us. She will keep watch. Otto, waiting below, will be able to tell us roughly where they are going to enter the wood. We'll conceal ourselves in a formation I will specify and rush them simultaneously. Each individual is to mark his man or men and attack before any one of them realises we are there. As I said, surprise is all. Is that understood?'

They nodded their agreement.

'We have a few hours. Otto please prepare a hot meal before you go and we'll go over the tactics again. Don't eat too much. It will make you sluggish.'

Kathryn and Joe sat together, their legs pressed one against the other, faces flushed with excitement, pretending that this was no extraordinary occasion, that life was continuing with its normal routine. They exchanged trivial remarks. The time for feelings, for words, had passed.

They put on boots and loose clothing and armed themselves with knives and axes already ground to a fine edge, then moved to the intended battleground at the edge of the wood, two hours distant from the house. As he retraced his steps to where he had so long ago waited for Randolph to return with Otto, Joe hardly recognised the boy he had been. Then, he had been frightened by a pig, now he was a man, his first major battle ahead. He felt light-hearted, confident. As did the others. No one hurried or panicked, all were calm, secure in their knowledge of one another. They waited, talking quietly of everyday things.

When Otto reported that Belinda had seen that the men were mounted on ponies a new plan was put into operation.

'We'll have to come at them from above,' Randolph said. 'Once we know roughly at which point they enter the wood each one of you will be designated a tree. Position yourselves so that you're immediately above the riders. I'll give a signal for all of us to attack at the identical moment. It's going to need accurate timing.'

More waiting. Joe felt the tension mount. Would Kathryn be safe from harm, was there a danger they might overpower her? Despite Randolph's warning he felt the need to be beside her, to protect her though, as he knew well enough, she was a better fighter than he could ever be, fast and sure. But the slightest slip...

Meredith, as though hearing his thoughts, passed by and said very quietly so that no on else could hear:

'She's a skilled fighter. As tough as they come.' And he grinned.

Otto appeared.

'About fifty minutes away. They're making straight for here.'

'Excellent.'

Randolph spread his meagre front on trees facing the enemy, Joe at one end of the line, then Meredith, Belinda who would be joining them once the horsemen were nearer, Kathryn, Randolph. Joe chafed at his distance from Kathryn. He could not even see her.

'OK,' Randolph said, 'to your positions now.'

The moment had come to part. Kathryn kissed Joe lightly on the cheek as she had done all those aeons ago when Joe had first declared his love. He kissed her back, a butterfly touch of the lips. He pressed her hand. They smiled at one another.

They heard them before they saw them, the jangle of harness, the steady beat of horses' hooves on hard ground, the crunch of twigs. Then they came into view, cantering towards the trees. There were twelve, the odds not as great as they might have feared. Joe could make out their faces, grey and unyielding. They were riding in pairs but, forced to slow down by the wood, they spread out in a line and approached at a slow trot. Randolph gave the signal, a hard rap on his tree. They dropped down as the horsemen passed below.

Their timing was perfect. The horses reared and the riders lost control of their mounts. Several fell. Unseated, the enemy prepared to fight on the ground. This suited the dissidents, trained as they were in guerilla tactics. Joe landed on an opponent and sunk a knife in his back. The man fell but another was immediately on Joe, wielding an axe. Joe gave a quick turn, avoided impact and slashed his opponent's back as the impetus from the axe hurled him forward. They seemed to be everywhere for another attacked. Joe parried with his knife and, using an old school trick, put his foot out. The man fell and before he could scramble to his feet Joe sliced his head from his body. At the same moment Joe felt a knife in his side. A man was standing over him. Joe's knees buckled.

Then anger took over. The Furies that had so long been his enemy became his friend. With a strength he did not know he possessed, Joe lashed out at the enemy. His speed and accuracy took his opponent by surprise.

and he lay dead at Joe's feet before he could even know what had happened. Joe looked up. Two men were running towards him, fleeing from Meredith who, blood pouring from a wound, was in pursuit. But Meredith was weakening. Joe ran after them. They recognised a fearsome enemy and fled but Joe caught them. The men were dispatched, their blood soaking the ground. He stood over them and his anger drained away. He had killed several men. He could hardly believe it and wondered if he looked different, a monster with two heads.

Things had gone very quiet. The enemy was lying in ungainly positions on the ground. All were dead. The horses, eased of their burdens, grazed in unconcern, as though nothing had happened.

They had won. Joe looked round. Meredith was limping towards him, pale but upright. Joe gave him the thumbs up sign and they grinned at one another. Victory tasted sweet.

Joe turned and noticed at the far end of the line of trees a group standing like statues in a semi-circle, Randolph, Belinda, Otto. They were looking down. His heart stood still. He walked slowly, deliberately, towards them, his intuition telling him what he did not want to know. 'No, it's not possible, not possible,' he told himself. He moved forward in a trance, everything happening in slow motion, his steps, Meredith coming up behind him, Belinda putting her hands to her face, Otto turning to look at him, slow, slow motion as though time had frozen.

He reached them and the circle opened before him. Lying between the two men she had slain lay Kathryn, her fair hair tumbled over her face, partly obscuring it. She did not move.

Joe knelt at her side. He felt as though the life had gone out of him.

—

Chapter Seventeen

THEY carried her on a bier, Joe and Meredith at the front, Belinda and Randolph at the back. All were wounded. Otto led the procession, past the house closed in on its mysterious self, up the grassy slope to the crest of the hill. Here they gave Kathryn one last sight of the beloved land below. They walked slowly to the farm, taking care not to jog her, they carried her into every paddock and every shed, stopping by each animal, and down into the fields where cows and oxen grazed. They rested the bier by the stream and sprinkled drops of water on her hair and face.

Then, satisfied that she had seen everything for the last time, the small procession moved to the cemetery and lowered her gently into her grave, freshly dug the night before by Randolph and Meredith. The amber necklace rested on her neck.

'You come from the earth and we return you to the earth. Your deeds live after you. We will never forget you.'

Joe took a knife out of his pocket and with desperate intensity hacked at chunks of his hair, leaving himself half bald. He spread them gently over her, then watched the clods fall, until nothing remained but fresh earth. They planted a sapling silver birch, elegant and lithe like Kathryn herself, to watch over her.

Joe was the first to leave. The others followed. They gathered in the kitchen, listlessly drank mead and toasted Kathryn in celebration of her life. They regarded one another blankly, each one too deep in sorrow to find words. No one knew what to say. They looked with sympathy at Joe but he had withdrawn into himself. They could not reach him. Tainted by the finger of death and sorrow, numb with shock and confusion, Joe felt like an untouchable, someone with a terminal illness who needed to keep the world at bay. He was superfluous, had no hold on life. His raison d'être had ceased to exist.

Ignoring his wounds, he wandered into the farmyard in the hope of finding something to do in this pointless universe, to replace loose tiles, rehang a stable door, all jobs that were outstanding. He got as far as the tool shed, collected the gear but when he looked at the repairs that had once seemed urgent decided they did not need doing after all. He put everything away, uncertain where to go.

The ordinariness of life overwhelmed him. Why had everything not stopped with this cataclysmic event, why did the animals go on eating, the grass growing, the sun shining? He realised with despair that the unheeding world would go on turning, indifferent to sorrow.

Randolph approached him with an oblique invitation,

'I've got a carving to complete.'

Joe followed him into the shed. He had started on a composite group of wolves standing proud, ears forward, listening. It was only partially sculpted out of the square block of wood he had prepared a lifetime ago. He studied its form and feigned interest in what he was going to do next but the emerging sculpture held neither meaning nor promise. He dutifully picked up a gouge but it lay limp in his hand. He watched Randolph busy and purposeful and then, muttering an excuse, wandered back to the top of the hill where so recently he had carried Kathryn on her last journey. His back against a tree, he absently surveyed the land, green undulations once as familiar as his erstwhile home. They now seemed like a foreign country.

Meredith limped up the hill and sat beside him, put out a comforting hand but then withdrew it. Joe was too distant. Meredith felt he was intruding but he stayed, a silent companion. Joe was only marginally aware of his presence.

'It must be time to milk the cows,' Joe said eventually. He rose wearily.

'Not till the evening. It's only morning now.'

'I've been here several hours, haven't I?'

'No,' Meredith gently said. 'It's still morning.'

Time had stopped, a minute passing like an hour, an hour like a day. The sun stood still, the world stood still, feeling ceased. That day passed like a year, the next day and the next like a slow, endless journey in a spiritual no man's land.

'This must be what hell is like,' Joe thought vaguely, not caring. Oblivious to the outside world, without emotion in the inner, he barely knew what had happened. No tears came, no outpouring of grief. He had the curious sensation that his body existed only in outline, the rest transparent, invisible. He clutched his stomach to make sure it was there, he was surprised to find his heart still beating when he placed his hand against it. He did not know it but his eyes had gone dead.

How he passed time he never knew, realised with hindsight that he had been like the walking dead for weeks on end. Only scattered memories remained. His only remedy was work, carried out with the mechanical gestures of old habit. He worked all day and took to wandering about the countryside all night, exploring further and further the wilderness that surrounded farm and house. He became familiar with the forest's night sounds and the furtive activities of busy night animals. Once, he came face to face with a pack of wolves. He looked them coldly in the eye and they fled and Joe ran after them in the grip of a boundless rage, the Furies lending him speed and strength. He wanted to kill but the wolves were too quick for him and disappeared into the trees. Joe stayed in the wood that night, his anger turned in on himself. He felt unclean, unworthy to have survived.

He returned to the carving shed and, choosing times when Randolph was busy elsewhere, gradually finished the wooden sculpture. The wolves were no longer looking forward, planning their next move, but were crouching, snarling, tongues lolling, teeth bared, ears lying back, one male wolf, behind him four wolverines. Joe was shocked at the ferocity he had brought to life. He hid it in a corner, and did no more.

*

Helmuth has waited in vain for the return of his troops and the captured boy. He cannot believe that his well-trained men have been vanquished. He sends two scouts to follow their trail.

The scouts return and tremblingly inform him that there is no sign of the men but they have captured all the riderless horses wandering in the countryside. They have brought them back in the hope that they will not be punished.

Helmuth is not accustomed to being thwarted. He lays his hands on the two scouts and throttles them. The Councillors watch impassively.

Helmuth storms out of the Meeting Room to pace in rage inside his own house. The refusal of the dissidents to be eliminated, to remain alive, is like a death-toll to his own existence. They personify who he once was and can no longer afford to be.

*

Joe no longer slept in the house. It held too many memories and he shunned it, sometimes lying in the hay barn all night, shivering. Meredith or Randolph would sit beside him, sometimes Belinda, occasionally Otto but there was little to be said. He felt estranged. He wanted to be away, anywhere except here where every dewdrop reminded him of what had been and never again could be. He felt his old world pulling him back but it was a lost land he did not know how to reach.

Late autumn turned to a bright early winter. Leaves eddied to the ground. He remembered how he and Kathryn would kick them into burnished spirals, how joyful they had been. He had lost Paradise. He turned away but there was no escaping memory, nowhere to hide. It waited to attack at every turn, from every crevice.

The temperature dropped and the nights turned too cold for Joe to remain outside. He did not enter the room that had witnessed his and Kathryn's passion and wandered round the house to find another, settling finally in a small cell facing the back courtyard and the hill. There was no view and no sunshine. This suited his blank mood.

Guard duty was now desultory for they were familiar enough with the townspeople to know that, despite their ignominious defeat, it would be some time before they gathered enough energy to attack again. Apathy would take over after so strong a burst of energy. It gave the community some respite and space in which to try and recover.

It was now their habit to collect at breakfast time and start the day together. It gave them strength. Joe did not join them. He preferred to be alone, leaving the house at dawn to feed the animals and milk the cows for he had taken to waking in the dark, early hours. He did not want to lie in bed and brood, to put out a sleepy arm to a form that was no longer there, to recreate Kathryn, how she had looked, how moved, how smelt, fragrant and clean, hear her voice and her infectious laugh. How they had laughed together! He had deluded himself into believing it would go on forever. Sometimes he was overcome with guilt. Had he used every minute, every second to its full? He thought with shame of his escape to the cave. All those precious days, hours, minutes lost. He would give the world to have them back and spend them with his beloved.

The early risings had the disadvantage of a long morning but Joe was perfecting the art of keeping him self busy and, under Randolph's tutelage, had taken to hunting whenever food was needed and even when it was not. This gave him the excuse for long wanders in the wilderness, close observation of the wild life and an occupation to stifle his bewilderment. He could not believe that Kathryn could be there one minute and not the next, could not visualise her unbeing. His mind perceived what his heart failed to absorb and he would turn automatically to speak to her about the most trivial event, about things that would amuse her; but his words met empty air.

One morning, his daily tasks completed, unable to immerse himself in other work, he wandered into the house while the others were having breakfast and sat down with them. They smiled at him and he began a random conversation about some fencing that needed repair. But as he spoke he felt hot tears fall down his cheeks, unbidden and unwanted; no sobs, no crying, only tears. He turned his head aside in embarrassment, wiped them away and resumed what he was saying; but they kept falling. He apologised self-consciously and ran from the room but Otto went after him and seized him gently by the shoulders.

'Come and sit down. You can't keep grief inside you forever, Joe. It will poison you. Let it out, share it. We need to cry too and for every tear we shed there is one less.'

Joe was not accustomed to crying but he found now that, whatever he was doing, no matter how mundane the task, even when thinking about nothing in particular, the tears would come as though a hidden spring was pushing to get out and wash away his sorrow. He wiped them away with his hand.

One blustery night he returned to Kathryn's grave. The silver birch had shed its tremulous leaves and the dug earth had darkened. He flung himself down with desolating cries, a last farewell. They brought him back to the house in the morning.

*

The guard brings into the dungeon a grim-looking man dressed in black, clearly someone in authority. The children are told to line up and he walks up and down, looking carefully at each child. Then he points at Rob and Margaret and says:

'Those two.'

'You're going somewhere else to work,' the guard says brusquely.

They are told to bundle up their meagre possessions and are marched out of the sewer, their hands tied behind their backs. They are pushed into the back of a cart.

'Take them to Star Farm,' the driver is instructed.

Despite the relief of leaving the dungeon, Rob and Margaret are certain that their last days have come. They lie inert in the cart, bruised and uncomfortable but at least in glorious fresh air. They gaze into the sky and wish they could fly into it for ever and ever, away from the hell that is earth. At least in their last days they will have seen and felt the sun. They smile at one another.

Soon they notice that the rooftops they have been passing have been replaced by trees. This is even more wonderful. They are in heaven and in hell.

Eventually the cart stops, the guards let down the tailboard and haul them out. They are tied together and locked inside a dark wooden shed, the only light seeping through knots in its wooden sides; but even this is a gift after the endless nights in the dungeon.

They listen to the noise of the departing cart. They are alone. Nothing happens. Mice and rats scuttle round the floor, the bolder of the rats inspecting these small shivering humans. One starts to nibble Margaret's big toe but she kicks it away. The children are used to rats.

Rob and Margaret try to break their bonds but they have been firmly tied. They are too weak to struggle effectively.

'Perhaps they're going to leave us to starve to death. Perhaps this is the end,' Margaret says.

They lean close to one another for support and fall into an uneasy slumber.

They are woken by the sound of footsteps outside, a fumbling at the lock of the door and moonlight outlining the silhouette of a large man, the same one they saw in the dungeon. They shrink back. He puts his finger to his lips to indicate they should not speak. Then he kneels down beside them, cuts their bonds and whispers,

'Don't be afraid. I've come to rescue you and take you to the others, Ian and Susie and two other children.'

Rob and Margaret can hardly believe what they are hearing. They had long ago given Ian and Susie up for dead but they dare say nothing. Is this man really going to help them or is he laying a trap?'

'I am William,' the man whispers, 'and I am a friend. Look, I've brought you some food and water. Don't eat too much in one go, you're not used to it.'

The two children look at him suspiciously. No one has been kind to them for a long time and they are uncertain how to react but the tempting look and smell of the food is too much for them. Despite his warning they wolf down what William has brought. He does not have the heart to stop them. He is talking quietly and explains that they cannot stay where they are for long, another day and a night at the most. He will come back for them tomorrow night and take them to the house where the others are. They must rest and be very quiet. Getting them through the town without being discovered is going to be hazardous.

He produces more food and water from a bag and leaves as silently as he came.

*

Joe noticed for the first time the drawn and grief-stricken looks on the others' faces and with a jolt of guilt realised he had been self-indulgent, had isolated himself without considering that Kathryn's death meant not just that of a loved and cherished person but a death-knell to the community. Only four people remained of the brave band that had first settled here. One more attack by the townspeople and none would be left.

One night he surprised himself by asking,

308

'Why don't you leave here and settle somewhere else, further away from the town?'

'We've thought about it,' Otto said.

But they no longer had the will. Too many years, too many deaths, their sense of defeat following Kathryn's loss too severe. The energy, Joe realised with an ache in his heart, had gone out of them. Even Meredith had lost his forcefulness and enthusiasm and no longer immersed himself in abstract studies. Randolph absented himself as often as he could and Otto sat in the kitchen, shoulders hunched, eyes half closed; Belinda had gone mute, speaking only when necessary. She and Randolph had drifted apart again. They were all in a parlous state of inanition and Joe feared that they were sinking into one of their sleeping periods; but they struggled on.

Conversely, their weakness became his strength for it seemed to him that he alone could save them from terminal decline; but he was frequently overcome by a sense of alienation, a rising doubt that hovered over every action. It reached its peak one windswept day as Joe walked behind the oxen, a firm grip on the double bladed plough, holding it to a straight furrow. This was a skill of which he was inordinately proud and, looking back at the long, shiny rows of upturned earth, birds scavenging in its rich profusion for worms and insects, he experienced a dislocation which tore him from the landscape. He felt the past two years slipping away as the smell of fresh, upturned earth assailed him with its somber memory. He left the row unfinished and fled from the field. Randolph was nearby, for they never left him too long alone, and he finished it.

He could no longer stay. This was no voluntary decision but a compulsion to flee, to leave this section of his life behind, consign it to the past; but the past, as Kathryn had once said, is not so easily shed. It had not finished with him.

In the long hours of sleepless nights, looking back, from his sudden expulsion from the known world to the present, his life took on the guise of a predetermined journey, himself as a wanderer on a quest, not for the Holy Grail as in days of old, but for a more indefinable prize. What it was he could not tell nor where to find it but he had come to believe in destiny and an irrational but fortifying sense that there was a purpose to be served.

Increasingly, the image of the skipping child returned, teasing him again with the possibility of her rescue, once planned on his intended foray for the drug. It became now an end in itself. A new, vibrant life might restore the community and bring back the energy that had abandoned the group since Kathryn's death.

Otto said to him one evening as they sat alone in the kitchen,

'You want to leave.'

'Yes.'

Otto nodded.

'Your business is no longer with us.'

'It is in a way.'

Joe explained his plan.

He told the others of his intention, pointing out the necessity of augmenting the community with new members. To do nothing but wait for the next attack even if it were several years away, anticipated defeat. He had elected to spearhead action before it was too late. He would bring the skipping girl back and other children and young people if he could.

'Others have been and not returned,' Randolph pointed out.

'I know the risks. One man alone may have more chance of infiltrating the town. I am not planning to attack, just find the girl and bring her here.'

Though of this he was not even sure. His sorrowing had turned into a deep and bitter anger, a burning desire for revenge. This too, like the rescuing of the child, was in the realm of fantasy, but it possessed him with overwhelming force. He was not master of his actions but their servant.

They had all known of the inevitability of his leaving. They had no hold on Joe. His world, his fate, lay elsewhere and they understood the urgent need for alteration to his life; but they mourned his going. They had travelled a long way together.

The parting from Meredith was going to be the most painful. There was so much to say, but it was impossible to say any of it. Joe admired Meredith, respected him, loved him. They had drawn close long before Kathryn's death and since, in the desolate days that followed, Meredith had been unobtrusively at his side, sharing his suffering with an empathy not available to the others. They were bound by their love for Kathryn and for one another. Joe feared that, when the moment came, all the emotion he had been suppressing would burst its bonds and he would weep again.

He packed his few belongings. His Gap jumper still lay under the mattress, the last remnant of his old life. He picked it up and stuffed it in his bag together with supplies prepared by Otto.

He set out early one morning, he shook hands with each one in turn. They kissed him on the cheek, a rare demonstration on their part. Belinda flung her arms round him. To Meredith he said goodbye in as nonchalant a manner as he could muster.

Meredith shook him by the hand. He appeared unmoved.

'Goodbye. Good luck. You never know when we'll meet again.'

'Perhaps. If I find the child.'

He did not count his chances.

They watched him go with sadness in their hearts. They felt dreadfully alone. Joe did not look back. He could not bear their desolation.

It was blustery and cold. High clouds scudded across the sky. He warmed up as he swiftly retraced his steps towards the river, anxious to put himself as far as possible from the house. It was tempting to turn back not leave Kathryn lying alone in her cold grave.

He reached the river by evening, lit a fire and made camp. He sat by the flowing water and wondered what would happen to him in this new phase of life; or was it death? He thought back on his time with the community for, among those friends, in that rambling house, in the fields and woods, above all with his beloved Kathryn Joe had begun to understand who he was. It was a though he had always worn ill-fitting outer garment which now he had shed. He owed this world a deb greater than he could ever repay but without Kathryn it had no meaning. And if he was returned to his own? He would be nothing but a stranger. He belonged nowhere.

The clearness of the air made the scene tremble, or was it tears coming unbidden to his eyes? The gentle flow of water, the wild life settling for the night along its banks, birds flying to their nests, were the only sounds to disturb the tranquillity. He could hear the earth breathing to the rhythm of his heartbeats, he felt its harmony, he understood that this landscape had become an indissoluble part of himself, his spiritual home. He knew it would sustain him forever.

He sat for a long while until night settled. When he pulled food out of his bag for his evening meal he was startled by a rustle, too loud for a small animal to make, possibly wild boar. They could be fierce and he whipped out his knife and crouched behind a nearby bush, ready to spring.

'Hang on a minute,' a voice said.

'Meredith!'

Joe was astounded to see him. He had not expected anyone to follow.

'What are you doing here?'

'Wasn't going to let you go alone.'

Joe clasped him in his arms. Never had he been so happy to see anyone though he at once assumed that Meredith would accompany him only as far as the cave, perhaps a little further.

Of this notion he was swiftly disabused.

'I'm coming with you. I mean all the way.'

'But the risks…'

313

'You're taking them.'

'It's different for me.'

'Why?'

He gave no answer but he knew what it was.

'What about the others, on their own? There's only three now.'

'It's been discussed. We made the decision unanimously. They'll manage and you can't rescue this child single-handed, never mind others. And…'

'Yes?'

'I want revenge. We've suffered too long.'

'Yes,' Joe said thoughtfully, 'so do I. I've discovered the desire to kill.'

They sat companionably round the fire and ate their food, tasting now like a feast.

'What if we get killed? What will happen to the few left behind?' Joe asked again.

It was a risk the remnants of the community was prepared to take. They had held a meeting while Joe was out hunting to decide what was to be done once he had gone. It was a dismal prospect, these few survivors clinging to their hold on life. They felt diminished. Their only hope was for Joe to succeed and bring back young people to swell their ranks; but they knew how unlikely this was.

'We've got to hold on,' Randolph had said. 'Once we have gone…'

'There's a prophecy,' Meredith had told them. 'Kathryn had a vision on the night of the eclipse.'

They had listened with rapt attention. They had no scoffed.

'You must go with him,' Otto had said.

'That's what I wanted to propose to you.'

It was agreed. Joe would be left to set out alone and Meredith would follow. Otto, though he forbore to point it out, perceived that the course of events was impelled by the vision itself, a circular, self-fulfilling prophecy. He did not know, though he may have guessed, the extent to which it had been the author of Kathryn's death.

They trekked to the cave next day. The thrush had left its nest. Joe missed its song but the tenacious tree had grown, its roots ribbing the small promontory. They cut bracken for bedding, hunted for food and built a fire. Joe was back in his old territory. He felt it enclose him in a warm embrace that made the prospect of leaving difficult. This Meredith understood. He too needed time to recoup before setting out on their expedition. They both had much to think about.

—

Chapter Eighteen

HIS epiphany by the river heralded the end of one section of his life, the beginning of another. Joe needed to adjust. He needed breathing space, a time in no man's land. The cave provided it.

They were sitting on the promontory on their second morning thinking their own thoughts when Meredith turned to Joe and said,

'Look at the waterfall behind you.'

Joe turned but found nothing unusual in the steady cascade of water trickling down the cliff face.

'Now blink your eyes.'

Had Meredith gone mad?

'I've got a theory….'

One of his mathematical conundrums. Joe smiled at him indulgently.

'About how you got here.'

This brought Joe sharply out of his reverie.

'It goes like this. The waterfall, it's not one continuous stream but a succession of drops. OK?'

'Yeah.'

"So, it's fragmented. Like time.'

'Go on!'

'Between the drops are other drops, hundreds of them, thousands. You can go on dividing them indefinitely. Between each one is the possibility of elsewhere.'

He paused.

'Look at it another way. You can go for hours without knowing that you're blinking regularly. Disturb the rhythm and you notice. Between the blinks...'

'You could move into another world.'

'That's it. Time is not what it seems - it lets two worlds share it. Perhaps more than two. An infinite number.'

Joe considered this proposition. Though it offered a possible explanation of how he had slipped into another world it was difficult to relate to himself. Here was now as real to him as 'there' had been; that this could be multiplied an infinity of times in unknown destinations in the universe was almost impossible to grasp.

'Have you just worked this out?'

'Yes.'

Clever Meredith. He was wasted in this wilderness.

But Meredith was no longer interested. His mind was on other things for he too felt overwhelmed by recent events. He had studiously avoided telling Joe about Kathryn's vision for it had been agreed that to inform him that his decisions and his actions were, or at least might be, foreordained would rob him of the most important element of his mission, free will, mastery over his life. That both he and Joe were already on their way to Bantage was corroboration enough of the truth of the vision's prophecy.

But Meredith was occupied with another, pressing conundrum that caused him grave anxiety and not a little misery. No matter how often he considered it, turning events this way and that, he could not comprehend why Kathryn had died in battle. It went against everything he knew about her. She had over the years won ferocious fights in hand to hand combat against the townspeople who were no match for her daring and skill. Yet at this crucial moment in her life, in the midst of her greatest love affair, when she had every reason to stay alive, she had allowed herself to be overcome.

Was that what had happened? Had Kathryn allowed herself to be killed? Was her death not a chance event, normal in the course of a bloody battle? Meredith was not someone who balked at reality but the fear that had shadowed his thoughts now revealed itself with painful clarity. He acknowledged in a moment of shock, horror, pity and respect what too late, he realised bitterly, he had subconsciously known. His beautiful, charismatic Kathryn had planned with iron resolve to take her life and remove Joe's reasons for obtaining the drug. The townspeople had saved her the trouble of a messy suicide. She had indeed 'allowed' them to kill her. He recalled her happiness and serenity interspersed by moments of introspection in the last weeks. These he now understood.

The irony of the situation was not lost on him and he railed against it. Kathryn's ultimate sacrifice, far from preventing Joe journeying into danger, was the reason for his so doing. The workings of fate were incalculable and impossible to gainsay. And could he defy the prophecy by saving Joe from his predicted death? Meredith had no ready answer, only an iron determination to put Joe's life before his own.

They left on the fourth morning as dawn was breaking. Joe looked round one last time at the cave, nodded and climbed to the top of the cliff. Meredith followed and took Joe by the arm.

'There's something I have to tell you,' he said.

Joe looked at him curiously. Meredith looked pale and strained.

'I've always been in love with Kathryn. Well, not always but for a long, long time.'

Joe looked at him with affection and placed his arm on Meredith's shoulder.

'It's OK. I knew that from the beginning. It forged a link between us.'

Meredith sighed with relief.

'How? How did you know?'

'You never caught yourself looking at her.'

They regarded one another sadly.

'I didn't expect anything in return.'

'You had her love. It was just different.'

The next day's walk brought them to the conifer forest. Joe listened for the mythological enemies that had so haunted him on his inward journey and heard them faintly in the distance, but they no longer had the power to frighten him.

They arrived at the edge of the town the following evening. Little had changed though the incongruous wasteland had expanded and threatened to spill into the wood where Joe and Meredith crouched, prospecting their next move.

'What now?' Meredith asked. He turned to Joe and was shocked to see him trembling all over, sweat trickling down his forehead, his face white. Joe was back in the territory of his chase. The old terror held him once again in its grip. He saw himself as in a dream crouching in the old furniture, wounded, frightened and lost.

Meredith sat him down and pushed his head between his knees until the colour returned to his cheeks.

'Sorry,' Joe muttered, abashed at this visitation from the past. 'Coming back. It hit me.'

Meredith was not surprised. Joe, for all his apparent resilience, was still in shock over Kathryn's death and this journey, undertaken ostensibly to rescue a child, had a deeper purpose. Joe needed to move on, to put distance and time between himself and his experiences. Meredith had watched him grow up and change, he had seen the depth of his passion for Kathryn, he had understood how their alien lives had changed this extraordinary boy and indeed how he had changed theirs. He suspected that Joe had been sent to them for a purpose that was now to be played out to its end.

The immediate problem was to find the skipping girl. This meant venturing into the town. As Meredith had never been to Bantage - lots had been drawn for taking part in the last fatal attack and he had, to his great frustration, lost - it was necessary for Joe to make the first foray alone.

'And if they catch you?'

'Wait until dawn. If I haven't returned come and find me; and if that seems hopeless go home. No point in two of us being killed.'

There was no moon. Dark clouds trailing shadows scurried across the sky as Joe found himself once again in Cat Walk, which now looked smaller than he remembered it. He emerged cautiously into streets still dominated by belfries but he gave them only a cursor glance as he moved silently past the shut-in and claustrophobic houses. A dog barked in the distance.

Keeping low, he ran across Woodberry Drive, waited at the corner of Berkeley Road and, when certain that no one was about, ran across into the park. The gate was locked and he vaulted over it and moved stealthily through the trees as far as The Field, where he had last seen the girl. There was no one there. This was no more than he had expected but he still nurtured the faint hope that the family were to be found in their house.

He was about to cross Bridge Road when he saw, going in the direction of the town centre, two guards dressed in the same threatening black uniform as before. Their step was determined, as though on a mission. Crouching in a dense hedge Joe was tempted to follow, see where they were bound, but he held back, reminding himself of the task in hand.

He could see number fifty six, Jarvis Road from the park's edge by looking down Rose Avenue. He watched for signs of life but there were none. This did not necessarily mean that the house was empty but it had a lifeless look, the garden overgrown, the paint peeling on doors and windows. Finding the girl so easily was too much to expect. Many things could have happened since he was last here, the parents might have been imprisoned, the child killed. Perhaps they had moved. Impossible to tell and impossible to find out. The house's implacable facade released no secrets and without breaking in there was no way of knowing if anyone was inside. Joe waited until the first dawn light and then swiftly, silently made his way back to Meredith. He had achieved nothing.

Rob and Margaret take it in turns to keep guard. One sleeps, the other stays awake and watches through the shed's knot holes. They expect any minute to be arrested. But the day passes and no one comes. Their first suspicion that they have been abandoned is confirmed.

'Perhaps we should try and get away.'

'That's probably what they're waiting for. Hoping we will lead them to other children. It's a trap.'

They are running out of food and water. Eventually, whether they want to or not, they will have to go outside to forage.

A few nights later they hear footsteps approach. They crouch in the dark and listen apprehensively. The door is unlocked from the outside and William comes in, dressed as a guard. The children draw back in terror.

'It's all right,' William whispers, 'I couldn't come before. Are you all right?'

They nod, afraid to speak.

'We're going to the house. I'm going to pretend you're prisoners. It's the only way. In case someone sees,' William says.

Rob and Margaret do not believe him but there is nothing they can do. William is a well built, powerful man. He understands the children's fears but cannot assuage them. Best get the whole business done as fast as possible and get them to safety. He ties them with ropes, first to one another, then to himself.

'Try and keep your footsteps as quiet as possible.'

They set out.

*

The failure of the first foray left Joe and Meredith downcast and uncertain how to proceed. Making contacts in the town was going to be even more difficult than they had anticipated. Joe blamed himself for lack of foresight and for dragging Meredith into this wild adventure.

'We'll have to break into the girl's house,' Meredith said

'And if there's hostile people inside?'

Meredith shrugged.

'No one said it was going to be easy.'

They stole together into the town the next night. At the end of Crown Road a dog barked but they pushed on before the owner could come out and find them. Another took up the warning and another but they reached the park safely and lay in the bushes, listening apprehensively to the cacophony of sound. Doors opened and men came out to patrol the streets. Meredith and Joe, knives ready poised, waited for a tracker dog to find them but none came. The strictly imposed curfew deterred most people from staying outside. Their only legal recourse to issuing warnings was to ring the bells; but as such alarms usually resulted in one or more of the householders being imprisoned it rarely occurred. The townspeople were only too fully aware of what was in store.

They waited until the streets had settled, then moved stealthily in single file across Bridge Road and down Rose Avenue to Susie's house. This was perilous territory but they were lucky. The garden gate of fifty six Jarvis Road was open and, to their astonishment, the back door unlocked. Someone careless must be inside.

'Let's go in,' Joe whispered.

They found themselves in the scullery, cold and deserted, and waited for sounds from above. When none came they pushed on into the kitchen. It showed no sign of recent usage; nor did the two downstairs rooms. Joe noted that the same portrait of Helmuth that he had first seen in twenty-two Fairfax Road hung on the wall. He pointed at it and looked questioningly at Meredith.

'They're obligatory in every house. No other pictures allowed,' Meredith whispered.

They stole up the staircase, pausing every few steps but if there was anyone upstairs they did not hear them. Nevertheless, both had coshes held ready to defend themselves as they slowly pushed open the bedroom doors. No one was there. One bedroom had recently been inhabited. Someone had left in a hurry.

*

It is with an overwhelming sense of relief that William leads the two children into his house. They are shivering with fright and he too is suffering from a state of extreme nervous tension. He had expected any moment to be stopped by patrolling guards or given away by vigilant dogs but, for once, fate was on his side.

324

He undoes Robert and Margaret's bonds and they rub their arms gratefully and look round in amazement. It is a long time since they have been in a house and its sparse comfort locks strange. But they are too tired to react. Gratefully drinking the hot milk William gives them and the hunks of bread and cheese, unheard of luxuries, they sink into beds and sleep.

William waits until early morning and then knocks on the dividing door.

'I've got two of your friends next door, Rob and Margaret,' he says.

The children look at him in disbelief.

'They're asleep at the moment. I have to go to work. Go in there later but don't forget. Absolute quiet.'

The children have not forgotten. They have learned to speak only as necessity demands and to move around silently. They are only too aware that the slightest noise can spell death. They communicate mainly by signs and have developed a hybrid sign language but they have also, under Susie's tutelage, learned to write, not normal writing but Susie's invented kind. It serves them well though writing materials are hard to come by. William brings them what he can, mainly pieces of charcoal and coarse sheets of paper that he picks up here and there. It will not do to be seen with such seditious material. Even so it is hard. The children are incarcerated and are finding their forced inaction strenuous. Disagreements break out. John turns out to be a belligerent boy who lets his frustration out on his small sister; and she silently resists him in subtle ways that drive him to greater fury. Either Ian or Susie is obliged to step in and keep the peace; but always the fear is that too much noise will be generated.

'Now that Margaret is here with the names of dissidents we'll be able to organise an uprising,' Susie tells William triumphantly.

'What will you do?' William asks.

'Kill the guards. Have all the people on our side come out of their houses at the same moment. There'd be a fight and we would win. We've got right on our side.'

There is no point in William trying to explain that their plans are hopeless. All he wants to do is to get the two new children strong and for all of them to escape. He is determined to get out of the town, into the country, to realise his dream.

*

Joe's intention, once the skipping girl had been found and rescued, was to accompany Meredith as far as the river and, as soon as he was sure they were safe, carry on alone across the hills on the further bank though he had little idea of what he could do in that wild and deserted country. He would be on his own again, and while the prospect did not frighten him it was not a choice he would voluntarily have made. But what alternative did he have? None. He pictured himself living like a hermit in a ruined village, growing old. Perhaps eventually he would return to the community. He could not tell, knew only that for the time being he had to move on.

They rose as dawn was breaking.

326

'What now?' Meredith asked.

'Look!' Joe said. He had found an old, dirty, torn shirt in the room. It was child size.

'She's been here!' Joe said jubilantly.

'Could have been anyone! And if it was her, where is she now?'

To find her in the maze of streets was daunting.

They did not think it wise to remain in Jarvis Road. Their plan was to make their way to Joe's old house. If it was empty they could use it as their headquarters. Joe dreaded the return to number twenty two, afraid that he would not be able to bear the load of memories from his past. If the wasteland had made him falter, how would he fare in his own home? He was faced with another trial of strength.

They stayed in Jarvis Road until night fell and once again crept through the town. At Leys Lane footsteps approached and they shrank back against a wall. Joe remembered seeing the man from number twenty two being marched away and wondered if this was going to be some kind of replay but the guard that appeared was alone, patrolling the streets. They waited until he was past. Then Joe led the way down the lane to the back garden, his heart beating in dread and anticipation.

Changes had taken place. The vegetable garden, so neat when he had first seen it, was ravaged and the garden shed, it was clear even in the dim light, had been used to live in. Piles of sacks were carefully folded to make two beds. The man-sized nets Joe had seen before still rested against the wall.

*

The children's reunion is full of joy though Rob and Margaret, bewildered by the sudden turn their life has taken, cannot quite believe in their good fortune. They are free, they are reunited with their two friends and with other children, there is new hope for survival. But it will take them time to adjust. For the moment they are too tired and weary to feel happy. They need food and rest but above all, they want to wash away the smell and the dirt from the dungeon. Susie and Ian cannot do enough for them. Susie, all caution laid aside in her anxiety to help, for once breaks the rules and goes outside in daylight to fetch water from the tub. She does this very quickly, darting back inside with a full bucket.

Margaret and Rob lather themselves all over with the gritty soap they have been given and watch the water wash away their imprisonment. It is a glorious moment.

*

Joe is mesmerised to see a young girl emerge into the garden. She looks remarkably like the one he is looking for though she is taller than she was when he saw her skipping, a thin, lanky child, pale skinned with straight mousy hair tied in two pony-tails. She makes a dash for the tub, fills a bucket and disappears inside.

'I think we've found her,' he tells Meredith in amazement, 'or at least someone who looks like her. A girl anyway, about twelve years old which fits with what I remember.'

Meredith is sceptical.

'You sure? It can't be that easy.'

'It was her, I swear it.'

They dare not emerge into the garden in full daylight. They wait in the shed for night to fall. Then they go to the back door.

*

No lamps are lit and the shutters are firmly closed, the chinks where light may escape filled in. The children touch one another as they quietly exchange news and make plans. As always when there is need to talk they are in the cellar, tight up against William's dividing wall. They have much to catch up on. Rob and Margaret are curious about William. They cannot believe that one of the townspeople is prepared to risk his life to save them.

'All we need now is the names and addresses of the dissidents you know,' Susie tells Margaret. 'Then we can contact them. William will find a way and we can at last take some action.'

There is silence.

'You do know some, don't you?' Ian asks, suddenly suspicious.

Margaret looks at them miserably.

'No. I was just pretending.'

Ian and Susie are angry and dismayed. They have been relying all this time on Margaret and promised William to give him a list of reliable dissidents. Now they will have to tell him that they know of none. They are as helpless as they were before.

'Wasn't a very clever thing to do, was it?' Ian says.

Margaret looks down.

'Why did you do it?' Susie asks indignantly.

Margaret looks miserable but says nothing. Rob too is shocked. He did not know that Margaret had been telling lies and fooling them all. He moves away from her.

'You never told me!' he says.

It is at this moment that they are interrupted by gentle but insistent knocking on the back door. They freeze in guilty silence. Have they been too loud, have they given themselves away in their excitement? No one dares open the door. Ian runs into William's house to fetch him. The knocking continues intermittently. This is what William has been dreading. He sends the children into his house and arms himself with a cosh. Then he goes to the back door, wrenches it open and without giving the two adults he sees outlined against the sky a chance to speak, attacks them, beating them over the head. They have no time to offer resistance. They fall and he drags them inside.

—

Chapter Nineteen

JOE struggled to consciousness, the threatening figure of a man looming over him.

'Who are you?' the man whispers.

'I think it's the boy,' Susie says, 'the one I saw.'

Through the gloom Joe can see that they are in his mother's bedroom, the largest of the three upstairs. Several people are bending over him..

'Where's my friend Meredith?' he asks.

Meredith's voice replies from somewhere to his right.

'I'm here,' he says. 'I'm OK but they've tied me up.'

'Can you prove who you are?' the man says. 'Speak only in whispers.'

'No. But I can tell you exactly when and where I saw that girl. The one I've just seen outside.'

'Susie.'

'I suppose so. I don't know her name.'

He recounts what he saw two years ago. Susie comes into his limited circle of vision and greets him. Willing hands untie him and Meredith.

'You didn't have to cosh us,' Joe says.

'Pretty stupid of you to knock.'

'We didn't know how else to attract your attention.'

William orders them not to talk, they have had enough scares for one night. Joe and Meredith have to be content with shaking hands with all six children though their faces cannot be clearly distinguished in the dark rooms. Not until daylight can they assess the group in hiding and are astonished to find so many children, not only more than they could have hoped for but unexpectedly young. John is a small underdeveloped seven and Issie only four. Susie and Ian are clearly the leaders, older, stronger, healthier than Rob and Margaret so recently rescued and still looking like stick insects, with pot bellies and gaunt faces, unsure that they have escaped the nightmare of their lives. Looking at their lacklustre eyes Joe wonders silently if they will ever recover.

'We used to be like that,' Susie says.

They spend the next day and evening finding out one another's histories' and catching up on recent events. Joe and Meredith are amazed at the children's resilience, especially Meredith. He is not used to children, has had no contact with anyone genuinely young since he was a child himself, and that is so long ago it is lost in the mists of time. He looks on them as though they were a different species. Joe laughs at him.

'They're just like us, you know.'

Meredith cannot take his eyes off Issie, the most beautiful being he has ever encountered. Such tender skin, such large dark eyes looking wistfully at him. He wonders what they conceal. Perhaps Issie notices his interest for she firmly attaches herself to Meredith. He finds her wherever he is, either trailing behind like a shadow or at his side, shyly seeking his hand. She never speaks but gradually, as Meredith gets accustomed to her presence over the next few days, he talks to her. He tells her stories, at first shyly, then with increasing confidence, about the moon and stars, about wild animals, he invents tales of fantastic complexity. As she listens Issie's eyes grow rounder and rounder. Soon Meredith is surrounded by an admiring circle. Joe is fascinated by this new aspect to his friend.

One night Meredith finds Issie asleep on the bedding he has arranged for himself on the floor. He lies down next to her and breathes in the intoxicating smell of a young child, fragrant and fresh, a new and wonderful experience.

Meredith does not want the other children to feel that he does not care for them; but it is difficult not to show partiality for this small child's surprising show of affection and trust. To make matters more even, he takes particular notice of John but John is not interested in being singled out. He has carried all the responsibility for his sister since they were thrown out of their home and it is a great relief to him that someone else has taken her over. It gives him the chance to associate more closely with the older children, though they do not find him easy. Meredith, used as he is to the changing dynamics among a small group of people, understands this shifting pattern.

All through his life Meredith has learned to walk alone, he has watched the ebb and flow of his friends' love affairs, considering them an ultimately vain attempt to breach the barrier of naked isolation and its attendant existentialist despair. He has distanced himself from pain and loss and fought against his feelings for both Kathryn and Joe. He wishes he had succeeded. One has gone and the other? Meredith has no illusions about Joe's intentions to leave him and the children once they are safe and on their way to the community. It is another loss he is going to be forced to accept. He wonders how many more there will be.

Their friendship, fortified by the death of the woman they both loved, strengthened by their hazardous incursion into the town, has bound the two men to one another with hoops of steel. But now, with the possibility of their mission successfully concluded and Joe planning to leave, Meredith is forced to look into the yawning abyss of life without either of the two beings he loves best, a loss that seems unendurable, a final blow of sorrow and pain. What would there be to live for? The temptation to seek the same solution as Kathryn has been, in moments of despair, overwhelming but it is not a realistic option. If Meredith survives the coming battle, he owes the small band waiting for him at home. He cannot turn away. So have The Fates decreed.

But all this has changed in a matter of days, his world turned upside down. A small girl has penetrated his armour, she has taught him that love lies dormant and cannot be denied. Meredith is bemused, jubilant and alarmed. So many years after the death of his first love of self-imposed emotional isolation, he has someone to love, someone who loves him back, a miracle he can't quite grasp. The world is, after all, pregnant with possibility, its sole demand enough patience to wait for fortune's gates to open and let one through.

One evening, as the last of the sunlight pushes its way through the gaps in the shuttered windows, giving enough light for the children to practise their letters, he watches Issie, her tongue sticking out, her hair falling into her face, concentrating hard, laboriously copying

Susie's alphabet. Meredith's heart gives a lurch and she gives him a secret smile as though she knows. He meets Joe's eyes over her head. There is no need for explanation.

With the children unconsciously forming into different camps, the atmosphere in the confined space of the house has become tense. While Ian and Susie have not openly accused Margaret of telling lies by pretending she had reliable contacts, they feel she has betrayed them. They now have no names of dissidents to offer William and few means of finding anyone who is prepared risk their life to fight the regime. There seems to be no way forward.

Joe and Meredith too have come into the town without proper planning. Everyone is relying on someone else, not thinking ahead, merely hoping for the best. Joe and Meredith confer and decide to take matters in hand. They call a meeting for the next night and in the cold and uncomfortable cellar consider all the possibilities open to them. There are few. Only one thing is clear - for eight people to remain in the two houses is inviting disaster.

Food has become a pressing problem. There are now many mouths to feed, stores in the two cellars are all but exhausted and there is a limit to what William can bring. He has foraged all over the town and it has been noted that he was taking into the house quantities of food that were excessive for one man alone. People are giving him suspicious glances and he senses that time is running out. He explains the urgency of the situation.

'We have to leave, at once,' he says. 'We can go to the dissident community. Joe and Meredith will lead us.

If Margaret and Rob are too weak for a long journey there's enough of us to help them. Go and pack up your things.'

Joe warmly concurs. It was, after all, what he and Meredith had come for, to bring new lives to the decimated community. Six children and a powerful adult are an unexpected bonus. He too is anxious to set out immediately. He gets up to prepare.

He is the only one.

'We have to go, at once,' William insists.

Nobody moves.

'No,' Ian states with unflinching determination, 'we can't go until the others are free. We can't just leave them. You agreed before.'

'Things have changed.'

William feels caught in a trap. Once he had decided to leave the town, the plan to escape, though fraught with danger, seemed manageable. He had not bargained on the children's firm refusal to co-operate. The situation was impossible. It was essential to force them to abandon their grandiose plans.

Joe is touched by the children's innocent enthusiasm but his patronising tone alters when he realises the seriousness of what they are proposing.

'No way,' he says. 'If we try and rescue everyone we'll all die. And what's the point of that?'

'You don't understand,' Susie tells him, 'We're going to topple Helmuth.'

'Very interesting. How do you propose to do it?'

'We'll think of a way.'

'You heard what William said. We have to leave.'

'No. You can go without us.'

It is all or nothing. Both Joe and William argue vehemently but to no avail. Joe admires the children's courage but feels increasingly frustrated. To have got so far and now to face failure because the children are stubborn and unrealistic is unendurable.

William is both frightened and angry. All the risks he has been taking, all the hopes he has invested in this desperate venture, are going to be destroyed, and he with them. He curses himself for his folly in ever getting involved with these illegal children. He now has six of them under his roof, holding him and the adults at bay, refusing the only way of escape. It is intolerable and, in a wild and despairing moment, he considers the possibility of handing them, plus Joe and Meredith, to the authorities, claiming to have collected them for just that purpose. This too is fraught with danger. The junta might not believe him and it could spell death for all of them. Nevertheless, he will have to risk it. It is his only chance to save himself. And there is no time to lose. There have already been questions at work and he has noticed an increase in patrols in the district. Every minute is terror strewn, every moment he expects the heavy tread of guards on his garden path. The situation is truly perilous and he no longer feels that, in the face of everyone's folly, he is prepared to sacrifice himself further.

But there is another William waging war against these thoughts, the William who did not betray the children, who took them in and sheltered them with little thought for his own safety. The action was not premeditated but spontaneous, an unknown nerve centre coming to life and commanding him to act against decades of compliance. He has astonished himself, did not know he had the courage to defy the machinery of which he has so long been a cog; but images of his wife dying of a broken heart, of a daughter lost, of the daughter herself, an adult unknown and unknowable, intrude constantly into his thoughts. He failed them. This he knows. Over the many years of brutal living he has lost his humanity, left it buried in his childhood village. By sheltering the fugitives and allowing them to burrow into his emotions he has unwittingly revived it. Is he going to deny it again and walk away from the one worthwhile act of his life? Would he ever be able to live with himself again? He doubts it.

Meredith remains strangely quiet during these discussions. He is torn by what he recognises as the immediate need to leave and what he alone knows destiny has, or may have, planned. It marries perfectly with his now heightened thirst for revenge. He has seen Margaret's and Rob's wasted bodies and has listened with horror and dismay to the children's accounts of their sufferings; but he can see no end to them. Even if they reach the community the children will remain fugitives, in constant fear of attacks from the townspeople. If the regime is not brought down there will be more deaths, its barbarous cruelties perpetuated indefinitely. Conditions now are as favourable as they will ever be. He and Joe have succeeded in infiltrating the town, are in a comparatively safe house with a junta official fighting their side. It is not an opportunity he is prepared to miss. He says so. Joe is astonished and dismayed at his partisanship and takes him aside shocked that they should differ at this urgent moment on so fundamental an issue.

'You're risking all our lives.'

'Our lives are at risk all the time. It's our destiny Joe.'

Meredith wonders once again if now is the time to make Joe aware of Kathryn's prophecy, to warn him that Kathryn witnessed events which are now unfolding, that she foresaw his death. He feels that he must give Joe the chance to escape. He tells Joe everything about the vision. He is astonished to find that this is not news to Joe. Close as he was to Kathryn, sensitive to her every subtle change of mood, he had intuited that something of the kind had occurred during her fit. But now, as then, he remains convinced that Kathryn was projecting fears about his safety into her dreams. He does not believe in the predicted victory and shrugs off the possibility of his death. His concern is for the children and the necessity to get them to safety.

'We have to leave,' he says.

'We have to liberate the town,' Meredith quietly insists.

They are at an impasse and both regret it but the niceties of relationships have to give way to the urgency of their plight.

William hears himself say,

'These young children are right, they understand what we don't - that the junta have to be brought down.'

Meredith is relieved at this unexpected support, Joe furious at what he sees as madness.

'Great,' he says. 'Can you tell me how?'

There is silence and Joe sees with dismay that they are all looking at him, expecting him to be their leader. The fact is, as Joe dimly realises, though none but Meredith knows his origins, they all sense a personality out of the ordinary. And indeed Joe, when he starts thinking more positively, recognises that he is in a unique position to plan a rebellion. He alone comes from a world where these are commonplace, where the overthrow of governments that deny liberty is considered not only normal but desirable.

Joe is not blind to what this can involve. Mayhem and death. He can see little chance of avoiding it, even less of success. The odds against them are overwhelming. He is puzzled and angry that he has been placed in a situation where so much, the fate of a people, has landed on his shoulders. He brushes aside the suspicion, long harboured, that the reason for his sudden appearance in this world has been to serve a purpose, that destiny has planned what only destiny can command; but he is not prepared to succumb to it dictates. Any decision he makes must be free, his own.

He thinks about Kathryn lying under the cool turf in the cemetery. What would she have him do? Turn tail and run or stand up and fight? He does not need an answer for he knows what it is and knows what he must do. And Joe sees what he has been blind to before, that it is possible to give gifts to people after they have died. This will be his gift to Kathryn, the liberty of her people so long desired, so long sought for. Meredith is right. They cannot walk away.

There were worse ways of dying.

'OK. I have a plan to offer,' Joe says.

The children are jubilant and Meredith clasps him in an embrace. He had feared a rift that would not easily heal had opened between them. He should have known better, should have trusted Joe.

Joe has recalled some of the video games in the arcade. One, which he and Martin played continuously, involved storming the army HQ of an alien race, conducting a shoot-out inside their octagonal building and hand to hand fighting in the stratosphere outside. Here, there are neither firearms nor stratospheres, no explosives, nothing that could be detonated. But there is the old friend and enemy of humanity - fire.

'You can tell us when the next meeting takes place? When Helmuth and his councillors are all in the Meeting Chamber?' he asks William.

'Yes.'

'We set fire to the building while they're in it.'

'What about the guards? It's impossible.'

'No it isn't.'

They had not reckoned on Susie.

'I know about them. They're lazy.'

Joe remembers Kathryn telling him of the townspeople's apathy. He could not have guessed how important a part it would play.

'She's right,' William says, 'they've never been challenged. They won't be expecting an attack and won't know what to do if there is one. They're not very energetic anyway. So we manage to set the place on fire. What then?'

'You, Meredith and I lie in wait and kill Helmuth and the junta as they come out.'

'They'll kill us first. They have guards on duty everywhere.'

'We'll have the advantage of confusion and surprise.'

It was a desperate scheme.

'All we've got to do is take Helmuth. No one else knows how to make the drug,' Meredith says.

'How do you know?'

'Stands to reason. If Helmuth shared the secret he'd lose power.'

'That may be so,' William concedes. 'Anyone got a better idea?'

None is forthcoming. William turns to the children.

'I thought you and the others could escape while the battle is going on. '

Ian squares up to him.

'No way. We intend to take part in the fighting.'

William looks at the determined figure confronting him.

'All the guards in the town will be called to the fire and while that's going on you can break into the dungeon and set the others free. That's what you most want, isn't it? And once you've got them we can all go.'

Ian considers this.

'Where to?'

'To my community,' Meredith says.

'Not before the town is liberated - and then we won' have to go.'

Susie speaks with absolute certainty and impeccable logic. The children have marshalled their facts with a simplicity that brooks no argument.

It remains only to work out their plan in detail and then to act.

Meredith has been occupied in the cellar for purposes unknown but that evening he signals everyone to troop down. Intrigued, they follow, surprised at what he has to show for it looks insignificant, a coil of rope made from dry straw, cocooned in tallow. He has placed it on escalating heights of bricks and various objects to hand so that it lies on a smooth slope.

'Now watch,' he mouths and taking a firebox, lights the lowest section. William is puzzled by Meredith's construction but as it starts burning, the fire gradually but inexorably snaking upwards along the rope's length, he understands its purpose. So does Joe. Meredith is demonstrating a fuse for reasons it is not hard to guess. The children put their hands together in delight. Later, after they have eaten a sparse supper, William gives them his news. A meeting of the junta is scheduled in three days' time.

The Meeting House stands in Weymouth Square, a considerable distance from Fairfax Road; to reach it involves crossing half the town, dangerous enough without the complication of laying fuses and preparing an attack. The building is constructed entirely of timber which would easily ignite but for an outer skin of brick that has been raised round the original edifice as an additional safeguard. A house within a house. It was necessary to get past the outside guards into the passageway that runs all round, separating timber from brick. Doors lead off into various rooms. These have no other exit. An underground passage at the back of the building leads to the centre, directly into the Meeting

Room. Beyond that, housed in a cast iron container that only Helmuth can open, is the drug. Where it was made William does not know, no one does, but rumour has it that it is in a laboratory far out of town. This is in any case irrelevant. Their target is Helmuth and his henchmen.

William draws a plan and they consider all the possibilities. Entry is going to be difficult. Apart from the guards at the main entrance, five others patrol the passageway, walking constantly round though William reckons that their numbers would, during this important meeting, be increased. Each guard inside the building has his own rota so that the changeover is perpetual. This means that those just come on duty are more alert than those towards the end of their shift. It is a well worked out scheme which leaves little room for manoeuvre.

'If there are five, how many minutes elapse between each guard passing the main door?' Ian asks.

William holds up two fingers. Meredith indicates cutting a throat.

'Yes,' William replies in a low whisper, 'so long as the one behind can't see what's going on in front; or the one in front does not hear what's going on behind; but we have to get past the outside guards first.'

'The building is a rectangle, right? Once we're in, we can use the two minutes one guard is alone.'

'So long as there aren't two visible at one time.'

'Can't be. Five men going round a rectangle must at some point leave one alone,' Meredith says.

'What's in the rooms that run off the passageway?' Joe asks.

344

'Some are empty, some occupied by personnel. Originally there was a huge staff but it's tailed off. Helmuth trusts no one. He's killed them off one by one.'

'OK. Here's what I suggest.'

Joe outlines a plan which is debated in a session that lasts all night. It is this:

William can supply uniforms but only Joe and Meredith are tall enough to impersonate guards. William will go as himself. Ian again protests as he feels he could qualify; but he cannot and his task to save the children from the dungeon is important and perilous enough to satisfy even him. William and Joe will set out on the morning of the meeting and walk the streets as though on their way to work. They will make their way towards Weymouth Square, taking the route via Rodden Road, Windsor Crescent, Streatfield Road and Catherine Street. Meredith will leave five minutes later and take the more direct route alongside the park, down Welshmill Road. They will meet outside the Meeting House while it is busy with the extra coming and going that accompany important councils. Two unknown guards will not be noticed, or so they hope. Then the dangerous part will begin. They will wait for the meeting to settle, William will divert the outside guards with a story of trouble round the corner while Joe and Meredith go in, one after the other. Meredith going ahead will garrotte the first man to come round the corner, drag him into an empty room - these William would identify beforehand - and Joe, following hard on his heels, deal with the next guard. They will then walk round as though they were guards on normal duty, one

345

laying the fuses in their purpose built wedges, the other lighting them. William will hopefully by then have joined them and at an agreed signal they will all three set light to torches concealed in their clothing and hurl them into the rooms as they pass through, ready to spring on Helmuth and the junta as they flee down the tunnel.

'What will be happening to us while this is going on?' Susie asks.

'You, Ian, will keep watch in the attic and the minute you see smoke on the horizon you run downstairs where Susie will be ready to leave. You'll take the quickest route to the nearest dungeon entrance in Lower Lennox Road. You, Rob, will wait ten minutes and if you think there is sufficient chaos outside for children not to be captured you'll go directly with John and Issie to Cat Walk and hide in the woods next to the waste ground. That is our meeting place. If outside is too dangerous you wait here.'

'I'll be back to fetch you,' Meredith says, giving the small figure next to him a squeeze.

'We'll gather in the wood,' William says. 'If anything goes wrong you'll have to use your initiative as I can't predict what's going to happen. But one thing I want to make clear - anyone reaching the wood is to leave for Meredith's community by dawn next day. You don't wait beyond that, not for a minute, not even if there are only one, two or three of you, though Issie is not to be left alone. OK John? Meredith or Joe will give you exact instructions how to get there. Is that understood?'

They nod, tired, cold, anxious but elated. Issie has fallen asleep. Meredith carries her upstairs.

A day later William gives Susie, Ian and Rob a cosh each and a sharp pointed knife. After that, there is nothing to do but practise with the weapons and wait.

Chapter Twenty

—

A sense of expectation and the prospect of action after a long and frustrating wait altered the atmosphere within the house. The children were subdued, the adults huddled together over last minute plans. Amid natural fears over the outcome, there was a sense of defying the odds; but waiting was difficult and tensions high, nerves stretched like trapeze wires.

The day of the attack dawned clear. Joe and Meredith had long been ready in their guards' uniforms, transformed into figures from which the children recoiled. Issie cried but there was no help for it.

William and Joe left first, their faces drawn into the vapid stare common to guards, as though they had no thoughts, like zombies carrying out orders. They waited until no one was about to see them emerge, then purposefully followed their planned route. People gave them a wide berth, crossed the street and looked the other way. It made them understand the fury with which guards attacked, the feeling of anger and resentment at rejection.

Once in the Square, they were met by a busy scene. People had congregated outside the Meeting House in expectation of they knew not what and large numbers of guards were on duty, far more than they had expected. Joe's heart sank. How could so few overcome so many? But he nodded briefly at William who went over to the main door while Joe stood at a discreet distance pretending to be on duty and hoping that no one would notice him.

Meredith meanwhile was on his way. Afraid of showing an emotion that he dared not feel he left the house swiftly, only giving a quick hug to Issie before putting her down. He was haunted by the look in her eyes but thought only of victory as he strode through the streets as though he owned them, looking neither to right nor left. He found, as had Joe before him, that he created a vacuum around himself. No one wanted to be near.

'Well and good,' he thought, relieved at reaching Weymouth Square without being accosted. He arrived in time to see William in urgent conversation with two officers in charge outside the entrance. Others stood around nonchalantly. As Susie had so wisely pointed out, they were unused to being challenged and gave no indication of expecting an attack. Joe noted that most were unfit and overweight. They took no notice of Meredith. New guards were not unusual and were often placed among them as spies.

William was gesticulating wildly, pointing round the corner of the building. Joe stood nearby, a blanketing calm replacing the nervous restlessness of the waiting period. He risked a glance at Meredith, looking with an air of menace at people passing, mutely challenging them to come near.

William was having some success. One officer ran to the next corner and disappeared, another scurried into the building. William followed. Meredith waited and, as no one seemed perturbed by his presence, entered the building. He had timed it well. The corridor was empty except for William hurriedly pulling the body of the officer into a side-room. Meredith ran past him and laid the line of fuses. William lit them.

The officer from the street corner, suspecting that something was not right, came in and, sizing up the situation, went for Meredith with knife and axe. Joe, hard on his heels, rushed to Meredith's defence at the same moment as a new guard came into the corridor on his duty round. All four were plunged into fierce hand to hand fighting, knives flashing, cutting into flailing bodies. Joe fell, blood seeping from a wound in his back but, surprised at feeling no pain, sprang up again. Meredith had pinned his opponent to the wall but the second guard was at his side, knife raised. Joe put all his force into an uppercut and sent him flying. Joe was on him, his axe plunged into the man's chest.

William meanwhile, was lighting more fuses and throwing burning torches into side-rooms.

More men ran in from outside. They formed a phalanx that filled the corridor and advanced on Meredith and Joe, pushing them further and further back. They fought side by side, but they were heavily outnumbered. Each time they killed a guard, another took his place. They were almost in the corner of the corridor when they heard guards running from behind. They were boxed in, no escape possible.

*

Nothing is amiss in the central meeting room. Helmuth, as always, sits at the top of the long table, his head raised in the usual commanding manner. He speaking slowly and deliberately to the ten men around him.

This is a special meeting Helmuth has called because of the failure of the last expedition to wipe out the community of dissidents. A larger, bolder one will be sent.

Helmuth has motives other than the one he is stating. Reports have come back to him that, despite the reign of terror which for so long has subdued the populace, there are signs of unrest, small and insignificant to be sure, but Helmuth is taking no chances. The knowledge of a major attack and victory will suffocate any movement against him. He gives orders for a new attack. Prisoners are to be brought back alive so that they can be paraded in a cage round the streets. No one need have doubts as to who is in charge.

Helmuth is elaborating his plan when he senses that something is not as it should be. He is not quite certain what it is but he notices that the men round the table are looking alarmed. They dare not rise while he is sitting but clearly want to do so. It is then that Helmuth recognises a familiar smell. Fire. The building is on fire. He orders immediate evacuation. The meeting breaks up in panic and the men, Helmuth at their head, fight to get into the tunnel.

*

As an acrid black cloud billowed towards them, the combatants dropped their weapons and, trampling over their wounded trying in vain to rise, turned and ran towards the main entrance. Joe and Meredith, caught between the fire and the enemy, followed but William, coming out of a side-room, pushed them through a door concealed in the outer wall at the same moment as Helmuth and ten junta officers emerged from the central tunnel, struggling to reach the open air.

The junta crowded round Helmuth, ready for further orders but Helmuth, transfixed, was too shocked to move. His erstwhile protégé, his long lost comrade, his bitterest enemy, Meredith. The two men stared at one another as painful memories came flooding back. Their old friendship, bathed in blood, was difficult to believe in now. But it had been real enough then, when the world was a different place, when they had hopes and ambitions to change it, to make it better. They had not known that it was already as good as it was going to get, that power corrupts, that the miracle drug that promised so much would be their undoing. For one wild moment Meredith wished they could roll back the years, return to where they had begun, map out a different course. Instead, they were facing one another, the bitterest of enemies, both knowing that this was to be a fight to the death. Did Helmuth, in that defining moment remember the man he had once been, did he regret the man he had become?

He was the first to move. He attacked Meredith like one possessed, as though wiping him out was to kill the shadow of his former self; and Meredith fought back with a ferocity born of disillusionment and despair. They fought body to body, naked in their hatred.

Helmuth's proximity, even in this tense moment, repulsed Meredith. The man smelled of decay.

The junta turned on the dissidents, eleven against three. Joe saw and knew that the end had come. The strength had gone out of his thrusts, only determination kept him upright, fighting off three guards. It was only a mattter of time. He briefly saw Meredith battling with a figure there was no mistaking. Meredith was beating him back, inch by painful inch. Joe cried out to him to beware, guards were coming at him from the back. At that moment he fell. Meredith saw and tried to position himself to protect him but he lost precious seconds, allowing Helmuth to gain ground, a look of savage triumph on his face.

Reinforcements appeared from the square.

'Kill! Kill!' Helmuth screamed in a demented voice.

Joe pulled himself up and using the building, now radiating heat, for support, parried attackers coming at him from every side. The crackle of fire grew stronger and flames leapt out of the roof. William lay in a pool of blood. It was a race between the collapsing building and the guards going in for the kill.

*

In Fairfax Road the children were gathered in the attic, Ian perched on a high stool, anxiously watching for signs of smoke on the horizon. The minutes passed but nothing happened. The sun shone in an unblemished sky. Susie and Ian conferred. Dared they go out? Both were wracked with uncertainty, terrified of making the wrong decision and giving them all away. But suddenly Ian gave a cry. Telltale wisps of black smoke were curling gently over the rooftops and they heard fire bells ringing in the streets. The children embraced one another and Susie and Ian tentatively opened the front door. They set foot on the garden path. It was a historic moment, the two children daring to show themselves in the open.

The townspeople in Bantage were used to silence; silence from their relatives, silence in their workplace, silence in the streets, silence above all from their government whose only communication was increasingly repressive laws. Few people had friends, for in this tightly controlled community it was dangerous to put one's trust even in those one had known since the beginning. Informing was the quickest way to curry favour and improve a precarious hold on one's position and informing was what they did. They had, indeed, little alternative. The slightest whiff of betrayal, and this could include not reporting the least suspicious trivial incident, meant imprisonment and death. And it had been noted by the original township citizens that, as more and more people brought up by the state joined the community, the situation grew more perilous. Head down, mouths sealed was the only way to survive.

But information flows on invisible currents. Even before the uproar from the battle, even before they smelled the fire or saw black smoke billowing into the sky, a silent line of communication informed the townspeople that something unprecedented was happening, that there was alteration in the air. They looked, hesitant at first, out of windows, they nervously opened their doors. And then, like champagne corks bursting from bottles, they erupted into the streets, men, women, the young, the old, the crippled, the fit, and boys and girls dazed by the light. They banged pots and pans, they brandished home-made weapons, they shouted and sang and, in one body, made towards the square, a river of chaotic but triumphant human beings.

'There's people in the street! They're going to kill us!' Susie cried in alarm, clutching at Ian's arm.

They stared open-mouthed.

'Come on,' Ian shouted and pulled her towards the gate. 'They're going the other way, to Weymouth Square. It's the uprising, it's begun!'

They held hands and pushed into the crowd. They had worked out their route and now followed it at a running walk, keeping low, stopping at corners to prospect the next stage. There were people everywhere but they took no notice of these two children as they ran down Stonebridge Drive, Rose Avenue and through the park to Lower Lennox Road. Unmolested amid the confusion, they plunged into the dungeon.

*

Joe fought with the last ebbing of his strength. He felt crushed by their defeat, by the ignominy of death. There would be no gift of victory for Kathryn, nothing to justify their sacrifice. He felt anger, shock, surprise.

Meredith too was being beaten back. He could no longer prevail against the number of attacking guards and the demonic Helmuth screaming orders to slay the dissidents. They had lost the battle, were doomed to die. His thoughts were with Issie, with the children and with the community who were waiting for news of victory. In vain. Everything was going to be as it had always been. Kathryn's vision had led them into a trap.

Blood trickling from his wounds, William tried to shield himself. He twisted this way and that, attempted to rise but he no longer had the strength. A guard stood over him, knife poised, his face twisted in vengeful fury. William prepared himself for death.

But death never came. The man's knife dropped to the ground and he fell dead at William's feet. William was seized by many hands, carried away. Weak and confused, he was unable to believe in his deliverance unable to comprehend that the incredible had occurred The town's citizens had rebelled, falling in a vicious swell on the enemy.

Helmuth saw the tide turning, his men falling back their weapons abandoned as they tried to escape. The townspeople ran after them, shouting and jeering Helmuth followed, hoping to be lost in the crowd bu Meredith, in a burst of energy born of hope, lunged towards him and pinioned his arms behind his back The crowd roared their approval and propelled victo and vanquished into Weymouth Square, now broilin, like a scene from The Inferno. Behind them blac smoke poured into the sky, burning particles fell to th ground and the building crashed into itself in a roar c broken masonry and flaming timber. But no one too notice. They were on a spree of bloodlust, the tyrann and hate of countless years finding release in bruta savagery. Corpses sprouted from trees, one man not ye dead, ignited by a piece of burning wood, bur shrieking into flames, a woman sank her teeth into a officer's neck until blood from his jugular spurted int

356

her face and she screamed, 'That's for my son!' Others dismembered men in uniform, not bothering to kill them first, ripping open and strewing innards on the ground. Blood spattered the paving stones, heads, limbs and torsos squelched underfoot.

Helmuth was seized out of Meredith's grasp, savagely hacked with knives, coshes, axes. His testicles were torn away, his eyes gouged out. Within minutes his eyeless head was poised bleeding on a high pole. The crowd let out a wild cheer and Meredith found himself hoisted on a phalanx of shoulders and carried to the centre of the square. He looked round desperately for Joe.

*

In Fairfax Road the three children in the house heard the tumult and ran outside. People were streaming past. A pregnant woman stopped when she saw them and offered her protection. She lifted Issie onto her shoulders, and holding John and Rob by the hand, ran with the crowd.

'Take me to my father,' Issie shouted in her ear. It was the first time she had spoken.

'Where?'

'He's in the square. He's the leader. He did it all!'

She was hysterical with excitement.

*

From the height of a wall on which the jubilant crowd had placed him, Joe watched the savagery below, saw bodies in their last agony, mouths open in unheard

357

screams; he saw women and children tearing at men half dead, pleading for mercy, he saw dismembered bodies cast aside like so much chaff. Out of this carnage a bunch of roses, red as blood, was thrust into his hands. Below, a woman smiled up at him, tears coursing down her cheeks.

Joe watched it all with both horror and a savage indifference towards the men who had killed Kathryn and perpetrated a reign of terror. This was what happened to tyrants. Rough justice. He scanned the crowd for Meredith, William and the children.

Meredith discovered him over the heads of the seething mass, Joe in an ecstasy of relief, smiling bloodied, upright and alive, clutching an incongruous bunch of flowers. And at that moment, through a sequence of events Meredith could not begin to unravel a woman carrying Issie was pushing through the crowd towards him. He grabbed the child and held her tight and waved to the others, milling below. He signalled frantically at Joe who waved back.

Meredith thanked fate for its bounty.

'We've done it, we've won. We're free and they're both safe, the two people I love most in the world.'

And he hugged Issie even tighter.

It was then that Joe heard Kathryn's voice. He heard her calling, 'Joe, Joe, I'm here, I'm here.' He looked round frantically and with amazement saw her, in moment of ineffable joy, standing on the erratic. She looked radiant, glorious, her face suffused with happiness. He did not question how or why she was there, vibrant and alive. He wanted to give her the flowers, put them in her arms.

He prepared to jump down. He heard Kathryn scream, his world turned black and he fell senseless to the ground.

*

The townspeople wanted to give Joe an honourable funeral. They searched for his body. They never found it and assumed it had been torn apart.

Meredith knew better. Joe had disappeared as mysteriously as he had arrived.

Chapter Twenty One

—

JOE heard traffic, the wail of an ambulance. Faces loomed above him, willing hands lifted him onto a stretcher, a red blanket covered him and he was travelling. He could not be certain but he thought he saw his mother's anxious face. Somewhere in the back of his mind he registered that he was back but he could not take it in.

They took him to what he recognised was the local hospital and people hurried past, some stopped and did things to him. They were kind. His mother's face came into focus and he tried to smile. At some point he noted that he was in a cubicle with curtains round, eventually in a side ward. He did not care. His mind was in one place, his body in another.

He lay for days, half asleep, half awake. His sense told him that he was in the ordinary world, the one that used to be his home. This it had long ago ceased to be. The other world was his reality, but he had been expelled. He dreamed he was imprisoned in a huge hour glass, beating its sides to be let out before it was turned upside down by some unknown, giant hand. He woke to find his mother dabbing his sweating forehead. He felt tight bandages round his head.

He was unable to do more than take sips of water. Mum kept speaking to him, her voice echoing as though coming from a hollow chamber, calling his name but he could not respond, he was occupied, travelling the long distance between two worlds. Doctors, nurses talked him as though he were an imbecile, calling 'Joe, Joe, can you hear me?' but still he would not answer. He wished they would leave him alone and turned his head away. Needles were stuck into his side, thermometers in his mouth, tight bands on his arm. He was pushed on a trolley down long corridors and the top half of his body stuck into a dark tunnel, then taken out again.

Mrs Harding was desperate.

'There must be something wrong. Have you done all the tests?'

'Everything. We can find nothing. He has a head wounds and a slight concussion. Leave him alone. He's had some kind of a shock. He'll get over it.'

She had no one to turn to and sat by Joe's bed day after day watching the tubes of liquid gently releasing nutrients into his arm. She tried to persuade him to eat but he could not or would not swallow. Another set of tests followed. Negative. She did not know whether to be glad or sorry.

'Get some friends in. See if that'll bring him round,' the doctor advised. She asked Martin and others to visit and in a desperate moment, Sally. It was a useless exercise. They sat, embarrassed when they failed to rouse Joe, and left. Eventually he started eating small amounts and the tubes were taken away. The hospital said he would have to recover at home. There was nothing more they could do.

'Get your GP to see him. Keep in touch.'

He was talking by now, only the bare necessities and could walk. He dressed himself slowly and got in his mother's cramped car. At home, for reasons she could not fathom, he asked to go into her bedroom. She

361

watched anxiously as he walked round it, touching objects and staring out of the window. He spent a long time looking into her long mirror.

'Do you want to sleep in here?'

He shook his head.

Over the next few days she found him exploring every corner of the house with an intensity that alarmed her. He spent a lot of time in the cellar. She thought he had gone mad and got an appointment at the out-patient's psychiatric clinic. Joe tore up the appointment card when she was not looking but in order to keep her happy went all the same.

They waited a long while and eventually saw a young woman who asked him what seemed to Joe inane questions.

'What's the date?'

He wasn't sure.

'What's the name of the Queen of England?'

He felt like saying 'Sheba' but desisted. They might lock him up.

'Do you hear voices?'

'Only yours.'

She looked up sharply.

'When?'

'Now. I can hear you talking to me.'

One question was not so inane.

'Have you ever thought of taking your life?'

He looked at her strangely and said,

'No. Never.'

She wrote out some notes and told him to come back in six months time.

He gradually regained a hold on life but refused utterly to finish his studies, go back to school or attend any other educational establishment. Mrs Harding cajoled, pleaded, threatened, pointed out drastic consequences, he'd just drift, never get a proper job etc. etc. He listened with patience but responded with obdurate stubbornness, reminding her of the time he had refused to be confirmed. She did not make the mistake of again suggesting her parents intercede but asked instead Joe's form tutor to come and talk to him, see if he could succeed where she had failed. 'If only....' she thought desperately. But there was nothing for it. She was a single parent dealing alone with a teenage boy.

Joe liked Brian Standish, had always got on well with him, was glad to see him but his gentle harangue about a clever, promising student throwing all his chances away had no effect.

'He'll catch up eventually,' the teacher told Mrs Harding, 'don't worry about it. It happens often. He's bright and there's plenty of time.'

He thought she was worrying unnecessarily.

Her parents came to see him, friends, neighbours. They were puzzled at the change in Joe, did not know what to say. He watched them with sardonic amusement and could not resist the temptation to play up so outrageously to his new image of mindlessness that they left, embarrassed. Mrs Harding did not invite them again but Joe heard her end of long conversations in which he repeated what Brian Standish had said.

'After all,' as her GP pointed out, 'you're not dealing with drugs, alcohol, teenage pregnancy or STD, like most parents. Think yourself lucky.'

Joe had changed and Mrs Harding had too much common sense not to bow finally to the inevitable. He had regained his health, she had done all she could to set him along the conventional paths but in this she had failed. He was in any case eighteen next birthday, a virtual adult who could do what he liked. But there were still things worrying her, such as her neighbour somewhat maliciously reporting that she and others had often seen him hanging about Weymouth Square, much of it spent near the erratic; and he'd been found wandering in the Council Chambers. She wondered again whether she should try and persuade him to seek help. He forestalled her by telling her he was perfectly sane, not a pervert hanging about to pick up young boys or girls and needed no one to interfere.

'What's so interesting about the erratic?' she enquired.

'I'm studying it from a geological point of view,' he lied.

She did not know that he was interested in geology but then she knew little about her son these days.

His constant presence in the house was in any case turning into a surprising pleasure. Instead of the normal diet of TV and videos, which he ignored as though they had never been, Joe busied himself with tasks that formerly were hers. He cleaned the house, he looked after the garden, he did the shopping, he prepared meals, he even did his own washing. He became a model son which she found slightly worrying and sometimes wished he was the old, uncouth Joe who did nothing to help, went to gigs and stayed out late. In a neat reversal of roles she often urged him to have a evening out with friends but beyond a few desultory outings he clearly was not interested. His life had taken a different turn though she could not tell what it was.

He took to going out alone for the day on his bicycle. She had no idea where but he often came in late; once or twice he camped out. And he spent a lot of time in the garden shed, listening to his CD's for she heard the familiar music beating across the garden, Beatles, Van Morrison, Bob Marley, Arethra Franklin, Tracy Chapman. She was too tactful to ask what else he did in there, for she heard sounds of energetic activity, hammering and sawing. She hoped he would eventually tell.

One Saturday morning when Joe was out her curiosity got the better of her and, finding the place where Joe kept the key to the shed, had a look. She was amazed to find it cleared, and an old hefty wooden workbench installed. Tools she had never seen before hung on the walls or were placed methodically on the bench.

Feeling guilty at her intrusion she asked Joe what he was doing.

'I'm taking up wood carving,' he said.

Life continued in its new pattern. She came home one evening to find on the kitchen table a fox carved in wood. It stood with its head raised, and down its back, instead of a sleek coat someone had worked an intricate configuration of patterns that were not mere decoration but enhanced in an abstract manner the essence of its foxy spirit, proud, predatory and fierce. She was afraid to pick it up.

'Where did you find it?' she asked Joe.

'I didn't. It's mine, I made it. I've been picking up wood from skips. Surprising what people throw away. Anyway, it's for you. A present.'

She was moved but puzzled. This was a new, extraordinary Joe.

The fox was the first of many. A wild world flowed from the garden shed, all carved with extraordinary striations that set them apart from any works she had ever seen. She surreptitiously went to the library and studied wood carving magazines to see if there were models from which he worked. There were none.

He got a job delivering papers in the early morning and worked at Woolworth's at night. She saw less of him and did not know how he occupied himself during the day.

Neither did Joe. He spent his days in a timeless zone. The gap between where he had been and where he was now was too great to cover in one leap.

One night he dreamed of Kathryn. He dreamed he was back in the community. They were waiting for the townspeople to attack. Events were jumbled. Then they came, the enemies on their ponies and the fight replayed itself. But not his fight, Kathryn's fight. He saw her drop down from her tree on one of the horsemen below, he saw them fall together, he watched the struggle on the ground, a second horseman falling on her, wielding his knife. Kathryn was up with a swift movement but before the first man could retaliate she had wounded him. He crawled away to die. The second one was tougher and fought back. They were fairly matched but Kathryn was faster and in the duel that followed he seemed to be vanquished. But suddenly unexpectedly, she fell to her knees and her opponent was on her, thrusting a knife into her chest. Her face was exultant.

The final tableau matched exactly what he had seen that fateful day.

Joe woke sobbing. He ran out of the house, into the street, he ran into the park and to Cat Walk. The furniture had gone, the cars remained.

He did not know how to go on living.

Chapter Twenty Two

—

Time has passed since then, time to absorb, to contemplate, to seek out the heart of my experience. Time out of time, two minutes in this world, two years in the other. There lies the paradox.

Time plays games; it pretends to run in a sequence, one minute following another, months, years, piling up in a relentless progression. We are born, we grow old, we die. That's the logic; but time conceals a genie in the bottle. Time is what we perceive, it alters according to where it is perceived and who is perceiving it. And who knows in what other dimensions it will work its magic. Only one thing is constant, the lifespan of an individual.

There is no explanation of how or why I blundered into a parallel world. None is needed. What happened happened and is happening still. It informs every aspect of my life, it has led me to what I now am, an artist, sculptor.

As for love? Love never ends, it is constantly renewed in ways surprising and mysterious. And so has been for me. I have found love again.

I think of the people I left behind. Sometimes I hear Meredith calling from the infinite and infinitesimal country 'in between'. There is always an in-between, in between dots on a line, in between the blink of an eye, in between life and death.

My arrival in the other world seems foreordained to alter it, a trajectory with all the appearance of deliberate and conscious decisions. But they were not mine, no

Kathryn's. Other forces were at work. Thus it was that while she thought she was dying to save me, she was dying to save her people; while she thought she was preventing me from venturing into Bantage, she was instrumental in my so doing. Fate is not without its touches of irony.

Perhaps all life is like that. Perhaps there is no free will, perhaps there is a 'divinity that shapes our ends, rough-hew them how we will.' It may be so but I have not left the other world empty-handed. I carry in my heart the knowledge that love, nobility and strength of spirit are the essence of our being. What was it Otto said?

'It's not comfort we're after, but the truth. That's all you've got to live by The truth.'

The End

I am indebted to a number of people who have helped me with this book. Regina Hallam Abel, Eleanor Hallam Abel, Bewick Abel Thompson and Cassie Coburn have tried to put me right about teenagers in all their extraordinary aspects; my husband Gregory Stewart has put me wise to many scientific and mathematical references and has tolerated the long hours I have been locked to my computer.

Jo Winter has supported me and made invaluable comments throughout the writing process. Andre Moore and Kit Gerould have given me incisive editoria suggestions and much encouragement.

Phil Abel of Hand & Eye has designed the book.
Steve Hardy did the hard technical stuff.

I thank them all.

My biggest debt is to my friend Frances Coburn, fellow writer, who has cajoled, bullied, edited commented unstintingly through the two and a ha years it took to write this book. It would certainly neve have been written without her. I owe her a huge debt of gratitude.

The front cover is designed by Henry Steadman.

October 2005.